Magic in His Kiss

SHARI ANTON

FOREVER

NEW YORK   BOSTON

Cover illustration by Alan Ayers
Handlettering by David Gatti

Forever
Hachette Book Group USA
237 Park Avenue
New York, NY 10017
Visit our Web site at www.HachetteBookGroupUSA.com

Forever is an imprint of Grand Central Publishing. The Forever name and logo is a trademark of Hachette Book Group USA, Inc.

Printed in the United States of America

First Printing: July 2008

10 9 8 7 6 5 4 3 2 1

To Denise and Ronald,
around whom center a mother's deepest
sorrows, greatest joys, inevitable regrets, and everlasting
pride. Love you, my darlings!

Magic in His Kiss

Chapter One

Wales, August 1153

Rhodri ap Dafydd skillfully wielded two weapons in the service of Connor ap Maelgwn, chieftain of Glenvair.

During supper, Rhodri had brandished the first one, his weapon of choice: his harp. To lift the gloom caused by grim news from England, he'd sung the praises of the Welsh princes who, after years of fighting, had reclaimed the Welsh lands once conquered by England's hated Marcher earls.

Now he sat cross-legged on the hard-packed earthen floor, tending the other, deadlier weapon. Within the central fire pit's flickering glow, Rhodri slid a whetstone along the edge of his sword, preparing for the possibility of gruesome battle with those same earls.

Connor paced a path in the manor's dirt floor and slapped the rolled parchment containing the bad news against his leg.

"If it is true that King Stephen's heir is dead," Connor said, "he may succumb to the earls' demands to bargain

for peace with Henry Plantagenet." He halted and stared
intently at Rhodri. "England at peace *always* means strife
for Wales. Better for us if the damn earls remain divided
in their loyalties between Maud and Stephen, continue to
fight among themselves, and leave us be!"

As the earls had done for the past few years. Empress
Maud and King Stephen had waged a fine war over
England's throne, occupying their supporters with attack-
ing and defending against each other, giving the earls no
time or resources with which to harass Wales. If Stephen
named Henry Plantagenet, Maud's son, as his heir, peace
might soon follow.

And Connor had the right of it. England at peace always
meant strife for Wales. Worse, Henry was said to be as
ambitious and forceful as his royal maternal grandsire, for
whom he'd been named, and during whose reign Wales
had suffered mightily. Since most of the Marcher earls had
rebelled against Stephen to fight for Maud, they'd happily
follow Henry wherever he led them, especially into Wales.

Connor waved the parchment scroll like a sword, as if
he signaled a charge into the enemy's heart. "The Welsh
princes must unite! If they do not, we may all perish."

Rhodri's gut knotted. During his apprenticeship to
one of the most accomplished bards in the land, Rhodri
had committed to memory the history of Wales, all the
way back to ancient times. Rarely had the princes banded
together under one leader to stave off invasions.

Rhodri pointed out the obvious. "Each prince has his
ambitions for expanding his own lands. For them to unite
for a common cause might require a miracle. Have you
one at the ready?"

Connor sighed and eased down onto a nearby stool,

placing his deeply wrinkled hands on his knees. White hair revealed his advanced years; a furrowed brow bespoke a troubled mind. Still, vigor and intelligence lit the chieftain's amber eyes, belying any belief that his mind might wither with age.

"No ready miracles," Connor admitted. "However, we may have time to conjure one. Even if Stephen names Henry as his heir, the lad will have to wait until Stephen dies to claim England's crown."

Rhodri scoffed. "We could both name several young men who sent fathers, uncles, and brothers to their graves before their natural life's end. Ambitious men tend to impatience when a great prize is within reach."

Henry Plantagenet, duke of Normandy and Aquitaine, count of Anjou, Touraine, and Maine, wasn't known for his patience.

Nor were the Marcher earls. They eagerly awaited the chance to punish the imprudent princes for believing Wales should be ruled by the Welsh.

Rhodri ran a thumb along his sword's edge, quite willing to cut down any Englishman who dared to attack Glenvair. "'Tis not Henry who is the immediate threat. If peace comes to England, the earls of the March will once again turn their thoughts toward Wales. Whether the princes unite or no, we will defend Glenvair, as we have always done."

"That we will," Connor stated firmly, then leaned forward, elbows on knees. "I am of a mind, however, to gain an advantage." He again waved the rolled parchment. "Though Gwendolyn kindly informs me of whatever news she hears of affairs in England, I wish to heaven above that when she and her sisters were orphaned, I had gone to Camelen to fetch my nieces and bring them to Glenvair. That mistake must now be made right!"

Rhodri couldn't see any advantage to Connor interfering with his long-dead sister Lydia's girls at this late date. Rhodri well remembered the day Connor received word that his Norman brother-by-marriage, Sir Hugh de Leon, along with his son, William, had died fighting for Empress Maud. The three orphaned de Leon girls had become wards of King Stephen.

Emma had been sent to King Stephen's court, where she'd been forced to marry Darian of Bruges, a Flemish mercenary. Gwendolyn had been forced to marry Alberic, the unacknowledged bastard son of one of the most hated of the Marcher lords—the earl of Chester. Nicole had been given to the Church and, as far as Rhodri knew, still resided in Bledloe Abbey, awaiting whatever fate King Stephen decided for her.

"The girls were out of your reach then, as they are now."

"Gwendolyn and Emma, perhaps, but not Nicole. Stephen holds her captive in Bledloe Abbey. He intends to wed her to a Welsh noble, preferably to a prince. Such a marriage would forge an alliance between the prince and English crown, possibly driving another wedge between the remaining princes. We must remove that weapon from Stephen's armory and use it to our own advantage."

Rhodri assumed Connor entertained his own notion of which high-born Welsh noble Nicole should marry. But for Connor to have any say in the matter of Nicole's marriage meant removing her from Bledloe Abbey, then quickly marrying her off to the man of Connor's choice. A good strategy, but he foresaw problems in the execution of such a plan.

To mount a raid on the abbey, located near Oxford, in the heart of England, might prove a disaster.

Connor ap Maelgwn was a cunning chieftain, a ferocious soldier, and—usually—an honorable man. How much was he willing to risk to wrest his youngest niece from English control?

"Kidnapping Nicole might be considered an act of war. And what of her sisters? Emma and Gwendolyn might not approve of your scheme, and their husbands would make formidable opponents."

Connor acknowledged Rhodri's concerns with a nod, saying, "I believe that, for a time, England's lords will be more concerned with the fate of the crown than with other matters. As for Nicole's sisters, I believe they will see that I act for other than selfish reasons. After all, our family's heritage must be preserved. The tree of Pendragon *must* bear a Welsh branch to remain strong."

Pendragon. The bloodline of King Arthur.

Rhodri knew every word of the ancient legends, could sing the tales of Arthur's conquests and his downfall. That revered bloodline flowed through the family of ap Maelgwn.

He'd been a young lad when his widowed father had become betrothed to Connor's younger sister. To everyone's sorrow, before the marriage could take place, the couple had drowned in the Severn. Connor had been kind enough to feed and shelter an orphaned boy.

Though Rhodri had been grateful for Connor's aid, he'd also felt insignificant, like a blade of grass within the mighty oak's shade.

'Twas one of the reasons he'd apprenticed for eight years with Cynddelw Brydydd Mawr, the acclaimed *pencerdd* to the prince of Powys, to become a bard like his father.

One day he would seize the opportunity to earn his chair and advance to the honored position of *pencerdd* to a Welsh prince. But until one of the princes held a contest to choose a new *pencerdd,* Rhodri could do little to advance in his profession. And at the moment, his duty as *bardd teulu* of Glenvair was to counsel Connor.

"You cannot march a band of Welshmen across half of England without drawing the enemy's attention. The raid would certainly fail."

"True, which is why I propose to send one man."

From the directness of Connor's stare, Rhodri knew whom he intended to send.

The prospect both excited and disturbed him. He was honored by Connor's faith and trust in him, and success would surely bring rewards—from both Connor and whichever noble he'd chosen for Nicole to marry.

Rhodri also foresaw problems. He wasn't one of Nicole's favorite people, as Connor well knew.

"You want *me* to kidnap Nicole out of Bledloe Abbey and bring her to Glenvair?"

"Better if Nicole comes to me of her own free will. You are one of the most persuasive men I know. Charm her with praises to her beauty. Remind her of her glorious lineage. Talk to her, Rhodri! Do whatever you must to convince her that coming to Wales is the best course for her and for her family's heritage."

"She does not like me. She may not listen."

Connor waved a dismissive hand. "Nicole was no more than a handful of years old when she was last here. Surely she is no longer a spoiled child but a mature woman and can now be reasoned with." Then his eyes narrowed. "And if reasoning fails, bring her anyway. The matter of her marriage is too important to me and to Wales to entrust to the English king."

Connor rose and strode off, leaving Rhodri to ponder how he might accomplish this difficult task.

Talk to her, Connor had said.

Rhodri dismissed attempting to appeal to her vanity, which Nicole most certainly possessed, in favor of the more practical course.

Could an appeal to Nicole's sense of duty to her Pendragon heritage have the desired effect? Perhaps, if she felt a sense of duty. Problem was, the Nicole de Leon he remembered cared only for her own concerns. A spoiled, headstrong imp of a princess who struck out physically when displeased.

Rhodri ap Dafydd rubbed his leg, remembering his last encounter with Nicole de Leon, fearing this time she might do far worse than kick his shin, the act of a petulant princess for which *he'd* been severely punished.

Perhaps Connor had the right of it. Surely Nicole's eight years in a convent had mellowed her temper and taught her humility. As a full-grown woman, maybe now Nicole could be reasoned with.

And if not, he now knew better how to guard against a kick in the shins.

∾

Your time here is done, Nicole. Come out.

Nicole de Leon bolted upright on her narrow cot, her eyes snapping open in the night-shrouded dormitory.

She recognized the voice from beyond the grave that woke her, startled over this unexpected contact. Her brother usually spoke to her only once a year, to rail and rage at her. *Never* had William spoken to her in so calm a manner.

She'd done her brother's bidding only once—the first time William had spoken to her—mere hours after his burial.

Every day, Nicole thanked the Lord she hadn't possessed the skill or strength to murder her now brother-by-marriage. Since then, she'd learned how to deal with William's yearly demand that she avenge his death.

But this time was different. William wasn't ordering her to do murder, just to leave the abbey. True, he'd arrogantly given an order, but he wasn't battering her with it. How unusual—and foreboding.

Warily, Nicole lowered the defenses she instinctively raised whenever she heard her brother's voice, trying not to hope that William's spirit was finally ready to converse with her, not merely give her orders she loathed to obey.

Why must I leave? she silently asked.

He didn't answer.

William?

Silence.

Confused by William's unusual intrusion into her thoughts, Nicole deeply breathed in the familiar scents of woolen robes hanging on their pegs and of the burning night candle near the doorway. A glance over the cots revealed she hadn't disturbed the nuns, who would soon rise for matins to begin yet another day of prayer, meditation, and service in God's name.

For eight years Bledloe Abbey had been her home,

these nuns her gentle companions and patient teachers. William wanted her to leave them behind. To go where? To do what? Not that she dared to escape the convent even if she wished to.

William, let me help you. Speak to me.

Silence reigned.

Angry at his abandonment during the one time she truly wished he'd speak again, Nicole tossed back the woolen blanket and silently rose, feeling the chill against her bare skin. She slipped on the white linen chemise that protected her skin from the black robe of prickly wool. When decently clad, with her bedding straightened and hose and boots in hand, she padded her way to the infirmary, where she knew Mother Abbess would be awake.

Mother Abbess rarely slept these days, too aware the heavenly reward she'd spent her life working toward was about to become reality.

Soon now, dear, soon!

This sweet, gentle voice, too, came from beyond the grave. Sister Enid's excited greeting made Nicole smile as she entered the herb-scented, tranquil infirmary.

Sister Enid had left mortal life behind a few days after Beltane. In life, the nun had considered the care of Mother Abbess her life's work, and so her spirit lingered to see her duty completed. The two old and dear friends would pass through the veil between this life and the next together.

Nicole swallowed the lump of grief that swelled in her throat. She knew it useless to pray for a miracle, to hope the woman who'd been both mentor and mother to her wouldn't die.

"What brings you to my side so early?" Mother Abbess

asked, the clarity of her voice belying both her advanced age and failing health.

The abbess looked no different this morn than she had last eve—frail and withered, her thin hair as white as fresh snow. In her gnarled hands she held prayer beads worn from years of use. Her green eyes, however, still often saw too much.

To hide both her confusion over William's unusual intrusion and sorrow over Mother Abbess's impending death, Nicole plopped down onto the stool beside the cot and bent over to put on her short hose and boots.

"I woke and could no longer sleep. I did not wish to disturb the others, so I came to see how you fare."

"Harrumph. We must usually pry you from your cot of a morn. What spoiled your slumber?"

Nicole smiled. "Perhaps I have at long last become accustomed to waking before the bell is rung."

Mother Abbess chuckled at the lie. "When sheep take wing." Then she sobered. "What ails you, child?"

Nicole grappled for something troublesome the nun might accept as a truthful answer and easily found one disturbing event that had floated in and out of her thoughts for several days now.

"Prince Eustace's death, and how his loss will affect King Stephen and the war."

Mother Abbess's fingers slid from one bead to the next, seeking solace and wisdom in the prayer that had sustained her all her life.

"You mean you fear King Stephen may now remember you are of an age to marry and can be of use to him."

Bluntly put, and all too true.

Nicole didn't care if the war went badly for Stephen,

whether he eventually lost his throne or not. But as his ward, she cared very much whether or not he would use her in an attempt to gain a desired alliance.

"I cannot say I am of a mind to marry as yet."

"You have always known the day might come. You also know how to avoid the king's machinations."

Nicole fingered the ends of her brown, waist-length braid. She could cut her hair short, cover it with a veil, and utter vows. She recoiled, as she always did, when she considered becoming a nun and spending her entire life in Bledloe Abbey.

"You well know I have no calling to the Lord's service, that I do not reside in Bledloe Abbey by any wish of mine own. 'Twould be no less than I deserved if God struck me deaf and blind the moment I uttered insincere vows. Nay, Mother Abbess, I have no wish to take clerical vows merely to escape marriage."

"Other women have done so."

Several of whom resided at Bledloe. One could tell the difference between the nuns who had taken vows because of a true calling from those who had done so for more selfish reasons.

"I will not. My fate lies in the world, not in the cloister. Whatever that fate may be."

"Then perhaps you should consult your sisters. They would come if you summoned them."

Emma and Gwendolyn would certainly make every effort to answer a summons, but they had husbands, children, and estates to care for. Too, Gwendolyn was in no condition to travel, awaiting the birth of her third child. Emma was at Camelen with Gwen, to assist at the birth.

And certes, at the age of ten and eight, Nicole was

reluctant to burden her beloved sisters if she could manage her problems on her own.

Truly, no problem yet existed. King Stephen hadn't decreed whom she should marry. And certes, if her only choices were to become a nun or marry a Welsh noble, well, there was no need to consult with her sisters. She'd accept the marriage rather than take vows.

Nicole wasn't opposed to the idea of marriage, even an arranged one. With the right man, marriage could be wonderful and joyous. Just look at how happy her sisters were with their husbands. She worried, however, that she might not be so fortunate in King Stephen's choice for her.

For now, worrying over the future would do her no good, and Nicole wanted no distractions from what she saw as her immediate and more important task: caring for Mother Abbess until the bittersweet end.

"I will consult Emma and Gwendolyn when the proper time comes," she said, more to ease the furrows on the abbess's brow than to quell her own misgivings. "Are you in pain? Need you a potion?"

"These old bones ache from disuse, but the pain reminds me there is life inside me yet. Go ready for prayer. The bell will ring soon."

Though Nicole preferred to remain in the infirmary, brewing potions and mixing unguents, she would attend morning prayers, if only out of love for Mother Abbess.

Nicole rose from the stool and kissed her friend and mentor's thin-skinned forehead, wondering if she should tell the abbess of the joyous reunion with Sister Enid awaiting her on the other side of life.

She would, she decided, but not until the very end, when the abbess had no time for questions or lectures.

Sister Enid, Nicole was sure, would let her know when that time was upon them.

"I will bring your morning repast after matins. Is there aught particular you would like?"

Another shift of fingers, another bead to hold between thumb and forefinger. Another prayer offered up to some good purpose.

"Nay. My hunger now is not for victuals. Ask the sisters to pray that I might see our Lord's face sooner than late."

The abbess had thoroughly accepted, even welcomed, her impending death. Nicole might have accepted, but she wasn't in any hurry for the event.

Nor was it in her nature to become morose, and Mother Abbess would be aghast if Nicole slipped into despondency.

She pulled a face of mock horror. "I will do no such thing! Our Lord will take you when He wills and not a moment before. Have pity on those of us you leave behind, dearest Abbess! We shall be like lost ships in a storm-tossed sea without you to guide us home."

The nun chuckled, as Nicole intended. "Oh, life will continue without me, and each of you will find your way."

"Rudderless, wind-deprived, becalmed ships, I tell you!"

Mother Abbess's hand rose, and Nicole took the hand that had gently but firmly guided a willful, brash, selfish girl into temperate, more peaceful womanhood.

At least Nicole hoped she'd grown up. She no longer ran through the passageways or giggled at inappropriate times. She no longer made unreasonable demands in a voice that echoed against the stone walls.

But, betimes, 'twas hard to be unselfish. Like now,

when she would rather King Stephen didn't remember her name or where she resided. When she wanted Mother Abbess to live.

Mother Abbess squeezed her hand. "The way is never easy, my dear. Remember this. When times seem the most confusing, point your bow to either sunrise or sunset and follow your heart."

Appealing images—in opposite directions.

And neither course guaranteed a welcoming shoreline or safe harbor.

Chapter Two

Midday sun streamed through the infirmary's open shutters, somehow brightening the prayers the nuns murmured at Mother Abbess's bedside. Kneeling on the plank floor, Nicole knew the perpetual vigil and the earnest invocations for God's mercy would do nothing to halt Mother Abbess's death. But since the Latin chants comforted the dying nun, Nicole strove to concentrate.

Unsuccessfully.

Chanting appeals to God, Christ, Blessed Mary, and every saint she'd ever heard of couldn't halt Nicole's restlessness.

Shifting on knees gone sore on the hard plank floor, Nicole remembered the day she'd first entered the infirmary. It was on the day of her arrival at Bledloe Abbey, her despair acute and her belly aching. Sister Enid, a short, plump woman with kindly eyes, had smiled at the distraught little girl of ten and given her a mint leaf to suck on. Ever after, Nicole had felt more at home in the infirmary than anywhere else in the abbey.

Immediately she'd been fascinated by the hanging

bunches of dried herbs, the mixing of unguents, and the brewing of potions. Over the years she'd tended the sick, held the hands of the dying, assisted at the birth of babes, and learned herb lore.

Unfortunately, nothing in the sacks of mixed herbs, little pots of scented unguents, or sparkling bottles of potions could cure Mother Abbess. Still, Nicole agonized over whether there was something more she might have done to slow the nun's decline.

Nicole struggled with the guilt even though she knew Mother Abbess was old, her earthly body worn out, as Sister Enid had been near her death. Though Sister Enid hadn't spoken to her in over a sennight, Nicole was aware the nun's spirit hovered nearby, waiting for Mother Abbess. Too soon both women would fully depart, and for their absence in her life, Nicole mourned.

A light hand landed on Nicole's shoulder, startling her. Sister Claire, who would become Bledloe Abbey's next abbess, bent down and whispered, "Come."

Nicole dutifully rose and followed the thin, sharply angled woman into the passageway, where Sister Claire stopped a few feet beyond the infirmary's door.

"You have a visitor," Sister Claire announced.

Despite Nicole's grief, excitement bubbled up. "One of my sisters?"

Sister Claire's mouth thinned. "Nay. A Welshman by the name of Rhodri ap Dafydd. Do you know him?"

Taken aback, Nicole swiftly sorted through memories of her only visit to Glenvair, her Welsh uncle's holding. When she remembered Rhodri—whom Gwendolyn had also mentioned in her letters a time or two over these past years—Nicole's cheeks warmed with embarrassment.

Their last encounter hadn't gone well. True, she'd been very young, but she'd also behaved very badly, and 'twas Rhodri who'd suffered the punishment for her show of childish, imprudent temper.

"I know him." Then her heart sank, fearful of the most likely reason why a Welshman would risk a dangerous journey so far into England. "Did he say why he came? Has aught dreadful befallen my uncle Connor?"

Sister Claire crossed her arms, her hands disappearing up into the wide sleeves of her black robes, her mouth twisting with ire. "He said only that he brings greetings. I shall take your place at vigil while you send him on his way. Be quick, Nicole."

Still apprehensive, Nicole rushed to the small receiving chamber near the abbey's main entry. Even if Rhodri hadn't come to tell her of Connor's illness or death, he surely brought news of grave import. A Welshman would not travel this deep into England merely to convey greetings, not even a bard, who might be afforded greater respect than his countrymen.

She felt a sweet pang for happier days, well before she'd been fully aware of the war that had taken her father's and brother's lives. She'd been all of five when Father had taken his children to visit their deceased mother's brother, Connor.

To a little girl accustomed to residing at Camelen—her father's intimidating stone keep, surrounded by a high curtain wall, efficiently guarded by gruff soldiers—Connor's manor at Glenvair had seemed a magical place of unobstructed freedom.

Barefooted, she'd chased butterflies in long, cool grass in the shade of towering trees along the banks of a bubbling stream. With a small smile she also remembered her brother William—then beloved, and golden, and recently knighted—who'd come upon her and the group of children she played with, sternly scolding her for setting aside her boots.

Beside William had stood Rhodri, a lad barely into his facial hair. He'd striven to follow William's stern example, and failed, which endeared him to her instantly. Unfortunately, by the end of her visit, Rhodri no longer found her childhood whims amusing.

Nicole opened the receiving chamber's door to behold the gangly youth of her memories, now grown into his full, magnificent manhood.

Sweet Jesu! The years had been most benevolent to Rhodri ap Dafydd.

Tall, wide across the shoulders, and narrow in the hip, Rhodri didn't need the sword belted at his trim waist to declare this bard was also a warrior—a *bardd teulu*. Garbed in the deep brown of a stately, solid oak, his imposing presence dominated the small chamber.

Long, raven-black hair skimmed his rough-woven long-sleeved tunic. His dark brown, amber-flecked eyes were deep set; his nose had been broken a time or two. His lips were firm and lush, and all the more beguiling when a slow, potent smile softened his squared, bold jaw.

She realized how thoroughly she inspected Rhodri when he returned the appraisal in kind, setting delicious sparks to tingling along his gaze's path, these becoming particularly unsettling where he lingered overlong.

Though she was garbed in a robe designed to conceal every womanly curve, she felt sure he'd taken the measure of each one. And liked what he saw.

Sweet heaven above, she tingled from hair to toenails at Rhodri's bold assessment.

Which only served to prove what she had known for many a year about her own nature. She thoroughly appreciated a handsome, solidly formed male far too much ever to be faithful to vows of chastity.

Not that every nun within Bledloe Abbey held to that particular vow. Only look at the number of births recorded in the infirmary each year, and how Sister Amelia disappeared for hours and hours every time a certain visiting bishop occupied the priest's hut.

"A princess in nuns' robes is still a princess," Rhodri said, his Norman French delicately flavored with the lilt of his native language. "Did I not know otherwise, I might mistake you for Gwendolyn."

A favorable comparison. Her sister was counted among the most beautiful women in the realm. Delight with the flattery battled briefly with the humility the nuns had toiled long hours to instill in her. Humility had never been one of her strongest virtues, either.

Nicole returned his smile. "Greetings, Rhodri. It gladdens my heart to hear your gallantry has not suffered."

He tilted his head. "I was not sure you would remember me. Many years have passed since we last met, and you were very young."

Thirteen years had passed, if she remembered aright.

"I was old enough to retain memories of Glenvair, and my uncle Connor, and you. Those were happy times for me." Except the last two days of her visit hadn't been pleasurable at all. But surely Rhodri hadn't come to take her to task for childhood mistakes. "How fares Connor?"

"He is well and sends his love and greetings. He also instructs me to invite you to seek refuge at Glenvair."

Shocked at the bittersweet invitation, Nicole wished Connor had tendered the offer immediately after her father's death, when she might have been able to accept. How much nicer to have been allowed to spend the past eight years at Glenvair instead of being banished to Bledloe Abbey! Sweet yearnings battered at her common sense, bringing her close to tears.

Useless tears.

Nicole sat on the bench beside where Rhodri had tossed his hooded brown cloak. Atop the cloak lay an oddly shaped sack made of soft, deep green wool. She touched the sack and felt the curve of his harp's wood frame beneath the wool.

"Your harp," she said, giving the instrument due reverence. "I remember you playing at supper at Glenvair."

"Do you?"

"Quite well. I always thought the music enhanced the magical feel of my uncle's holding. Gwendolyn told me you finished your training and are now *bardd teulu* of Glenvair."

He nodded, his rugged chin dipping in a manner worthy of a court poet as well as a warrior. "I am. Connor kindly allows me a place at his manor until I am able to compete for my chair."

"I wish you good fortune in your ambition, Rhodri ap Dafydd. Not all bards are skilled enough to become a *pencerdd*."

"My thanks, but I did not come to talk about my future, but yours. Connor's invitation is not an idle one, nor a whim. He is in earnest."

Nicole withdrew her hand from the harp, still a bit incredulous at the offer. "You truly came all this way to invite me to Glenvair?"

"Aye."

The men had surely lost their wits!

Not sure if she was more annoyed with Rhodri or Connor, Nicole rose from the bench, her ire growing at her uncle's desire for her to accept the impossible offer.

"Then you have come far for naught. King Stephen has twice denied my sisters' petitions for me to return home to Camelen, even for a short visit. If the king will not allow me to go home, he will certainly not permit me to visit Wales! I thank my uncle for his kindness but must refuse."

"I fail to see why King Stephen's wishes should affect your decision."

Nicole tossed a frustrated hand in the air. "I am the king's ward! I have no choice but to do his bidding!"

"I hear the Norman in you speaking. What says the Welsh?" His amber-flecked eyes narrowed. "Or have you abandoned the better half of your heritage? You are of *Pendragon,* Nicole, and yet you bow to the wishes of an English king. I should think your lineage sets you far above his whims."

How dare Rhodri reproach her for disregarding a lineage that had not earned her or her sisters a dram of sympathy or regard?

"When my father was killed, the king gave Camelen to Alberic of Chester, who forced Gwendolyn to marry him. Also on the king's order, Emma was sent to court and forced to marry Darian of Bruges. I was sent here to await my fate, which will also be decided by the English king! What good is the Pendragon blood if no one gives it reverence?"

"I do," he said softly, sincerely, bursting her bubble of anger over how heartlessly she and her sisters had been treated after her father's death.

In Rhodri's expression she saw respect for her Pendragon lineage, a thing she'd never witnessed from any other person save one—Rhys, also a Welsh bard, who resided at Camelen.

'Twas Rhys the bard who'd honored Nicole's mother's wishes by singing the ancient tales, telling stories of valiant kings and honorable knights, of King Arthur, keeping their Welsh heritage alive for all the de Leon children.

Naturally, Rhodri had heard those same tales from his father, then learned to relate them to others from a revered *pencerdd*.

Still, his respect for her lineage did her no good.

"I cannot leave Bledloe Abbey. Were I to take refuge in Wales, my sisters' families might suffer for my audacity. I will not bring the mallet of royal ire down on their heads."

He huffed. "Right now Stephen can barely lift a mallet, much less wield it. Have you heard of his heir's death?" At Nicole's nod, he continued. "Stephen is far more concerned with keeping hold of his crown and throne than with the whereabouts of one Nicole de Leon. Nor, I believe, would your sisters suffer. From what I have heard of Alberic and Darian, I dare say both would make powerful adversaries, and Stephen is needful of all the good will and allies he can convince to remain his supporters." He stepped forward, a hand outstretched, palm up in an offer of succor. "Think on it, Nicole. The time for you to escape is now, when your absence will barely be noticed. By the time King Stephen is aware you are gone, you will be safely in Wales."

The door swung open and Sister Claire burst into the chamber, her eyes wide with concern. "I heard shouting! Nicole, have you been harmed?"

With Rhodri's reasoning swirling in her head, Nicole absently shook her head at the distressed nun. "I beg pardon for my outburst, Sister Claire. I did not mean to disturb you or the vigil."

Sister Claire took a calming breath. "Well, then, if you are finished, you may again take your place at vigil and I will accompany your visitor to the door."

Except Nicole didn't want Rhodri to leave just yet.

Could he be right? Could she leave Bledloe Abbey without worrying over what the king might do to her or her family? Could she escape a marriage that might not be to her liking?

Dare she take the risk?

She needed more time to further ponder her uncle's unexpected and wickedly tempting offer of refuge. Nor could she abandon Mother Abbess in these last hours before her death.

But how to keep Sister Claire from banishing Rhodri from the abbey until she could further ponder Connor's offer?

The answer to Nicole's dilemma popped forth and rolled off her tongue before she could question its wisdom.

"Sister Claire, Rhodri ap Dafydd is a bard. Might he be allowed to play his harp for Mother Abbess?" She spun to again face Rhodri, not caring if he saw through her ploy to gain more time. "Mother Abbess weakens hourly, and I doubt that in all of her life she has heard an accomplished bard play the harp. Would you do us the honor, Rhodri?"

His answer was immediate, his graciousness genuine. "I would be most pleased to play for all who care to listen."

The nun chewed on her lip in indecision. "This is a most uncommon request, Nicole. Men are not allowed within the depths of the abbey."

"For the past sennight we have allowed men into the infirmary to visit Mother Abbess."

"Two priests and a bishop who came to give comfort and say final prayers. One can hardly compare the circumstances!"

"Rhodri's music can also give comfort," Nicole countered. "I know my request is unusual, but consider the joy you could give Mother Abbess in her final hours. I beg of thee, Sister, give her this one last gift."

Nicole held her breath while Sister Claire hesitated before relenting.

"You must leave your sword behind," she ordered Rhodri before leaving the chamber, no doubt headed for the infirmary to warn the other nuns that she'd broken one of the abbey's rules.

Delighted, Nicole let loose her breath.

Rhodri laid his sword and scabbard on the bench and unsheathed the beautiful harp. The silver strings caught bits of light and flung them throughout the room, like tiny stars whirling brightly in the night sky. The harp's music would sparkle as brightly. Oh, how she'd missed a harp's music!

"Sister Claire must have been very near the door if she heard you shouting at me," Rhodri commented.

Nicole couldn't remember *ever* shouting since entering Bledloe Abbey. Embarrassed at her lapse of good manners, she explained, "Loud sounds carry far down stone passageways. Surely she heard me from the infirmary."

"Or she hovered outside the door to spy on you."

The very idea that Sister Claire had lingered outside the door apurpose, to overhear Nicole's conversation with Rhodri, was preposterous.

"Sister Claire is to be the next abbess. Never would she do such a thing."

"So you say."

"You have a most suspicious nature, Rhodri ap Dafydd."

He smiled without a hint of humor. "Then that is to my advantage. A good trait in a warrior, is it not?"

Nicole conceded the point. "Then I should be suspicious of your purpose, should I not?"

Now he laughed. "Be assured, my lady. Had not Connor sent me to convey his offer, I would not have stepped foot on English soil, much less journeyed so far into enemy lands."

That she could believe. He'd risked his neck by playing messenger for Connor. Did that make Rhodri brave, or a fool?

Brave, she decided. Welsh bards weren't fools.

Rhodri had never before played his harp for a group of nuns, one of whom lay prone on a narrow cot, beads in her frail hands.

He sat on a stool near the head of the cot, delighted the merry melody he'd chosen to play brought a soft smile to the abbess's thin lips.

The power of music, whether to calm an upset child or stir men into battle frenzy, had always intrigued Rhodri. As a boy, he'd sat at his father's feet, watched those nimble fingers pluck at the strings, and felt the force of each song played.

He'd craved that power and learned his craft well. When playing the harp he'd inherited from his father, Rhodri was confident in his ability to stir whatever emotion he chose to draw forth in whatever audience he played for.

Today was no different. As he intended, Mother Abbess smiled, and the nuns kneeling on the floor had given up their praying and listened, enthralled, to the music.

Except Nicole de Leon.

She stood on the other side of the cot, paying him utterly no heed, her gaze steadfastly fixed on Mother Abbess. Rhodri doubted Nicole heard a note but blamed her lack of enchantment on her concern for the abbess and her familiarity with harp music. Unlike the other women, whom he now held in thrall, Nicole had spent her childhood in a household blessed with its own bard, so the music wasn't new to her.

He hoped she also pondered his suggestion that she should take refuge in Wales. Nicole had declared the offer impossible to accept, but while still in the receiving chamber, he'd sensed her plea for a bit more time to decide.

And now, in the infirmary, Rhodri saw who truly bound Nicole to Bledloe Abbey. Mother Abbess. No royal command, nor religious conviction, could bind her as thoroughly as her devotion to the dying nun. Nicole would balk at leaving the abbey while Mother Abbess yet breathed.

Nicole's loyalty might be commendable, but he hoped the abbess wouldn't take much longer in her dying. A day's delay in removing Nicole from the abbey he could countenance. But longer?

Rhodri plucked the song's final note, allowing it to fade before beginning a gentler, softer tune. His heart beat a little faster when Nicole turned her head slightly to reward him with an approving smile. The glint in her large brown eyes confirmed that he played a favorite song.

A man could become entranced by those lovely eyes, lose all sense of time and whereabouts. They'd fascinated him as a youth and held no less appeal for him now.

When Nicole entered the receiving chamber, he'd been briefly stunned to see how the adorable little girl had bloomed into a beautiful young woman.

Not even the black of Nicole's robe could dim the ivory-hued glow of her heart-shaped face. Nor could the unshapely garment completely conceal the allure of her up-tilted, firm breasts or her nicely rounded hips.

And when, as now, her rosy mouth blessed him with a smile, he felt a tug on his innards he thought he'd possessed more wisdom than to feel.

Even as he attempted to pay more heed to the harp than the temptation to further notice Nicole's charms, he conceded that if they weren't deep in an abbey at the bedside of a dying woman, he might well be tempted to play a different sort of song.

One of seduction.

Nicole's body was made for a man's hands to caress. Her mouth fair begged kissing.

Even as his loins stirred, Rhodri acknowledged the danger of luring this particular captivating woman into his bed. Nicole de Leon was the object of his mission— and he couldn't fail in his task.

Best to think of her as the petulant little girl who'd kicked him in the shins and caused him three long months' worth of punishment, not ponder overlong on her womanly enticements or on the benevolent smile she turned his way. Except she was no longer a little girl, nor violently petulant, nor utterly selfish.

Mother Abbess's hand shifted. Nicole was quick to notice. She covered the nun's hand with her own soft-skinned, delicate fingers, bending low to hear whatever the nun whispered.

Giving him yet another perspective from which to contemplate the jut of her bosom beneath the habit. He almost groaned aloud in pain, fighting the nearly over-whelming urge to reach over and take the weight of a breast in his hand.

When she straightened, Nicole's eyes sparkled with amusement. "You play so beautifully, Mother Abbess believes you must be an archangel sent to ease her way heavenward."

He'd been called many things in his life. Stalwart, brave, and loyal by his friends. Dangerous, a conniving cur, or debased devil by his enemies. Charming, wonderful, and talented by his previous lovers.

No one ever had compared him to one of the heavenly host. If the nun only knew how the bulge in his pants urged him to commit unholy decadence, she'd be shooing him off to hell.

"I am no angel, Mother Abbess, though I would appreciate your recommending me to Michael or Gabriel should you happen to meet up with them."

Nicole's smile teased him, charming him so completely his fingers almost fumbled on the strings. "I could tell Mother Abbess a tale or two to disabuse her of her mistaken notion."

What tales could Nicole tell of his not-so-angelic nature? She'd certainly been too young to remember much of what had happened during her visit to Wales. But then, she might have heard stories from her sisters or her brother, William. Tales he certainly didn't want a nun to hear.

"You could," he allowed. "But then I would have to tell a tale or two of my own, would I not?"

Her smile faltered but didn't disappear. "Mother Abbess already knows I am no angel."

Rhodri could have sworn he heard a snicker from one of the flock of nuns kneeling on the floor.

During his journey to fetch Nicole, he'd given brief thought to the rightness of taking Nicole away from the abbey, wondering if perhaps he'd be tearing her away from a true calling to the Church. Not that her calling mattered to Connor, or to Rhodri, who was duty bound to follow Connor's orders. Still, he gladly set his mind at ease that Nicole didn't belong to the Church and that at least one nun in the crowd agreed with him.

Rhodri refused to feel guilty that Nicole still looked a bit worried that he might inform Mother Abbess of just how unangelic Nicole could be. Instead, he revealed his own devilish tendencies with his harp.

The song was a common one, heard at every hall, tavern, or campfire where men downed ale. Out of respect for where he was, he didn't sing the words, but he drew expected reactions all the same.

From the flock he heard soft gasps and saw a few disapprovingly arched eyebrows. Mother Abbess breathed a soft "Oh" before gracing him with a beatific smile.

And Nicole—she crossed her arms under her sweet breasts. Her reproachful look failed. Then her boot tapped the rapid beat against the plank floor.

Her decorum suffered further when she began to mouth the words, even the bawdy ones.

Sister Claire stood, her expression thunderous, her intent clear. Rhodri stared at her hard and played on, willing her not to interrupt the song he'd chosen with deliberate care.

She blinked when he finally sang.

"The journey is upon us."

Nicole joined him, in a clear, sweet voice too angelic for his peace of mind.

"To faithful fellows farewell."

His eyes locked with Nicole's, and he surrendered the lead to provide harmony.

"Until next we raise an ale.
All hail! All hail! All hail!"

Sister Claire's thunder never rumbled. Tears streaming down her face, she sank back down to her knees and bowed her head. Others softly sobbed while still others worked their prayer beads faster.

"All hail," Mother Abbess said, her voice thready and faint, and Rhodri inwardly breathed a sigh of relief that for this woman, at least, he'd chosen his song correctly.

Nicole's chin rose, her gaze peering over his shoulder, her stare so intense one would think someone stood behind him. Her lips parted slightly; her eyes welled with tears. With a mixture of sadness and an emotion he couldn't quite identify, Nicole uncrossed her arms and bent toward the abbess.

What Nicole urgently whispered into the nun's ear he couldn't understand. He merely noted a look of surprise and—concern?—on the old woman's face.

"Oh, Nicole," the abbess whispered.

Nicole mustered a smile. "'Tis true. You will see."

"But how—"

"You will know all soon. Be at peace, dearest Abbess. Heaven and friends await you."

Which didn't sound like a platitude to him. The confidence in Nicole's voice said she knew for certain what awaited the nun on the other side of life.

"Oh, my. Praise . . . the Lord." And with the words on her lips, the nun's eyes closed for what Rhodri was certain was the last time.

Nicole kissed the abbess's forehead and arranged the prayer beads around still hands. When satisfied, she turned those beautiful, moist eyes his way. He saw resignation and grief, but there was also peace and, somehow, joy.

"Pray, one more song, Rhodri," she requested, then took her place among the kneeling nuns.

Rhodri swallowed the lump threatening to close his throat and again chose his music carefully. Not for this nun a mournful tune, but one of victory, triumph, and celebration.

Near the end, he noted the abbess's chest failed to rise and fall. He played on to the glorious end, then quietly left the room to allow the nuns to mourn privately and prepare the body for burial.

To his surprise, several of the nuns followed him out, two of them rushing off down a long passageway. Nicole wiped away tears on her wide black sleeve as she approached him. For the briefest of moments he considered spreading his arms to offer her comfort, invite her to cry on his shoulder. But her tears were gone by the time she reached him.

"My thanks, Rhodri," she said, her voice steady. "You so impressed Sister Claire she invites you to evening meal and asks if you will play at the burial on the morn."

Oddly disappointed Nicole didn't require the use of his shoulder, Rhodri would far rather have grabbed hold of her hand and removed her from the abbey. But she'd fight him, and as much as he wanted to be away, he reasoned that waiting one more day wouldn't matter. As a bard, he also knew Sister Claire awarded him a singular honor.

"I would be most pleased to play at the burial. Is there aught else I can do to be of service?"

"Nay, I can think of nothing . . ."

Her voice trailed off as she stopped to listen to the deep, mournful drone of the chapel bell, announcing the abbey's sad news to the countryside.

After a deep breath, she continued, "Let us gather your belongings, and I will point out the priest's hut, where you may spend the night."

Chapter Three

Nicole's knees ached from kneeling on rough, cold stone. The air in the abbey's chapel had become both stale and odoriferous, a result of Sister Claire's bad judgment, in Nicole's opinion.

Last eve, not long after the tolling of the bell, people from leagues around had swarmed the abbey. So many pleaded with Sister Claire for a last glimpse of Mother Abbess that the doors were thrown open and all allowed to enter. *Mon dieu,* Sister Claire had decided to completely ignore the ban on males within the abbey, and so entire families were given free rein. Too many mourners spent the night in vigil with the nuns, and so too many prayers had been accompanied by the harsh rasp of snoring.

Nicole truly couldn't blame the tenant farmers and villagers for wishing to bid farewell to one of the most fair and compassionate overlords they might ever know. Nor could she hold these simple people to the same rules of suitable behavior that she'd learned as a child in a noble household, the same rules practiced here in the abbey.

And perhaps, now well after dawn, heart sore and

body weary, she simply couldn't muster the tolerance necessary to contend with too many people in too little space. She needed sleep, and a bite of bread to calm her protesting stomach, and knew she couldn't have either for several hours yet.

Nicole glanced at Sister Claire, who hovered near the bier where the body of Mother Abbess awaited burial in the great maw of a hole that had been dug in front of the abbey's altar.

Sister Claire had been Mother Abbess's assistant for longer than Nicole had resided in the abbey. The nuns would surely elect her to the position of abbess. Did the woman have doubts about her ability to assume the burden of responsibility for the welfare of her fellow nuns and of the many people who depended upon the abbey for their livelihood?

Nicole swiped at her eyes, moist from grief and lack of sleep. Sweet Lord, she would miss Mother Abbess. Her kindness, her steadfastness, and her sometimes irreverent humor had enlivened conversations until the very end.

That Mother Abbess enjoyed a drinking song hadn't surprised Nicole. Rhodri chose his songs well, comforting Mother Abbess in a way no prayers and no priest could.

Mother Abbess no longer needed comfort. Indeed, all these prayers for the repose of her soul weren't necessary. On one breath the woman died and, forswearing another breath, she'd gleefully greeted Sister Enid before the two of them fled swiftly through the veil between earth and the heavenly kingdom beyond.

Without a glance back. Without a word of farewell.

Spirits, Nicole acknowledged drolly, had no use for the

living unless they required the living to perform some service. Having lived a long life, rich in service, Mother Abbess required naught of the living and left behind her mortal life as swiftly as she could. Leaving Nicole bereft. What good was the ability to hear the dead if not to receive a final, private fare-thee-well?

Nicole knew she shouldn't be upset with Mother Abbess for doing what a spirit ought to do—sever earthy bindings and depart for the glorious beyond. Still, Nicole had yearned for a private parting word from the woman she'd adored.

With a sigh, Nicole admitted that more than Mother Abbess's swift departure, more than the lack of sleep or food, more than a snoring farmer, what had bothered her most throughout the night was Rhodri's ill-timed arrival at the abbey.

Certes, there would be changes at Bledloe Abbey. Sister Claire simply didn't possess Mother Abbess's commanding presence. Not that Nicole thought the nuns would suffer for it, but life at the abbey would be . . . different.

Sister Claire might require more frequent attendance at chapel, perhaps rein in the freedoms Nicole enjoyed in the infirmary. Without Mother Abbess as an advocate, Bledloe Abbey might feel more like a prison than a pleasant place to reside until the king decided what to do with her.

Damn Rhodri! Why had he appeared the very moment when her life was about to suffer an upheaval, making her vulnerable to Uncle Connor's offer of refuge?

But then, she truly didn't have a choice of whether or not to leave. No matter what her uncle wished her to do, she couldn't leave Bledloe Abbey without the king's consent.

To do so meant putting her sisters in an untenable situation and probably angering both of her brothers-by-marriage.

Rhodri might be right about Alberic and Darian being well able to take care of themselves and her sisters, but Nicole saw no good reason to put them at risk over her uncle Connor's whim.

And especially not over William's. Her brother had said no more to her after giving her the ominous order to leave. She had yet to discern the precise reason for his order, other than to decide he'd done so to somehow further his quest for revenge against Alberic. She would *not* be used again in such fashion.

So she dared not leave the abbey, no matter how much running barefooted through long grass to chase butterflies appealed. When the burial was over, she would thank Rhodri ap Dafydd for playing his harp for Mother Abbess and send him back to Wales, to give her thanks and regrets to Connor.

A stirring near the chapel's door snapped Nicole from the musings she'd wrestled with for too many hours. A few of the nuns were urging the villagers and tenant farmers to their feet and shooing them out the door, which likely meant the clergy from Oxford had arrived. Soon they'd be lowering Mother Abbess's body into that cold, dark hole.

Nicole shivered and struggled to her feet, intending to help with clearing the chapel and, 'twas to be hoped, sneak a breath of rose-scented air from the cloister garden. She touched the shoulder of the woman who'd knelt beside her most of the night, the potter's wife, who held an infant, the youngest of her six children. The woman looked up, seeming to come out of a trance.

"Madam Potter, time to leave," Nicole said quietly and looked about for five small bodies, which were nowhere to be found. Puzzled, she asked, "Where are the other children?"

Madam Potter handed Nicole the sleeping infant before also struggling to her feet. "They are here, somewhere."

Somewhere? Upon further inspection of the chapel, Nicole realized that not only had the potter's children disappeared, but not one small body capable of walking remained within.

Sweet mercy, had all of the children left the chapel? She nearly groaned aloud, aware of the mayhem a group of untended children could cause. The abbey could very well be in shambles!

Since Madam Potter seemed in no hurry to reclaim her babe, Nicole carried the small, warm bundle out of the chapel, with the mother close on her heels.

"I wonder where they are?" she asked, more of herself than of Madam Potter.

"My eldest, he left the chapel to take a pee, then came back for the others. Said not to worry over them."

Madam Potter's eldest was a male of no more than ten summers. The children's mother might not have been worried, but Nicole certainly was. Then she heard the faint sound of silver strings, and her worry waned as she headed toward the source of the music.

Seated on a bench in the garden, surrounded by enthralled children, Rhodri ap Dafydd smiled broadly when he spotted her under one of the arches.

She handed the infant back to Madam Potter, who absently took the babe while gaping at the children, every one of them sitting still, entranced.

"Saints be praised! What magic is this?" the woman asked, only half in jest.

"No magic, merely a Welsh bard. I have witnessed the power of his harp on grown men. These wee ones were likely no challenge."

Charming the nuns of Bledloe Abbey yesterday had presented no difficulty for Rhodri. Lightening her grief and weariness now was easily accomplished. Rhodri performed no magic, just wielded a harp with great skill.

How long had Rhodri entertained the children? She'd not seen him since he'd retired to the priest's hut last night after supper. When had he returned and watched over the bored little ones?

Not that he seemed to consider the task a hardship. His wide smile attested to his pleasure, as well as a decided hint of triumph.

"I do not suppose he intends to settle in our village," Madam Potter said on a wishful sigh.

"Rhodri returns to Wales on the morrow."

"A pity. We mothers would welcome a man with such a way with the children. Faith, he is not hard to look on, either. Some village maiden should set her claim to him right quick!"

Aye, Nicole knew of at least two maidens who would take one look at Rhodri's handsome visage and broad shoulders and swoon straightaway into his bed. Even Sister Gertrude, at whom the visiting priests' sermons on fornication had no effect, had gazed lustfully on Rhodri while he'd played his harp for Mother Abbess.

Nay, he'd not lack for female adoration wherever he went.

Who could blame the women? Not her, not when her

woman's places stirred with wanton curiosity whenever she looked on Rhodri overlong.

With a discordant note, Rhodri put aside his harp. Softly he told the children, "Your elders seek you out. Pray go quietly. Remember this is a house in mourning."

Madam Potter shook her head in disbelief as the children rose to obey his command. "'Tis nigh unbelievable," she muttered, wiggling her fingers to beckon her young ones. "Ye have a care today, my lady, and give our thanks to Sister Claire."

With that, Madam Potter herded her children down the passageway, and Nicole made her way across the garden to where Rhodri stood, his smile now soft but no less exultant.

Irritated by the wanton thoughts he could evoke, she said accusingly, "You look pleased with yourself."

"My father once said that when he could no longer hold the attention of the children, he would give up his harp. They are a difficult crowd to please."

He'd enticed the children for selfish reasons, not to be of service. But wasn't that the way of men, seeking always to gain some satisfaction or reward from their actions? Not bothering to hide her disapproval, she waved a hand at the archway.

"You will have a new crowd on which to test your skills shortly. I believe the clergy have arrived."

"Lead on, my lady."

She briskly led him through the now full passageway and into the chapel. Indeed, Father Gregory from St. George's-in-the-Castle, and Prior Robert from St. Frideswide's had arrived, along with Lord William de Chesney, the castellan of Oxford Castle. Nicole also recognized many of the town's merchants, including the apothecary and the wine merchant. Monks mingled with several town officials. The chapel was nigh on as full as it had been last night.

Nicole followed Rhodri to where Sister Claire waved him to a stool placed below the north window, where the Virgin Mother and infant Jesus reigned in stained-glass glory.

"No drinking songs," Nicole warned Rhodri.

He settled on the stool and set the harp on his thigh. "So now the princess commands the bard on what songs he may play?"

"Certes not, but be forewarned that Father Gregory lacks Mother Abbess's sense of humor."

Rhodri set the harp strings to singing softly in a sweet melody, one she didn't recognize, lulling all to silence. When the last note faded into the chapel's rafters, Father Gregory and Prior Robert stepped up to the altar and began the Mass.

The Latin chants were familiar. The priests sprinkled Mother Abbess's body with holy water and, to the irritation of Nicole's eyes, wrapped them all in a cloud of incense.

Father Gregory was about to begin the homily when a rustle from the back of the room narrowed his eyes, then fully widened them. The crowd parted, like the Red Sea for Moses, to allow a tall, burly, handsome young man to swagger to the front.

"My lord," William de Chesney said with a slight bow. "I did not realize you were coming to Oxford. Had we been aware of your intent to so honor Mother Abbess, we would have waited for you."

Rhodri leaned in close and whispered, "Who?"

"Aubrey de Vere, the earl of Oxford."

"Truly?" he asked, clearly impressed.

As well he should be. De Vere, one of the wealthiest men in the kingdom, was both a powerful ally and close advisor to King Stephen. Few men were his match.

"The earl's father founded Bledloe Abbey, and Aubrey continues the de Vere family's patronage. Without his financial support, Bledloe Abbey would not long survive."

The earl stepped up to the bier and gazed down at Mother Abbess, his visage reflecting his sorrow. The earl and the abbess had been great friends, despite their differences in age and temperaments. The formidable earl truly mourned.

De Vere stepped back to stand between de Chesney and Sister Claire. "I arrived in Oxford after you left and was most aggrieved to hear the reason for your departure." De Vere waved a long-fingered hand the priest's way. "Proceed, Father."

Nicole heard nary a word of the priest's continued rambling, disquieted by the earl's presence in the abbey's chapel.

Sometimes called Aubrey the Grim, de Vere spent most of his days either at his grand castle of Hedingham in Essex or in King Stephen's entourage. How odd that the earl should visit Oxford at any time other than a fortnight or so before Michaelmas. There could be any number of reasons for his visit, she supposed, but his sudden and unannounced appearance hinted at urgency.

What pressing business required the attention of an earl? Most likely it concerned the war, a very quiet war of late. But Prince Eustace's death might have sparked intrigues on both sides. Oxford might be threatened. Chiding her imagination for taking flight without good reason, Nicole forced her attention back to where it belonged.

The remainder of the Mass passed without interruption, and when it ended, Sister Claire and Sister Mary stepped to either side of the bier. With great reverence, they gathered up the white linen that draped the bier and folded it over the woman who lay upon it. Two more nuns joined them, large needles and heavy thread in hand.

Nicole had seen shrouds sewn shut before, but not since her father's and brother's burial had the sight caused such sharp heartache. Mother Abbess had lived a long, full life. Her spirit had joyfully departed. Nicole wanted to rejoice, but overwhelming grief made it impossible.

Her throat closed up. Her eyes burned. Cursing her weakness, she crossed her arms tightly over her middle, pressing back threatening sobs. As Sister Claire tied off the last stitch, Rhodri's hand touched Nicole's shoulder and her composure crumbled.

Nicole spun and hid her vulnerability in Rhodri's chest.

Rhodri realized he shouldn't have touched Nicole, but 'twas too late now to undo his mistake. With his arm resting atop her shoulders, she tucked perfectly into his side, her face buried in his woolen tunic. She was pressed so close he could feel her inhale great gulps of air, hold her breath, then exhale in a rush before repeating the actions.

To his chagrin, he also caught her scent. Delicate, yet

as captivating as a bouquet of roses. He breathed her in and savored the heady aroma, scolding himself for taking sensual pleasure in her nearness when all she sought was comfort.

Nicole made no sound as several men lifted Mother Abbess from the bier and lowered the revered nun into her final resting place in front of the altar.

Indeed, no one noticed Nicole's distress, their attention too fixed on the proceedings.

Rhodri felt her rally, her breathing no longer as labored. Still Nicole remained warm against him, her arms wrapped tight around her middle to contain her grief. Only now and again a slight hitch of breath revealed the depths of her upset.

Father Gregory broke the silence with a final blessing while Prior Robert swung the incense burner over the grave. With a sniff so indelicate Rhodri had to smile, Nicole turned her head to the side to observe the ceremony.

She'd always possessed the ability to amuse him. Even as a child she'd known she was a princess and, as the youngest of the de Leon children, had been doted upon. While Nicole had delighted in getting her own way, she'd also been earthy, not as aloof as she could have been. Nice to know that in some ways she hadn't changed too much.

'Twas then he noticed that Nicole's upset was no longer private. The earl, his eyes narrowed and head tilted, frowned on Nicole's failure to control her emotions. His ire pricked, Rhodri tightened his hold on Nicole, as if that small action could shield her from the earl's disapproval, knowing damn well that the earl was right—Nicole shouldn't be pressed up against him in so intimate a fashion.

However, what Aubrey de Vere thought of Nicole didn't matter to Rhodri as long as the man kept his displeasure to himself, not adding embarrassment to Nicole's grief by taking her to task for a momentary lapse of proper behavior.

When de Vere finally looked away, Rhodri's own breathing eased.

Nicole hadn't moved so much as a hair, and he felt a measure of satisfaction knowing she was comfortable turning to him when distraught. Clearly she trusted him somewhat. A good omen.

He would need her to trust him fully in the days ahead. There were dangers on the road between Bledloe Abbey and Wales, and their survival might depend upon her willingness to trust him and take orders.

She glanced up at him with a wobbly smile. "I believe your part in the service has come," she whispered and stepped out of his embrace, taking all her lovely warmth and scent with her.

Rhodri sank onto the stool and plied his harp, as Sister Claire expected of him. Since his fingers knew the strings intimately, he allowed them their freedom and observed the relaxing crowd. Most of the people would soon depart for the refectory, where the nuns had prepared a light repast to fortify all for their journey home.

The earl and the highest ranking of the clergy and the city officials should have been the first to leave. For some reason the earl refused to budge, keeping Sister Claire, the clergy, and Lord de Chesney with him. De Vere still frowned, and whatever he was saying was directed at Sister Claire.

Rhodri suppressed a chuckle. Poor Sister Claire must be aghast at how many males had invaded the abbey's depths in recent days. The nuns would surely be pleased to reclaim their feminine sanctuary, though right now most of them would be delighted just to catch a few hours of sleep.

For all he believed the English bishops too rich, and the Church laws too strict and unyielding, he had to admit Bledloe Abbey a fine place. The abbey itself wasn't ostentatious, built of timber in clean, unadorned lines. Spacious, yet cozy. Though the stained-glass window was an expensive ornamentation, and the jewel-encrusted gold chalice evidence of wealth, for the most part these nuns lived without excess comforts—or so he judged from what he'd seen.

Nicole still stood close by, weariness slumping her shoulders, exhaustion and the aftermath of weeping dulling her usually sparkling eyes.

Rhodri silenced the harp, intending to escort Nicole out of the chapel and into the refectory for a meal. Soon afterward they'd leave Bledloe Abbey and head swiftly westward. The sooner away, the better.

His intention was thwarted by the earl's order. "Lady Nicole, pray attend us."

After a sigh audible only to him, Nicole crossed the chapel. Having nothing better to do, or so he told himself, Rhodri followed close on her heels, deepening the earl's frown.

Here was arrogance.

Rhodri knew much about England's Marcher earls but little of the others whom the Welsh didn't consider a threat. Such a one was Aubrey de Vere. He struck Rhodri as too damn overbearing for a man of so few years. The earl could be no more than twenty and five yet believed it his right to order about everyone within the sound of his voice.

Perhaps that was what happened to a man when handed so much wealth and power at so young an age, and the conceit of it proved irritating.

Nicole dipped into a deep curtsy. "My lord de Vere. Mother Abbess would have been pleased to know you attend her burial."

The earl held out a hand, helping Nicole to rise. "My condolences, Lady Nicole. I know how much you loved Mother Abbess."

"As did you, my lord. She always enjoyed your visits. We shall both miss her mightily, may she rest with the Lord."

"So we shall," the earl agreed before *finally* releasing Nicole's hand and turning his narrowed eyes on Rhodri. "Master harper, I find it right strange to find a Welshman so far away from his native land. What do you here?"

The demand for an explanation didn't sit well, but Rhodri saw no compelling reason to withhold an answer. This wasn't the time or place for a confrontation with an English earl. That place was on a battlefield, not an abbey's chapel.

Rhodri bowed as shallowly and swiftly as he dared before answering. "I am *bardd teulu* to the lady's uncle, Connor ap Maelgwn. He bade me visit the Lady Nicole and report on how his niece fares."

De Vere's glance darted from Nicole to Rhodri and back again. "I cannot believe King Stephen would condone your having contact with your Welsh uncle, particularly now. Does it not seem strange to you that your uncle would send an emissary to inquire of your welfare after so many years of neglect?"

The back of Rhodri's neck itched in warning. De Vere had been doing too much pondering during the Mass instead of paying heed where he ought. And he dearly hoped Nicole wouldn't take offense at the earl's inferences and blurt out the reason for Rhodri's visit.

To his relief, she tossed a dismissive hand. "Since our father's death, Gwendolyn has kept my uncle Connor informed of mine and my sisters' well-being. Apparently my uncle thought it time for a more direct report. I confess I am glad he sent Rhodri. His music has lightened our sorrow."

"All well and good, but I cannot help but wonder why a Welsh chieftain is so curious about you at a time when you may prove valuable to our king. 'Tis now obvious that Lady Nicole cannot be properly guarded at the abbey. Until I am assured this visit is as innocent as you say, you shall both become my guests in Oxford Castle."

Nicole paled.

Rhodri clutched his harp a bit tighter. "My lord, I assure you, I mean the lady no harm, nor does her uncle. Connor merely wishes assurance of her health and happiness."

De Vere crossed his arms. "When the uncle is a Welsh chieftain, and King Stephen is in the midst of negotiating the lady's marriage, then I would say mere concern for her welfare is not reason enough for your visit."

Rhodri nearly winced at how close the earl had come to the truth.

"Marriage to whom?" Nicole asked, clearly surprised by de Vere's revelation.

"I am not at liberty to say," de Vere stated. "I suggest you partake of the meal and gather your belongings quickly. We leave before the sun marks midday."

Obviously stunned, Nicole said naught as they followed the earl out of the chapel, and Rhodri had no opportunity to reassure her that she need not worry over the king's negotiations or the earl's audacity. But even as he looked for an escape route, he realized he must bide his time.

The earl hadn't come to Bledloe Abbey alone. In the passageway outside of the chapel stood four knights, each of them armed with swords and daggers even in this holy house. Rhodri had left his own sword in the priest's hut, anticipating no need for it during a burial! Too, there was likely a large contingent of soldiers in the yard guarding the horses.

Damn!

Upon his arrival, he should have grabbed Nicole and hustled her out of the abbey. Adhering to Connor's wish to convince Nicole to leave the abbey of her own free will had been a mistake. Now, instead of fending off an upset nun or two, they must escape a fully armed escort of knights and guards.

'Twas his fondest hope that an opportunity for escape would present itself somewhere on the road. If not . . . Rhodri preferred not to ruminate on the difficulty of getting both himself and Nicole out of the royal castle in Oxford.

Chapter Four

Nicole awoke, cocooned in a soft woolen coverlet atop a down-stuffed mattress. Dim light from the narrow window barely reached the corners of the bedchamber's gray stone walls.

Familiar with her surroundings, Nicole tried to enjoy the simple pleasure of waking in a bed more comfortable than her cot at the abbey, until the sound of someone rustling the rushes on the floor told her she wasn't alone.

Blinking away sleep, she rose up on an elbow to identify the intruder.

"Ah, you are awake, my lady!" Lucy, a slender, well-endowed maidservant whom Nicole had known for several years, set a platter of food on the small oak table under the window. "'Tis sorry I am about the abbess, may she rest with the Lord. She was always kind to me, an undemanding soul."

Nicole swallowed hard to dull a sharp pang of fresh grief.

The last time she'd visited Oxford Castle, she'd slept in this same chamber. Mother Abbess had occupied the bed, and Nicole and Sister Claire had taken pallets on the floor. That had been this past winter, before Mother Abbess's health began to fail.

"My thanks, Lucy." Determined not to wallow in grief, she glanced at the platter. "Have all broken fast already?"

"Long ago, my lady. 'Tis after nooning. The earl said to allow you to sleep as long as you might, but I knew you would not want to sleep the whole day away, so I brought victuals and ale. Did I do wrong?"

Sweet mercy, after nooning? But then, having been awake from sunrise to sunrise and far beyond, by the time she'd arrived at Oxford Castle late yester noon, she'd been hard pressed to keep her eyes open and her legs from collapsing.

And she understood Lucy's concern. The servant had taken liberties she truly ought not.

"You did right to wake me, Lucy. The earl will not hear of your transgression from me." She eased her legs toward the edge of the bed, wincing at her entire body's stiffness. "I swan, I would be in less pain had I walked all those leagues from the abbey. The cart's driver had no notion of how to avoid ruts. My bottom will be sore for a sennight!"

Lucy gave a mew of sympathy. "Do you wish me to brew you a potion? Willow-bark tea, mayhap?"

"Your offer is kindness itself. My thanks."

"The bread is from this morn's baking, and the ale is the village brewer's finest." Lucy paused by the door, putting a hand on a gown of light blue that hung on one of the pegs. "This is one of Lady Julia's castoffs. If it does not fit you aright, I shall send for the seamstress to make the needed changes."

Nicole saw her white shift on the same peg, partially hidden by the gown. On another peg hung her cloak.

"Where is my habit?"

"The earl ordered it sent to the laundress to clean before it is returned to Bledloe Abbey."

Nicole clutched the coverlet a bit tighter. "I should like the robe returned to me. Can you fetch it?"

Lucy's brow scrunched in confusion. "I can try, my lady, but beg pardon, why would you want it? The laundress is readying an entire chest full of Lady Julia's garments for your use. Most should be in good order by this eve, and certes, Lady Julia would not disapprove of your use of them."

Julia de Vere, the earl's niece and a dear friend of Nicole's sister, Emma, now resided at the earl's castle in Essex and wouldn't begrudge Nicole the use of her old garments. Nor did Nicole oppose wearing castoffs. The earl's presumption, however, proved most irritating.

"I hope to convince the earl to allow me to return to Bledloe Abbey. I should rather do so in the habit in which I left."

Lucy tilted her head. "You wish to go back?"

Her wishes aside, Nicole knew she must return.

"The abbey is where the king expects me to reside. The earl should not have brought me here."

Nor should de Vere have forced Rhodri to come to Oxford!

Sweet mercy, if the earl ever learned of Connor's offer of refuge in Wales, Rhodri might not see Glenvair again in a very long time. If ever.

Before she could ask after Rhodri, Lucy left, closing the door behind her, leaving Nicole both worried about Rhodri and resentful of the earl's impudence.

After Mother Abbess's burial, the earl had made his shocking announcement about the king negotiating her marriage. Then he'd turned an unhearing ear to her protests, forcing her to leave Bledloe Abbey and suffer being bounced on the hard plank seat of the cart.

Upon arriving in town, she'd struggled to shut out the cries of the spirits in St. Peter-in-the-East church's graveyard. She'd heard the pleas of these spirits before and refused to aid them, because their ties to earth involved inflicting harm on a living person.

The climb up the steep outer stairway of St. George's Tower—the central keep of Oxford Castle—had wrung out the last drop of her vigor.

The last thing of yester noon she remembered clearly was watching Rhodri being led away by the castle's soldiers, suspecting she was more than partly to blame for the earl's decision to take Rhodri captive.

If she hadn't turned to Rhodri for respite and solace during the burial, the earl might not have paid the harper much heed. She feared her moment of weakness had set the earl to wondering about the relationship between a king's ward and a Welsh bard. Not liking what he saw, the earl had decided to further investigate.

Nicole sighed, unable to summon uninhibited sorrow for turning to Rhodri. His touch had been all the invitation she'd required to seek succor. Sweet mercy, she'd felt so cosseted and sheltered within the circle of his arms, as if while within his protection nothing more could hurt her.

Even now she could feel his strength, warmth, and compassion, and she couldn't allow him to suffer any longer than necessary for her ill-timed vulnerability.

Praying the earl treated Rhodri with respect for his

profession, but fearing he didn't, Nicole cast aside the coverlet and pushed herself off the bed.

She quickly used the chamber pot and, from the pitcher on the side table, poured tepid water into the washbasin. The splash of water against her face banished the last traces of sleep. The quarter round of brown bread was indeed freshly baked. The yellow cheese proved mellow and the ale robust.

The gown, the blue of a clear summer sky, was truly lovely, the weave finer than Nicole had worn in many a year. The wide sleeves and generously cut neckline allowed enough of her shift to show to give a striking, fashionable contrast. The hem brushed the tops of her boots.

Vanity might be a sin, but sweet mercy, she couldn't help wishing for a polished silver platter in which to see how she looked.

She was beginning to tighten the gown's side laces when Lucy returned with a mug of steaming tea.

Lucy's smile went wide. "Heaven have mercy! Will you look at what you were hiding under that habit! The knights will stumble over each other for the favor of your company. Allow me, my lady."

Nicole smiled at the insolent servant's flattery, a confirmation of how well the gown suited her, though she doubted any of the knights would fall at her feet. She took sips of tea and transferred the mug from one hand to the other while Lucy pulled the gown's laces snug.

"Did you speak to the laundress?"

"The habit is cleaned, but you will not wrench it from Tilda's hands without the earl's consent. Certes, my lady, you have no need of the habit here, and if you do return to the abbey, it will be waiting there for you."

True, but the habit was one more thing that had been taken from her in the short space of two days, and she found the earl's lack of consideration for both her person and belongings irksome.

Still, Nicole admitted she rather liked the way the blue gown hugged the curves of her body. Though she didn't possess the fullness of Lucy's bosom or the blatant outward thrust of hip, Nicole believed she wouldn't be found wanting.

Lucy eyed her critically. "Lady Julia was wont to wear a gold chain around her waist with this one. I do not suppose you have one in that satchel of yours."

She'd had no need for any type of belt in the abbey. Indeed, Nicole possessed so few personal items they all fitted in a small satchel with room to spare.

"Alas, no gold chain, but I do have my gold circlet."

Lucy fetched the satchel and opened it. "Blessed saints, my lady! What would you be doing with a dagger!"

Nicole gingerly eased onto the stool that stood next to the table. She put down the mug and began to undo her waist-length braid, remembering her childhood banishment from home while she'd still deeply mourned her brother. She'd pilfered one of William's old daggers, wanting to take something of his with her to keep his memory alive.

Little had she known that she wouldn't require a reminder, that once every year William's revenge-needful spirit would spoil her family's Easter visit to the abbey.

Damn! She'd inadvertently obeyed William's latest command when she'd left Bledloe Abbey. One more reason to return as soon as she was able.

"'Tis merely a keepsake, Lucy. Find my ivory comb, too, if you please, as well as my circlet."

"As you say, my lady. Oh, this be lovely!" The maid-servant set the emerald-studded gold circlet on the table. "I remember Lady Emma's circlet. Hers is adorned with topaz, is it not?"

As Gwendolyn's circlet was adorned with sapphires. The circlets were gifts from their father, who'd fondly dubbed his daughters his jewels. Then Father had been killed in battle, along with William, and the girls had been left with little to call their own but their circlets.

In answer, Nicole merely nodded and closed her eyes. While Lucy attacked the snarls with the ivory comb, Nicole pondered her next move. Somehow, she must convince the earl to allow both her and Rhodri to quit Oxford.

"Is the earl in the hall?"

"Last I saw, he were in the solar. An odd thing, too. Lord de Chesney invited the earl to fly the falcons, which the earl dearly enjoys, but the earl said he was waiting on some messenger and wished to be in the castle when he arrived. Must be important, that message."

William de Chesney knew his duty as a royal castellan and kept a mews full of excellent hawks and falcons for visiting royalty and nobility to enjoy. The awaited message must be important, indeed, for the earl to foreswear a chance to hunt.

Nicole suppressed a shiver, then chided her foolishness. She'd been here less than a day. Surely the message the earl expected didn't concern her and an impending marriage.

"Do you know the whereabouts of Rhodri ap Dafydd?"

Lucy sighed. "Is it true this Welshman is a bard?"

Apparently, castle gossip spread as efficiently as ever, which Nicole hoped would work in her favor. "Aye."

"A damn shame, then, that the earl ordered him locked up in the north guard tower. 'Twould be a fine thing to listen to a harp at supper."

Nicole's heart sank at the news she'd expected to hear but had hoped for better. Locked in a tower—not good.

"I need to see Rhodri. Can you take me to him?"

Lucy tied a strip of leather to the end of Nicole's braid. "The guards are under orders to allow no one to see him but his lordship. If you can get the earl's consent, then I can show you where the bard is being held."

Nicole voiced her greatest fear. "Is he being treated well?"

"Cook says his platters come back to the kitchen empty."

Which didn't mean Rhodri ate the food sent to him. Soldiers were notorious for taunting captives. Eating Rhodri's food might be the least of the soldiers' abuse. A Welsh captive in Norman hands might suffer far more than most prisoners.

Nicole drank down the remains of the willow-bark tea, then stood to pluck stray hairs from her gown.

"Am I presentable enough for an audience with the earl?"

Lucy set the circlet in place. "You have the look of royalty about you, my lady. I do wish we had a gold belt to hang on your hips. A woman needs all the advantages she can muster when dealing with a man, be he field laborer or earl. Shall I inform the earl you wish to speak with him?"

"My thanks, Lucy."

The maidservant sped out the door.

Needing to keep her hands busy for the few moments

she must wait before following, Nicole put her comb back in the satchel and pulled out the dagger she truly should have sent back to Camelen years ago.

The dagger was a soldier's unadorned weapon, solid and sharp, beautiful and deadly.

Nicole bit her bottom lip when the thought occurred to her that if she couldn't convince the earl to release Rhodri, then Rhodri might be able to make good use of the dagger to effect his own escape. She hesitated only briefly before slipping the dagger into her boot, hoping she need not give it over.

She knew escape from Oxford Castle was possible. Everyone had heard the tale of how, in the early years of the war, Empress Maud and four of her knights had tossed a rope made of bed linens out a window and climbed down to escape King Stephen, who'd besieged the castle. Of course, that had been during winter when the river Thames, which surrounded the castle, had been frozen.

Certes, she wouldn't needs climb down a rope of bed linens or swim the Thames. Surely the earl could be made to see reason and allow both her and Rhodri to leave.

She'd never begged favor of so high a ranking noble before but had watched Mother Abbess bargain with earls and abbots, bishops and barons, with a mix of flattery and sound reason.

Praying she would find the right words to set her and Rhodri free, Nicole scurried down the torch-lit passageway and the tightly winding stairs to the solar.

Both the earl and the castellan were seated at a heavily carved oak table, a large sheet of vellum spread out before them. Two knights—Sir Etienne, one of the earl's men, and Sir Walter, the captain of Oxford's household guard—stood behind their respective lords. All of the men wore somber expressions, as though they'd received ill tidings.

Had the messenger the earl awaited already come, then? Likely not, or Lucy would have said somewhat of the messenger's arrival.

Nicole squared her shoulders and crossed the room, her boots clicking softly against the stone floor. The earl saw her first, and once he took notice, so did the others. Their bold stares made her insides squirm until she ventured close enough to recognize signs of admiration.

Her rank, proclaimed by the circlet, might account for some of their regard, but Nicole suspected the snugness of her gown, leaving no female curve hidden, earned her the greater attention.

The earl rose from his chair, smiling. "Lady Nicole, 'tis pleased I am to see you rested and in full bloom."

Ignoring the knights for the nonce, Nicole gracefully curtsied low to the highest-ranking men in the chamber.

"Greetings, Lord de Vere, Lord de Chesney." Rising, she smiled at the castellan of Oxford Castle, her host. "As always, your hospitality is above reproach, my lord. Pray give my compliments to your housekeeper and cook for providing excellent bed and board, particularly when they are forced to accommodate a guest without warning."

The earl's smile faltered, but the castellan's widened. Apparently he understood and approved of her attempt to discomfit the earl. Had she found an ally in de Chesney? Would he aid her cause?

"You must know the servants hold you in affection, Lady Nicole, so they do not mind providing for you for as long as you may be with us."

"'Tis my hope their service shall not be required long." A slight shift of stance faced her square before Aubrey de Vere. "My lord, while I appreciate your kindness in the lending of Lady Julia's garments, I must protest the necessity. Truly, my habit, though old and unfashionable for so esteemed a court, would have done me fine."

The earl crossed his arms. "You are the first woman I have heard protest the gift of a fashionable gown, and certes, the time has come for you to put aside the habit."

"You may be right, my lord," she conceded, mindful of not angering the earl. Calmly presented reason would carry the day, as it had for Mother Abbess. "However, I am uneasy over leaving Bledloe Abbey without the king's consent. 'Tis where he has commanded I reside, and I have yet to discern an urgent reason for my displacement. Though I am not averse to residing in Lord de Chesney's care, I fear we may all suffer the king's displeasure over my removal from the abbey."

De Vere sank back down in his chair. "You are kindness itself to concern yourself over my good standing with the king, but I believe he will understand my unease over leaving you in the care of the nuns, unprotected. I would be remiss in my duty to our sovereign if I did not take action to assure your safety."

"Safe from what threat, my lord?"

"Your Welsh uncle, my lady. And his bard."

The bard whom de Vere had locked up in a guard tower. Who was denied his freedom because she'd unwisely wished time to consider her uncle's offer of refuge in Wales, even though she'd known she couldn't possibly accept.

"My Lord de Vere, I do not make light of your concern.

However, you must consider that Rhodri, truly, is merely a messenger from my uncle Connor. Indeed, had I not asked Rhodri to play his harp for Mother Abbess, and had not Sister Claire requested he also do so at the burial, Rhodri would have come and gone the previous day without incident. I beg you not to hold him at fault for consenting to my whim."

"Lady Nicole tells the same tale as ap Dafydd," de Chesney said, and Nicole was so grateful for the castellan's support she could have hugged him. "I still believe we should have left Lady Nicole to the nuns and allowed the bard to go his way."

Apparently the earl and castellan had argued over this earlier, given the tension she now sensed between the two men who usually got on well together.

The earl shook his head. "I cannot ignore the disturbing presence of a Welshman within the walls of the abbey, no matter his intent. Faith, the king's negotiations for Lady Nicole's marriage are in a delicate state. She should not be allowed within ten leagues of any of her kin, most especially the Welsh."

Not any of her kin? Not even her sisters? Sweet mercy, whom was the king planning to marry her off to that necessitated such secrecy? Nicole bit her bottom lip to halt the question de Vere said yesterday he wasn't at liberty to answer, determined to first gain the concessions of foremost importance—her return to the abbey and Rhodri's release.

Before she could utter another plea for mercy, de Chesney leaned toward the earl.

"No harm was done," he said. "Making prisoners of them both makes no sense."

The earl sneered. "Does it not? I cannot be assured the encounter was, as you say, innocent. But even if it was, the situation has changed. I dare not allow Lady Nicole to return to a place where I can no longer feel certain she is safe. As for the bard, if I allow him his freedom, he will but return to Wales and inform Connor ap Maelgwn of the king's intentions, who will in turn inform the prince of Powys. That man will do his utmost to cause mischief with the negotiations, and that is a risk I dare not take."

Now de Chesney shook his head. "The Welsh have known for years that King Stephen intended Lady Nicole for marriage to a Welsh prince, or at least a high-ranking noble. What matter if they know our sovereign now makes good on that intention, so long as they do not know the identity of the groom?"

"Perhaps, but until I receive word from King Stephen to do otherwise, both the lady and bard remain in our custody."

Vexed with the stubborn earl, Nicole pondered over what to do next. Good manners and sound reasoning hadn't moved him, but she doubted he would be budged by tears or a fit of temper, either, ploys she hadn't used since childhood and refused to resort to now.

With an inward sigh, Nicole conceded she had no choice but to await the king's decision, which might not come for several days even if the messengers were swift. For herself, she could abide, being in no immediate danger. But Rhodri was locked in a tower cell, and she wanted him out and on his way back to Wales before anyone discovered that the reason for his visit hadn't been as innocent as they were claiming.

Too, this matter of her marriage wasn't right. The

king should have, at the least, informed her brother-by-marriage, Alberic. Camelen bordered Wales, so Alberic should have some say in the matter of any proposed alliance with a Welsh noble. Neither the earl nor the castellan would be willing to allow her to send a message to her family, but if she could help Rhodri escape he might be willing to carry a message to Camelen before returning to Glenvair.

Her brother's dagger weighing heavy in her boot, Nicole gathered her composure once more.

"My lords, since I am at your mercy in this affair, I ask a boon. I am concerned for Rhodri's welfare, as I am sure he is concerned for mine. Might I be allowed to see him, for a few moments only, to banish our common fears?"

The men looked to each other, silently debating the wisdom of granting the request. De Chesney shrugged a shoulder, as if to say he saw no harm in granting the boon, but left the decision to the earl.

De Vere rubbed at his chin for a moment before relenting. "I shall grant the boon, but do not linger. Walter, pray escort Lady Nicole to the Welshman's cell, and ensure she returns in short order."

"As you say, my lord." The captain of the castle guard waved a hand toward the door. "My lady?"

Nicole curtsied to the earl once more, hoping her delight in his concession didn't show overmuch. "My thanks," she said before scurrying out of the solar.

Short of stature, round of build, Sir Walter had always reminded Nicole of a bear, rather lumbering in his movements and lacking in social graces. All thought of judging him ineffective, however, had ended when she once observed him in the practice yard. As with a bear, one would not wish to come up against Sir Walter without warning or in the dark. And as captain of the guard, he expected his men to match his high standard of physical ability and proficiency with weapons.

Walter said not a word as he arrowed across the bustling bailey on this brilliant afternoon, the air warm and redolent with the odor of the earth beneath her feet and of horses and hay from the stables. Nicole clutched her skirts, hiking them up to avoid soiling the hems of either shift or gown, but not high enough to expose the hilt of the dagger.

Heads turned as they passed, and she noted the surprised looks on those few who recognized her in her new finery. Later, she might visit the gregarious blacksmith and the always amusing stable master.

Too, she must arrange another meeting with the earl. Nicole consoled herself by remembering that Mother Abbess hadn't always won battles during the first foray into the field. Sometimes several skirmishes were necessary before gaining an opponent's surrender. She just had to think of the most effective argument to gain the most advantage.

But for now Nicole shifted her focus to her destination, the northernmost guard tower along the high, thick curtain wall.

While still in the bailey, Nicole heard the sound of a harp and, from the unholy noise, knew the harp's master didn't play it. Her ire pricked, she entered the circular tower, where a rotund guard sat on a stool, his filthy, untalented fingers abusing the silver strings of Rhodri's precious harp.

Furious that the guard dared to toy with the harp, she

snatched the heavy instrument away from the stunned guard.

"A toad could play better!" she snapped. "By whose leave do you possess it? Most certes you have not permission from the harp's owner!"

The guard's eyes widened as he stood, his mouth agape. "Uh, my lady, uh—"

Nicole cradled the harp with one arm, holding it firmly against her hip, and pointed to the floor. "Give me the sack."

The guard obeyed swiftly, and not until she'd covered the harp and pulled the sack's strings securely shut did she notice neither the guard nor Walter had said a word while she completed the task.

She glared at Walter. "Well?"

Mercy, milady, mercy!

Nicole's breath caught at the sound of a male voice intruding into her thoughts. Gor, she had no time now to converse with a spirit but couldn't ignore the man's wrenching plea for mercy.

Who are you?

Thomas Thatcher, milady. I beg your aid!

Sir Walter waved at the stairway that hugged the tower's wall. "Lady Nicole is allowed a short visit with the prisoner. Unlock the door."

The guard's eyes narrowed. "The earl said not to let anyone in there but him or Lord de Chesney."

"The earl will be pleased to know you remembered your orders. He will also be very displeased if you do not allow Lady Nicole entry. Good God, man, would I give you an order you could not obey?"

"Humph. Suppose not, Captain. This way, then."

Her attention divided, Nicole knew she must free Rhodri from the tower before all else.

Hear me, Thomas Thatcher, she ordered the spirit. *I will aid you if I am able, but you must give me a few moments to complete my errand.*

The spirit sighed mournfully. *I have waited more than a man's natural lifetime for one with the gift of hearing to come my way. I can wait a few moments more if I have your oath not to forsake me.*

I will not forsake you.

With the oath given, Nicole nervously followed the guard up the stairway, Walter a few steps behind her. They stopped on the small landing of the tower's middle floor—on the next floor up, she knew, the stairway opened out onto the wall walk where the guards patrolled the curtain wall.

From around his neck the guard removed a necklace of thick string, from which dangled a large iron key. As he unlocked the windowless oak door, Nicole hugged the harp, fearing the condition in which she might find its master.

Chapter Five

The cell was half the size of Nicole's bedchamber, furnished with only a thin pallet that would do little to cushion a body from the hard floor. Dim sunlight from the defensive arrow slit didn't ease the dreariness of the cell, and the stench of a piss bucket nearly gagged her.

Nicole pushed past the guard. Rhodri uncurled his legs and stiffly rose from the pallet. His distrustful glance flickered between the guard and the captain behind her. She took the two steps necessary to put her within arm's length of Rhodri.

Not until she held out his harp did Rhodri look at her fully, beginning with the circlet on her head and moving down the length of her snug gown. His gaze left her as unwarrantedly, improperly tingling as had his inspection of her in the abbey's receiving chamber.

Except this time he didn't smile or offer compliments on her appearance. Now that she actually looked like a princess, he seemed not to appreciate the change.

She tried not to be miffed.

"Ah, my lady," Rhodri said on a hearty sigh. "My

undying thanks for rescuing my harp. The indignity of being held captive 'twas naught when compared to the torture of hearing those sweet strings suffer violent ill-treatment." He held up his hands, palms outward, refusing her offering. "I prefer you hold the harp safe for the nonce."

Understanding his fear that the harp would be taken from him again, Nicole once more hugged the harp to her bosom, wishing she could as easily remove Rhodri from this wretched place as she could the harp. Words of apology didn't seem adequate to compensate for being the cause of his imprisonment. Sweet mercy, if she hadn't asked him to play for Mother Abbess, he'd be on his way home to Glenvair instead of trapped in this wretched cell.

Then Rhodri turned his head to again look past her at the guard and captain. Being closer to him now, she saw the ugly bruise on his jaw that hadn't been there yesterday.

Her heart fell at the evidence of his mistreatment. She placed gentle fingertips on the physical indignity he shouldn't have suffered.

"Oh, Rhodri," she whispered.

He grasped her shoulders, giving them a squeeze as if in reassurance. "'Tis nothing, Nicole. I have suffered worse. Make no more of it."

The last was an order he expected her to obey. Damn it, did he truly expect her to keep silent over the violence done to him for no good reason?

The urge to reach into her boot and give him the dagger, if naught but for his own protection, nearly overcame her good sense. Too many eyes watched. She'd never get the dagger out of her boot secretly, and she might then, too, be imprisoned, if in more comfortable quarters.

To gain Rhodri's freedom she needed to maintain her own, be free to roam the castle grounds to find the least observable way out and devise a plan to liberate Rhodri.

Hoping he could sense her determination, she whispered, "With Archangel Michael as my witness, I will secure your release."

His mouth quirked with humor at her reference to the angel Mother Abbess had mistaken him for. All well and good, except she also sensed Rhodri didn't believe her. Well, let him doubt. She'd prove him wrong! She'd convince the earl to give Rhodri his freedom. She would!

Nicole squared her shoulders, but not sharply enough to displace his hands.

"Are you receiving the food sent to you?"

His attention again fixed on the guard and captain, he said absently, "Enough of it."

"Time to leave, my lady," Walter ordered, his voice gruffer than what she thought it needed to be.

She loathed leaving Rhodri, but heaven help her, she didn't want to linger in the cell any longer than she must, either.

Nicole turned to leave. Rhodri grabbed hold of her around the waist and pulled her hard against him. His other hand clenched her throat, tilting up her chin, almost choking off her breath. Her panic absolute, she wouldn't have moved if she could.

"One cry from either of you," Rhodri told the men in a low, menacing voice, "and I shall break the lady's lovely neck."

Heart pounding, Nicole didn't doubt that with the merest twist of his wrist she'd be dead.

Damn him! She'd been distressed over his welfare, nearly wept over his mistreatment, completely forgetting he was not only a bard but a warrior, as well. A Welsh warrior so intent on escaping a Norman earl that he'd do whatever he must to save his ungrateful hide!

"Release the lady, Welshman!" Walter ordered. "You have no hope of gaining your freedom if she is harmed."

"Whether she is harmed or nay is now your decision. The lady shall serve as both my shield and my writ of safe conduct out of the castle. Step aside, Captain."

Walter huffed and, much to Nicole's dismay, drew his sword.

Her back pressed tightly against Rhodri's unyielding length, she could feel him chuckle, an evil sound.

"Your weapon does you no good, sir, unless you intend to run the lady through, too. Might be rather difficult to explain to the earl why her blood stains your sword."

The captain spat on the floor. "I had heard you Welsh are a barbaric lot! To hide behind a woman is dishonorable."

Walter waved the sword. Rhodri tilted her chin higher, and her high-pitched, pleading gasp for mercy reverberated through the chamber.

"Good sirs, pray make yourselves comfortable on the pallet before the lady can no longer breathe!" Rhodri commanded.

Walter growled his displeasure, but her desperate plea had the desired effect. To Nicole's relief, both Sir Walter and the guard sidled along the wall, obeying Rhodri's order.

Dear God in heaven, was Sir Walter truly allowing Rhodri to escape?

And wasn't Rhodri's release precisely what she'd set out to accomplish this morn?

Not like this, however, with his hands at her throat, threatening her life. Certes, she didn't approve of his method of escape, of being used in such harsh fashion!

Except . . . his scheme seemed to be working. And certes, she might not have arranged his escape, but she'd given him a weapon—herself—that he'd used to his advantage. Resourceful of him, she reluctantly admitted. Later, she would ensure Rhodri fully appreciated her cooperation in his escape, but not until they were safely away from the tower.

Surely, if he managed to get beyond the castle grounds, then through the town and beyond the town's walls—a daunting task—Rhodri would soon be on his way back to Wales.

"Give the lady the key," Rhodri told the guard.

The guard looked to Walter, who grimaced as he nodded. "Do as he says."

Nicole gingerly reached out a hand, not wishing to test Rhodri's grip on her throat. The guard looped the string over her fingers and stepped back.

One slow step at a time, Rhodri guided them out the doorway and kicked the heavy door shut. He released her, and while she drew in a much-needed, ragged deep breath, he snatched the key from her hand and locked the guard and Walter in the cell.

She was rubbing at her throat when Rhodri did the completely unexpected. With a huge smile and no forewarning whatsoever, he grasped her upper arms and kissed her thoroughly, banishing all thought from her head but the glory of his lips on hers, before just as suddenly and dismayingly releasing her.

"Well done, Nicole! Now let us depart this place," he said, still smiling. "'Twill not be long before they raise a cry."

Stunned, she could only stare at the man who'd in one moment threatened to break her neck and in the next kissed her in so sublime a manner her mouth felt ravished and her knees had gone wobbly.

After a mental shake to clear the fog that seemed to have formed in her head, she asked, "Have you a plan?"

"Nay. We are devising as we go." He waved a hand at the stairs. "Swiftly, if you please."

"Not we, you. Hurry! Go!"

He arched an eyebrow. "You wish to remain in Oxford?"

"Nay, I wish to go back to the abbey."

"Surely you do not believe the earl will allow you to! Come, Nicole. You cannot be so naive."

She winced at the accusation, admitting Rhodri was likely correct about the earl. De Vere had already refused to allow her to return to the abbey. He'd be as steadfast if she asked to go home. Likely, after learning how Rhodri escaped, the earl wouldn't allow her out of her bedchamber until the king arranged her marriage.

The prospect of being shut away in the bedchamber for who knew how long churned her insides. Escaping Oxford with Rhodri suddenly seemed the least objectionable choice.

Irritated beyond measure at this turn of events, Nicole descended the stairs as quickly as she could with the bulky harp in her arms, belatedly beginning to wonder at the wisdom of attempting to flee an efficiently guarded castle at midday. Surely they should wait until the cover of darkness before attempting an escape so daring. But because of Rhodri's impulsive action, they'd now be forced to risk an escape with the garrison on alert.

Upon reaching the lower floor, she stopped and shoved the harp at him, giving him no choice but to take it.

"Are you angry with me?" he asked.

She gave him credit for noticing. "For a time I was not sure whether or not you would break my neck."

He shrugged. "I know, but I also knew the moment you realized what I was about and lost your fear."

She had? "When?"

"You leaned into me, so I need not hold you so tightly. I knew then you were willing to cooperate. Are you familiar with the castle grounds?"

She didn't remember willingly leaning into Rhodri. But she supposed she must have if Rhodri had taken the movement as a sign of her cooperation.

"I have been in Oxford Castle often with Mother Abbess, when she came to confer with the prior of St. Frideswide, which we passed on the road coming into town, or with the abbess of Godstow Abbey, which is a few leagues north of Oxford. Mother Abbess was also friendly with Lady Julia, the earl's niece. 'Tis one of Julia's old gowns I wear."

Nicole crossed her arms over her middle, an effort to contain her nervousness. She'd babbled enough nonsense. Rhodri certainly didn't give a fig about Mother Abbess's friends or care whose gown Nicole wore.

He snatched off her circlet and, along with the key to the cell, stuffed her precious possession into the harp's sack, an attempt to make her less noticeable, she supposed.

From the cell above came the sounds of fists pounding

on the door and Sir Walter's muffled shouts hailing his soldiers.

Nicole reached into her boot and drew out the dagger. "I am sure you can use this in more efficient manner than I. You take the dagger and give me the harp so your hands are free."

He raised a questioning eyebrow as they exchanged possessions.

"My brother's," she answered his unspoken question—then remembered her promise to another dead man, Thomas Thatcher.

The poor man must have died in the upstairs cell for his spirit to have lingered in this place. Despite the need for haste, she'd given the spirit her oath not to forsake him.

"Lead on, my lady," Rhodri ordered.

"A moment."

Nicole closed her eyes and silently summoned a spirit, something she hadn't done in many a year, not since she'd learned that most spirits remained tied to this earth for unconscionable reasons. Thomas, however, had seemed a reasonable sort.

Thomas, why do you linger? Why do you not pass on?

My friend, John the cobbler, died by my hand. An unintended mishap, I swear. Still, I cannot seek God's mercy until I have obtained earthly forgiveness.

Heaven help him, Thomas had killed his friend and sought absolution! Which she couldn't give him.

I cannot help you, Thomas. Only a member of the clergy can grant absolution.

I did not die unshriven, but my heart failed before I could express my bitter sorrow to John's family. 'Tis their forgiveness for my misdeed I require before I can seek my peace.

The pounding on the cell's door became louder. Soon one of the guards patrolling the wall walk would hear.

"Nicole?"

She held up a hand to hold off Rhodri a moment longer.

You seek the forgiveness of the cobbler's family?

Aye, and I will be grateful to you for an eternity for this one small service.

Nicole bit her bottom lip in indecision. She knew where in Oxford to find the cobbler's shop. Would she have time to not only pass by the shop but convince a member of the cobbler's family to forgive a death of long ago?

Poor Thomas might linger here for another man's lifetime if she didn't try.

Will you be aware if I am successful?

I will know.

Nicole opened her eyes to find Rhodri staring at her, stricken with alarm.

"Did I harm you?" he asked. "Truly, I tried to be careful not to hamper your breathing."

She couldn't very well tell Rhodri she'd been speaking silently to a man long dead. Rhodri would be shocked, and they didn't have time for explanations that he probably wouldn't believe anyway.

"I am fine. We can go now."

∾

Rhodri wasn't accustomed to following a woman's lead, especially a woman who seemed so distracted. Still, Nicole wound her way through the dusty, crowded bailey, cradling his harp, staying as close to the wall as possible, her chin high and body erect. No one observing her would question her absolute right to pass through the bailey.

Nor, thank the Fates, was anyone taking an inordinate interest in the man at her side, too engrossed in their own purposes to pay others much heed. While he doubted many of the castle folk would recognize him, he longed for the concealment of his hooded cloak, which, along with his horse, sword, and money pouch, he hadn't seen since yester noon.

Resigned to the loss of his belongings, Rhodri gave thanks for the one possession they'd allowed him to keep with him, his harp. Which he'd feared he might lose, too, until Nicole rescued it from the tower's guard.

And he'd repaid her by threatening to break her neck. With a wince, he admitted his hastily devised plan for escape had been roughly executed and smacked of dishonor.

Still, the scheme had worked, and he didn't give a damn about what the captain thought of his methods. However, Nicole was probably due an apology for his uncouth manner, especially for the celebratory kiss he shouldn't have stolen.

Nicole hadn't seemed to mind his forwardness overmuch. He'd startled her as much with the kiss as when he'd grabbed her in the cell. The kiss had been quick but long enough for him to enjoy the sweet taste of her mouth. Her surprise hadn't been so acute to prevent her from kissing him back.

While he didn't know precisely what had ailed her so intensely in the tower, she now seemed to have recovered from both the ailment and the kiss.

Determined to put both disturbing events out of mind

until he and Nicole were well out of danger of capture, Rhodri cautiously glanced up at the wall walk, noting the garrison hadn't yet been alerted to his escape. However, someone would soon hear the captain's shouts and the soldiers would swarm the wall walk and bailey.

"Do we merely walk through the gatehouse and over the drawbridge?" Nicole asked, her uncertain tone at odds with her confident stride. "Escaping cannot be that simple."

He could see the gatehouse now, and the throng of people passing through, some leading oxen-yoked carts.

"'Tis possible. Until the garrison is alerted to our flight from the tower, they will not be looking for us. If we edge through alongside one of those carts, the guards might not notice us at all."

"What if they stop us?"

He briefly considered drawing from his boot the dagger Nicole had given him. A fine, solid weapon she'd claimed once belonged to her brother, William. One had to wonder why she possessed the dagger at all. 'Twas hardly the type of thing a woman needed in an abbey.

He was glad to have the weapon at hand, but best to leave it be, for the nonce. No sense drawing attention by carrying the blade openly.

"The guards do not seem to be stopping anyone. If we give them no reason to do otherwise, they should leave us be. How many gates in the city?"

"Seven. Two to the south, one east—"

"Lady Nicole!" hailed a female voice.

Nicole slowed and began to turn her head. Rhodri put a hand on her back to keep her moving.

"Do not stop."

"But Lucy—"

"There, the cart stacked with sacks of grain. Get beside it."

"Lucy may follow me."

In the shadow of the stack of grain sacks, Rhodri slowed to keep beside the cart, hoping that whoever Lucy was she had the sense to believe Nicole hadn't heard her. The rumbling cart churned up dust, the grit invading his nose and eyes, but not so badly that he couldn't see and smell freedom but a few steps ahead.

From the wall walk above came the sound of men running. All hope of uneventful passage through the gatehouse fled. His heartbeat rising in rhythm with the increasing danger of capture, Rhodri grabbed the harp's sack from Nicole and slung it over his shoulder.

"The garrison has been alerted. If we do not pass over the drawbridge quickly, they will be on us." He reached for her hand, which she immediately took. "We must run. Stay close."

"Lord have mercy," she muttered. "I knew we should have waited until nightfall."

Rhodri saw no sense in arguing. He took advantage of a narrow opening in the throng to break into a long stride, pulling Nicole behind him. They passed under the gatehouse to a shower of shouts to halt. The guards' cries grew more insistent when Rhodri's boots hit the plank bridge.

"Left!" Nicole ordered.

Deciding she must know where she was going, and in no position to question her now, Rhodri turned left at the end of the drawbridge, running as fast as he could without overly straining Nicole's shorter stride.

He recognized the broad street that ran east and west through town as one he'd been on yester noon. Naturally, they drew a few stares from the townspeople, but Rhodri chose to ignore discretion in favor of speed.

They'd gone no farther than a few blocks when Nicole again ordered him to turn left, onto another broad street. He almost hesitated, knowing that if they turned right, they'd come to the southern gate through which they'd entered Oxford. But again he obeyed, trusting she had a plan in mind.

Not until a bit farther on, when she tugged him onto a narrow lane, did he begin to question her intent. Before he could ask where she was headed, she slowed, nearly jerking him off balance.

Nicole pulled her hand from his.

"There, the cobbler's shop," she said, moments before she ducked through the shop's door.

What the devil was Nicole about? They didn't have time to have a sole mended or heel repaired! He entered the shop after her to hear her address the young man seated on a stool, a boot with the heel up between his knees, an upraised hammer in his hand.

"Are you descended of John the cobbler?" she asked.

From a mere step inside the doorway, Rhodri glanced back down the lane, looking for signs of a patrol.

"I am," the man answered, setting aside the boot and hammer. "John was my grandsire, may he rest in peace."

"Was your grandsire a forgiving man?" Nicole asked, much to Rhodri's confusion.

The cobbler's brow furrowed. "He was a God-fearing man. Why do you wish to know?"

Precisely Rhodri's question, too!

Nicole shot Rhodri a disturbingly anxious look before she blurted out, "Had your grandsire lived, would he have been able to find the mercy in his heart to forgive Thomas Thatcher his unfortunate misjudgment and allow Thomas's soul to rest in peace? Can you?"

The cobbler's mouth twisted in disgust. "Forgive the friend turned murderer? I hope he suffers the fires of hell!"

"Thomas meant to express his deep sorrow over what happened, but he died before given the chance. I assure you he is eternally sorry for the unintentional wrong done your grandsire and your family. Pray, sir, is there no mercy in your heart?"

"Hrumph. You would receive a better hearing from my mother. She forgave her father's murderer—"

"She did? Why, that was most kind of her! Pray thank her for her understanding."

The poor cobbler looked as dumbfounded as Rhodri felt.

Nicole had acted strangely in the tower, and now . . . he shouldn't have held her throat so tightly, tilted her chin so high. Surely he'd deprived her of enough air that it had affected her wits. God forgive him, what had he done to her?

The cobbler's eyes narrowed. "Who are you, milady? Why your concern over my family and matters best left in the past?"

Rhodri understood none of this, but he'd heard enough. He lunged for Nicole's hand and hauled her out of the shop.

She was smiling. "In which direction do you wish to leave Oxford?"

Rhodri took a deep breath, guilt over the instability of

Nicole's mind weighing heavy on his soul, unsure if he could trust her mind at all.

"The nearest gate will do."

She pointed northward. "That church spire is St. Michael's-at-North Gate."

Rhodri squeezed Nicole's hand. "You are sure?"

"Certes. Should we not hurry?"

He feared they'd stopped too long for speed to do them any good. Surely by now the castle garrison had altered the guards at the city gates, which might explain why no patrol had come down the lane. The soldiers would ensure the outer gates secured before beginning a search in the town.

Still, he set a quick pace, winding through the unfamiliar, narrow lanes. Both he and Nicole breathed rapidly before he stopped within sight of North Gate. As he'd feared, the guards were many and halting everyone who wished to pass through, going so far as to search the carts.

Were he alone, he'd push through the crowd and take his chances with the guards. But he wasn't alone, and he wasn't about to risk either Nicole's safety or chance them being parted.

"I fear we must abide for a time," he told Nicole, glancing around for suitable shelter. Hell, any unoccupied building would do for the nonce while he came up with a less risky plan to escape Oxford.

"When King Stephen burned the city several years ago," she said, "the area around St. Ebbe's suffered the worst damage. Recent flooding has taken a toll, too. Most of the buildings left standing are in ruins and for the most part abandoned. We might find a place there to hide."

Nicole seemed so reasonable now, when only a short time ago she'd been speaking nonsense. Perhaps her ailment wasn't permanent. Maybe he hadn't done her irreparable harm. A few hours' rest might do her good.

Besides, they truly had no choice but to hide if they were to avoid capture. Since he didn't have the vaguest notion of St. Ebbe's location, once again he must trust Nicole to take the lead.

With too many misgivings to contemplate, he reluctantly said, "Lead on, my lady."

Chapter Six

Sheltered in a burned-out, abandoned building in an almost equally deserted area of Oxford, Nicole used a stick to draw a large oval in the dirt floor—a rough map of the high, thick stone walls that fortified the town.

"'Tis simple, really." She drew an X with a circle around it on the far west end. "This is the castle. The town has two main roads. One runs through the middle of town from the castle to the east gate. The other cuts the town in half north and south. At the end of those streets are the larger, most-used gates. The smaller gates are here."

Nicole drew several more X's, one of them in the southwest corner of Oxford, not far from where she and Rhodri took shelter.

"The bridges?" he asked.

Outside of the town's walls, she drew a long, winding line—the river Thames—and marked, to the best of her memory, the bridges' locations.

She glanced up at Rhodri, who loomed over where she'd hunched down, his arms crossed, frowning mightily.

He'd been frowning since leaving the cobbler's shop.

Understandable, she supposed. She'd cost them time, and Rhodri certainly didn't approve of what she'd done. Nor did he understand why she'd done it.

She should probably explain the importance of her errand on Thomas's behalf, but first they must decide how to get beyond the city gates. If they didn't escape Oxford, naught else mattered.

"Will they set guards on the bridges?" she asked.

"Not likely. They will hope to catch us at one of the gates. Once the gates close for the night, they may begin searching the town."

Nightfall wouldn't come for several hours yet. The small building Rhodri had chosen as a hiding place, with its gaping holes in the walls and blackened support beams, probably wouldn't fall down in the next few hours. Still, she would prefer not to remain in this part of town any longer than she must.

Among the charred and rotting shells of former dwellings lurked many of the town's disreputable folk, the beggars and brigands who would as soon rob you of your boots than earn an honest wage to pay for them.

Nicole dropped the stick in the dirt before rising and dusting her hands together. "Which gate do you think best?"

"I wish I knew which gate was the least guarded."

She had no notion of how many guards were posted at any of the gates.

"Would our chances of getting through be better at a gate with fewer guards, or at one with more people passing through so the guards' attention is more divided?"

"Truth to tell, both would give us a better chance to slip through. However, I would not wager a halfpenny that we would be so fortunate."

Not that either of them had a halfpenny to wager. In their haste, they'd left most of their belongings behind, and right now Nicole would give most anything—except capture—to retrieve a few of those possessions.

"I wish we had our cloaks. They would afford us a measure of protection."

"How so?"

"As a disguise, if only to cover my hair and gown."

"Aye, that gown is rather noticeable, is it not? 'Twould be best if you still wore the habit."

Heretofore, Rhodri had given no indication he'd noticed her change of garb, or whether or not he liked the difference in her appearance.

Unwarrantedly peeved at his lack of appreciation, Nicole was forced to agree with his assessment. In a habit she would be far less noticeable.

"Mayhap we could disguise ourselves in some way."

"With what?"

She tossed her hands in the air. "I do not know, but at least I am trying to find a solution to our dilemma! If you have one, pray share it with me!"

"Not as yet."

Which she took to mean he hadn't thought of a good plan, either, and so had naught to share. Infuriating man.

Disgruntled, Nicole glanced around for a length of wall she deemed solid enough to lean against, plopped down in the dirt, and shifted to get comfortable, thankful the building had burned so long ago that it didn't stink of smoke. A small thing to be thankful for—and that apparently no spirits lingered in this place. The very last thing she wanted to deal with was another spirit.

She wrapped her arms around her upraised knees,

wishing she could have another talk with Thomas, but she dared not return to the tower to find out if he'd passed on or not. All she could do was hope he knew the cobbler's mother had forgiven him and that the woman's forgiveness was enough to allow Thomas to finally rest in peace.

"Nicole? Are you all right?"

The concern in Rhodri's voice was as genuine as before. This was the second time today he'd asked that particular question. The first time she'd assured him nothing was wrong.

Well, devil take it! This time he might as well hear the true answer to his question!

"I shall hereafter count today among the worst days of my life, and it is not over. We may yet be captured and hauled before the earl, who will not allow our escape to go unpunished. You, he will likely hang. Me, he will confine to my bedchamber until the king decides what to do with me, and I shudder to think of how long that might be! Does that answer your question?"

Rhodri strode over to the door and glanced up and down the eerily quiet street. She'd known this part of town hadn't seen much improvement since its burning and that honest folk rarely ventured near. She hadn't known that even the birds and mice tended to shun the area.

Apparently satisfied they were safe for the nonce, Rhodri quit the doorway to ease down beside her and lean against *her* wall, stretching out his long legs, crossing them at the ankles.

'Twas both disconcerting and comforting to have him so near, especially since he appeared to be in an uglier mood than she.

"Had you not pulled us into the cobbler's shop," he grumbled, "we might have reached a gate before the guards were alerted."

She couldn't refute the truth of his accusation. But she'd not had the heart to forsake Thomas.

"I had no choice."

He raised an eyebrow, expecting further explanation.

Few living beings knew of her ability to hear the dead. Only her sisters—who both possessed unusual talents of their own—and their husbands. The Easter after Nicole had been sent to Bledloe Abbey, Alberic had brought Gwendolyn to visit. Distress at her brother's reaction—again battering at her to kill Alberic—had forced Nicole to reveal her ability to hear the dead.

Gwendolyn had informed Emma and Darian.

Nicole hadn't told anyone at the abbey, for fear of being scorned for possessing an admittedly unnatural ability.

Whether Rhodri believed her or not truly didn't matter. He could think as he wished, accept or scoff. She heard what she heard, and nothing he could do or say could change that.

"I possess the ability to hear the dead whose spirits are bound to this earth, who for one reason or another cannot pass on to eternity. In the tower, the spirit of Thomas Thatcher begged my help in his quest for forgiveness, and I could not leave Oxford without giving it."

Rhodri's eyebrow rose higher, as did his voice. "You risked our lives because you thought you heard some spirit?"

His ire and disbelief stung more than it should. So why did she find herself telling Rhodri the whole of Thomas's tale of remorse over John the cobbler's death and his quest for forgiveness?

Through the telling, Rhodri didn't blink an eyelash, simply stared at her as though seeking to judge her sanity.

So when he had the whole of it, she asked, "If Thomas's spirit had pleaded mercy from you, would you have denied him knowing he might linger yet another lifetime in that wretched tower, losing hope of ever passing on?"

He hesitated but a moment before stating firmly, "Nicole, dead is dead. The soul goes to heaven or hell or purgatory and does not roam the earth."

Little he knew!

"Truly? Did you happen to note the cobbler knew who I was talking about, even though both his grandsire and Thomas have been dead for many a year! How would I know about either man, or how both had died, if Thomas had not spoken to me?"

Rhodri shrugged a shoulder. "Perhaps you overheard the tale long ago, and being in the tower where Thomas died reminded you of it, and you thought you heard—"

"If you are about to suggest that my wits have fled, you had best hold your tongue!" Her outburst took her by surprise. Perhaps she cared what Rhodri believed more than she ought. Forcing her ire to calm, she continued.

"This is not the first time I have answered a spirit's plea for help. With God as my witness, I have told you true why I spoke with the cobbler. Believe as you will, but do not *dare* say I risked our safety on a fanciful whim. Each of us has a purpose in life, and I believe helping spirits is mine."

He sat quietly for several moments, his expression reflective. "For how long have you believed—beg pardon—have you heard spirits?"

Nicole wasn't sure if he made an honest attempt to

understand or merely humored her. Still, his tone was less reproving, so she answered.

"Since childhood. I was all of ten when my father and brother died. William was the first spirit to speak to me."

"William? For what reason?"

Nicole inwardly cringed at the memory of how she'd tried to murder her now beloved brother-by-marriage, goaded unmercifully by a dead brother who desired revenge.

"Have you heard the story of my brother's death at Wallingford?" At Rhodri's nod, she continued. "William could not accept that he died so young, and he wanted revenge against Alberic for happening to be the man holding the sword that took his life. My brother begged me to kill Alberic, and in my youth and grief, I tried to do as he bade. To my everlasting relief, Alberic easily swept the dagger from my hand before I could do him an injury."

Rhodri glanced down at the weapon in his boot. "This dagger?"

"Nay. That dagger now hangs in the keep's great hall, among the weapons of other of Camelen's lords. I took this one to the abbey with me as a keepsake, as a reminder of my brother. It has since become a reminder to never aid a spirit who wishes to do harm to the living."

"These . . . spirits. They seek you out, begging your favor?"

"They speak to anyone within hailing distance of wherever the spirit is bound to earth, which is usually the place where they died or are buried. I know of no others but me who can hear them, so I try to help those I can."

Except William. Him she couldn't help, because he wouldn't let her.

Nor did she understand why she could hear him at the abbey. William had died in battle near Wallingford Castle, several leagues south of Oxford, and been buried at Camelen, in Shropshire, nigh on the Welsh border. Perhaps it was because he'd been the first spirit she'd heard— and she'd often wondered if William hadn't forced upon her the ability to hear spirits—or because during his life she'd so adored her brother with all of her being that his voice could reach her no matter where she might be.

"If what you say is true, and beg pardon, Nicole, but I am not convinced you hear spirits, then you did Thomas a great service. May he now rest in peace."

Rhodri's concession wasn't as complete as it could be, but she admitted that what she'd told him might be difficult for anyone to believe. At least his anger for pulling him into the cobbler shop had ebbed.

For as elated as she'd been at her success when coming out of the cobbler's shop, now doubts began to prick at her conscience.

"Was it enough, do you think, that John's daughter had forgiven Thomas? The grandson certainly wasn't in a forgiving mood. I must wonder if the grandson's opinion matters, since his grandsire must have died long before his birth." She sighed. "Always before I have known if a spirit's bonds were broken and it passed on. With Thomas I am not sure."

Rhodri's eyes narrowed. "We are not returning to the tower."

"Nay, that would be foolhardy."

His expression said he still considered her pulling him into the cobbler's shop foolhardy, but she was grateful he didn't voice the opinion. He leaned his head back against the wall, and a soft smile touched the lips she'd recently discovered were both warm and enticing.

"I remember a time, princess, when you would not have taken a step out of your way to show anyone a kindness."

Nicole groaned, knowing precisely when she'd been unkind to Rhodri. "Is it your intention to *now* take me to task for the horrible thing I did as a child?"

His smile widened. "I merely state that I believe you may have changed—somewhat—since our last encounter."

"You mean to say you no longer believe I am so pampered I am unable to strap on my own sandals?"

"'Twas ungracious of me to have said so."

"'Twas mean of William to repeat your words to me. Still, I should not have attacked you."

Kicking Rhodri in the shin had been bad enough, but when her sandal-shod foot slipped, sending her sprawling in the mud and ruining her best tunic, she'd shunned his efforts to help her up, crying and calling him a horrid beast.

Naturally, her unleashed rage had drawn a crowd, including her uncle Connor, and she'd done nothing to soften the reprimand Rhodri so stoically accepted for the offense of pushing a little girl into the mud. An offense he hadn't committed. Connor had denied Rhodri his harp and the privileges of the hall for an entire summer, further assigning the lad to muck out the stables for the duration of the punishment.

"Why did you not tell Connor what truly happened, that 'twas all my fault?"

Rhodri shrugged a shoulder. "Given your upset, I did not think Connor would believe me. Besides, you were the princess and I was nothing. Best to take the punishment and be done with it."

Said as though he'd found it to his advantage to accept the reprimand rather than accuse an overindulged girl of five for tossing a fit and muddying her own tunic.

"Never did it occur to me to beg your pardon until I was older and realized I truly ought to make amends. I never did, so I will offer my apology now. I also ask your forgiveness for getting us into this mess. Had I sent you on your way when I ought have, you would not have been tossed into that dreadful tower." She waved a hand at the crumpled building in which they took shelter. "And we would not be sitting here wondering when the guards will search this area of town."

Without comment, Rhodri rose and again eased his head out the doorway, apparently with the same result as before, seeing no one and hearing nothing to alarm him.

"This is not all your fault, Nicole. On the road from the abbey to Oxford, twice I could have escaped."

"Why did you not?"

"Connor sent me to fetch you, and I could hardly allow the earl to shut you up behind castle walls without my being nearby. So I stayed, though I would have preferred a pallet in the hall, to which I am accustomed when in noble houses, than to being locked in the tower."

"So now we are merely trapped in the town." She rubbed her arms, telling herself the sudden chill came from the breeze allowed in by the cracks in the walls, not from a jolt of fear. "We should not tarry here overlong. We need a plan to get past the gate before the guards close it for the night."

"I am thinking on it, but you are right, we should try to

escape before we fall prey to less gentle talons than those of the guards."

Rhodri hovered near the doorway, keeping watch, his thoughts bouncing between how to escape the town and what Nicole had told him about hearing spirits.

Aware of many tales of ghosts and dragons, and various other strange sightings and beings, but never having seen or heard them for himself, he believed them all stuff of myth and legend.

There were no dragons left to be slain. Ghosts didn't exist.

Still, Nicole seemed so sure she'd heard the voice of a dead man speak to her in the tower. Though he couldn't fully explain how she'd known so much about John and Thomas, he reasoned there must be an explanation other than the one she'd given him.

If she'd truly heard a spirit, 'twould explain her odd behavior in the tower. He wanted to believe her, if only for the relief of knowing he hadn't hurt her overmuch with his ill use of her throat. Damn hard to accept her story as true, though.

He shifted his stance and glanced up at the sky. Only a few hours of daylight remained. Nicole was right about not spending the night in this place. Though the building was sound enough to provide shelter, he didn't trust the local ruffians to mind their own business. The few he'd seen on the street didn't inspire the least sense of safety.

The way to best safeguard Nicole from both the ruffians and the earl was to leave Oxford.

But how to get past the guards at the gates? Without his horse and sword, he couldn't make a fast, bold run at them. Without coin, he couldn't bribe the guards. Without their cloaks, they couldn't hope to sneak through.

A cloak to cover Nicole would be more than welcome. She looked damn fine in her blue gown, the fabric soft and so snug it hugged every lovely curve. Those curves would tempt a eunuch, and he was a healthy male, possessed of all the normal, base urges of his sex. He couldn't help but be aware of Nicole's bountiful charms—breasts large enough to fill a man's hands, a slender waist, and a nicely rounded bottom.

Did she realize how temptingly her bottom swayed as she walked? The gentle yet provocative swish from one side to the other made it impossible to ignore that the adorable child had become a beautiful woman.

Even now, as she sat on the dirt floor, leaning back on one of the building's few sturdy planks, her pert chin tilted upward to expose the throat he was glad he hadn't bruised, the temptation of the feast beneath the gown beckoned.

He quickly squashed the pangs of a hunger having naught to do with food, forcing his attention back to facing the next obstacle on their journey to Wales.

With other options too dangerous to consider, they must resort to guile. Except the one strategy he thought might work involved using Nicole in a ruse that could prove disastrous if it failed.

At least, disastrous for him. Nicole was right. The earl could simply hang him to be rid of him.

Should the worst happen, Nicole wouldn't suffer unduly. From the moment he'd decided to use her in his escape from the tower, he'd taken care to make it appear as though Nicole were being forced to accompany him. The earl would hold her gently, if well guarded, until the king finished his negotiations and married her off to a Welsh noble.

Connor planned to do the same with Nicole once she was within his grasp. But at least Connor would marry her to someone who supported the unity of Wales, not someone who supported the rule of England's king.

Did Nicole have any notion of the reason for Connor's offer? He didn't think so, and he didn't believe it a good time to mention it now.

"Rhodri, I want to go back to the abbey. I should never have left. Not with you or the earl."

So that's what she'd been mulling over all this while. Most definitely not a good time to give her more reason not to go to Wales. Better to point out the advantages.

"Once the earl is aware you have passed beyond the town's gates, the abbey will be among the first places he will search, and you would again become his guest in Oxford Castle."

The twist of her lips affirmed her distaste for being the earl's guest.

"But as you say, this gown makes me conspicuous. At the abbey, I could exchange it for a habit, and perhaps Sister Claire would provide us with cloaks."

"Then the earl could accuse Sister Claire of aiding us. If the abbey is beholden to the earl for support, then we should not put the nuns and abbey at risk of reprisal."

Her next suggestion came swiftly and more firmly. "Then take me home to Camelen. Alberic will find a way to shelter me. He might even provide you with the means to return to Wales."

Taking her home was an even worse idea.

"Sheltering you and aiding me would set Alberic in opposition to the earl of Oxford and the king. Why cause Alberic trouble if there is no need?"

"Will he not have problems anyway if I hie off to Wales?"

"A bit, perhaps, but no one can accuse him of defiance if he can honestly declare he had no part in the matter. Nicole, so far as anyone at the castle can attest, I forced you to leave with me." The only resident of Oxford who might question it would be the cobbler, but Rhodri doubted the earl would call upon every citizen of the town for interrogation, so the earl might never learn of that one digression.

"As long as the earl believes you were forced to leave with me, neither Sister Claire nor your sisters and their families are in danger of reprisal for my actions."

Her lush mouth thinned, her eyes tinged with sadness as she realized he'd left her with the one option she likely considered the least harmful to those she cared for. "So we go to Wales."

The resignation set hard on her and, moved by the upheaval he'd wrought in her life, Rhodri was on the edge of apologizing when movement in the corner of the building caught his attention.

Through one of the gaps in the walls appeared a slow-moving hand—male, large, and dirty—reaching for the sack holding Rhodri's harp and Nicole's circlet.

Furious at the possessor of the hand for his audacity, Rhodri silently sprinted toward the sack and stomped hard on the thief's greedy fingers, pinning them to the earth.

Their owner yelped, startling Nicole into rising to her feet.

Stupid thief! The gap wasn't big enough to pull the sack through, but that hadn't stopped the villain from trying.

Rhodri lifted his foot. The thief's arm immediately retreated through the gap in the wall, and judging by the sounds coming from outside, he swiftly sped down the lane.

Rhodri grabbed the sack. "We need to leave Oxford. Now."

Nicole rubbed at her arms. "Have you a plan?"

He did, and though he disliked once again exposing Nicole to danger, he knew they must press forward or become victims of the denizens of the area or, worse, be captured.

"I do. Think you can carry out a deception?"

Nicole glanced upward at the charred beams, then at the now menacing gap in the corner. "What do you want me to do?"

Chapter Seven

Rhodri squinted through a gap in the wall of yet another burned-out, abandoned building, one with a decent if not complete view of Little Gate.

"How many guards?" Nicole asked.

"Six on the ground. One more up on the wall walk." He shifted to get a better view of the area in front of the gate. "No other people around."

'Twas a better situation than he'd hoped for. Granted, most people would leave town through the larger gates, on the roads that led into the countryside. He'd feared some might decide to use the smaller gates to avoid the crowding at the larger ones. Apparently, that hadn't happened yet.

"The gate is open?"

"Aye."

Again as he'd expected. Towns closed their gates during daylight only to keep out an invading army, not to prevent a person or two from leaving.

"Have you heard the tale of how Empress Maud escaped Oxford?" she asked. "We should wait until nightfall and try something similar."

Rhodri came away from the wall.

The tale of Maud's escape was legend throughout the kingdom, and impossible for them to emulate.

"We have no bed linens to tie together, and even if we could find a rope long enough, I doubt the guards on the wall walk would stand aside while we tossed it over the wall and slid down. Nicole, this is truly the only way for us to escape Oxford."

Nicole didn't look convinced, and Rhodri felt as if he faced a youth about to engage in first battle. Uncertainty marred her doe-brown eyes. Her lips were pressed together tightly, a further sign of worry. For a moment, he considered kissing those lips to ease their tenseness.

He put a finger under her chin and gently nudged it upward.

Her skin was so soft and smooth, so touchable. Other places on Nicole's body would be just as soft. Intrigued by the thought of touching those other places, he almost forgot his purpose for raising her chin.

"You know what to tell the guards. Leave the rest to me. We will be out the gate and over the bridge in a trice. You can do this, Nicole. I have every confidence in your ability to play the ill-used princess."

She huffed. "'Tis not my part I worry over, but yours. You have no proper weapon."

Rhodri was torn between being flattered that Nicole worried for his safety, and chagrined that she doubted his skill as a warrior.

He picked up the stout, almost sword-length piece of wood he'd found among the ruins and slashed it through the air to again test the weight and balance. Not perfect, but it would serve the purpose.

"Between this and the dagger, I am armed well enough. Are you ready?"

She still looked dubious, but she picked up the harp's sack and clutched it to her lovely bosom. "You have a care. I will meet you on the other side of the gate."

With that welcome bit of confidence in their plan, Nicole strode out the door. Rhodri scurried back to the gap in the wall to watch her run toward the gate, the end of her braid bouncing rhythmically against her beautifully shaped rump.

Rhodri hated using Nicole this way but knew no harm would come to her if the plan failed. 'Twould be his neck in a noose if he'd not judged the reactions of the guards rightly.

As expected, every guard watched in wide-eyed wonder as the beautiful woman ran toward them, screeching at them to chase after the cur of a bard who'd audaciously kidnapped her from the tower.

Nicole didn't bother to hide her nervousness from the guards. She was supposed to be afraid. The guards just needn't be made aware of what she feared.

She had made her plea for succor to the guard who'd stepped forward, seeming to be in charge. Now she pointed down the road behind her.

"I broke free of him in a building two streets down and around the corner!" she informed her would-be savior. "If you hurry, you can capture the beast!"

As she hoped—or feared, she still had yet to decide— the guard drew his sword from his belt. She need not have worried if several guards would give chase. They all knew a reward would be forthcoming from *someone* for whoever captured the Welshman. Soon four of the seven guards were following her directions, quickly passing by the building where Rhodri hid.

"Milady," said the taller of remaining guards, "they will have the cur soon. Shall I take ye to the castle? The earl will be right glad to have ye back."

Nicole forced a grateful smile. "Oh, I should like that above all else, but my legs are about to fold. Might I rest first, there, in the shade?"

She gave him no time to object, hurrying over to the stone arch and settling beneath it.

The guard rubbed at his beard, not quite knowing what to do with her. Which suited her fine.

"Edgar, stay with the lady," he told the other guard, who carried a long pike, the sharp iron end a cause for further concern. "I will inform those at the castle of what goes on."

Edgar nodded his assent and came to stand beside her while the other guard sprinted off to give a report.

Only two guards left. The one hovering over her and the other up on the wall walk. Better odds for Rhodri. Nicole blew out a relieved breath, her part done. So . . . where the devil was—

"Holy hell!" Edgar spat out. "Get yer ass down here, Odell! Here he be! You stay well back, milady, you hear?"

Nicole didn't need the command to stay out of range of flying weapons. Any fool knew better. Still, neither could she back away, awed by the sight of Rhodri racing toward the gate.

He was glorious, his stride long and perfectly balanced, his arms pumping in natural rhythm with each footfall. The ominous, intimidating look on his face frightened her silly. A glance at Edgar told her he didn't like the looks of the Welshman bearing down on him, either.

Edgar raised his pike, swallowed hard, and set his heels.

Nicole slid along the ground to the far side of the archway, covered her face with her hands, and awaited the collision.

Wood struck wood in a sharp clap of thunder. Again. And again. Wood cracked and splintered. A man grunted.

Nicole peeked through her fingers. The pike had broken in two, and the guard lay sprawled facedown on the ground.

Rhodri spun to face the second guard, who'd reached the bottom of the stairs. This guard possessed a sword. Rhodri grasped his board with both hands and used it as a stave to fend off two blows. The guard circled to find a better vantage point; Rhodri didn't yield one.

The guard feinted left, then swiftly circled the sword to come at Rhodri's right. Rhodri wasn't fooled, bringing the board up to block the swinging sword at an angle. The blade bit deep into the board. With a mighty heave, Rhodri sent the board and sword flying, then ducked low and threw a fist toward the guard's jaw.

Nicole was sure she heard bone crunch before the guard went down in a heap and didn't again move.

Not until she stood up did she realize she was shaking, but not with fear. The violence had been alarming, but also exciting. Elation that Rhodri had won the day overcame her good sense.

He'd no more than yanked the sword from the board when she hit him breast to chest and tossed her arms around his neck.

"Well done, Rhodri!" she exclaimed, just before she kissed him.

He smelled of sweat and tasted of victory. His free arm came around her and pulled her up onto her tiptoes, saving her from melting into a puddle at his feet.

Heat flowed through her, banishing the delicious tingling with molten desire for more than a kiss.

She mewed a protest when he set her back down on her feet.

"The other guards will return soon," he said, and Nicole took some satisfaction in his not-so-steady voice. "We must go."

She said nothing while he tucked the sword under his belt, fetched the harp's sack, and slung it over a shoulder. Not until then did she realize Rhodri had never drawn the dagger from his boot. He had vanquished two armed soldiers with only a board as his weapon.

Rhodri held out his hand; Nicole slipped her small hand into his large, capable one. Together they ran for the bridge over the Thames, intent on reaching the woodland beyond.

∽

Little Gate came into view, and Aubrey de Vere's heart fell at the sight of two guards sprawled on the ground, a gaunt man in tattered clothing tugging at one of the guards' boots!

Vexed, he broke into a run, shouting obscenities at

the thief, who quickly decided he didn't need new boots, after all. The thief sped off into the streets of Oxford's most notorious area, several of de Chesney's men hot on his tail.

De Vere bent over the first of the fallen guards, who breathed but couldn't be awakened. A second guard, supported by de Chesney and another of his men, was now sitting up, his fingers gingerly probing his nose and mouth and coming away bloody.

To his distress, de Vere saw no sign of Lady Nicole or Rhodri ap Dafydd.

The earl bent down and snatched up the wooden remains of a pike. The sharp, pointed end and two hand-spans of shaft lay a few feet away. A quick check of the guards' scabbards revealed that Rhodri ap Dafydd had absconded with a sword.

De Vere stepped to the outer edge of Little Gate's stone arch. From here one could see the nearest bridge over the Thames and the countryside beyond. His anger rose upon seeing no hint of a tall Welshman or a lady in a light blue gown. The pair must have already entered the woodland, where they would be damn hard to find.

De Chesney's men returned, having caught the thief who'd tried to steal the guard's boots. One of the men grabbed the thief by the scruff of the neck and pushed him down to his knees in front of the earl.

"This one says he knows somewhat of the Welshman, my lord."

De Vere tapped the now useless shaft of wood against his palm, staring down at the wide-eyed thief with the misshapen hand, two of the fingers obviously broken.

"Does he?"

The thief nodded, now all atremble, as well he should be. "I 'eard 'im and the lady talkin'. Didn't 'ear all they said, but seemed to me the lady was wont to go to some-place name of Camelen. The Welshman, 'e weren't havin' none of it, sayin' they needed to go to Wales. 'At's all I know, milord, I swear."

'Twas no less than de Vere might have guessed. Natu-rally, Nicole had probably first asked to be returned to the castle and, when refused, begged to be taken to the bosom of her family, as any young woman would. Her appeals had fallen on deaf ears.

From the moment he'd seen the Welshman at the ab-bey, de Vere had known something was amiss. Rhodri ap Dafydd might well have brought greetings from Nicole's Welsh uncle, but more, he'd planned to remove Nicole to Wales.

De Vere flung the pike's shaft away, knowing he couldn't go after the Welshman himself. Not even de Chesney knew the messenger he waited for was actually Theobald, Archbishop of Canterbury, the man chosen to negotiate a peace between King Stephen and Duke Henry. Escorting the bishop to Nottingham to meet with Duke Henry took precedence over chasing after ap Dafydd and Lady Nicole.

'Twasn't often an earl felt powerless against so incon-sequential an enemy as a bard, and Aubrey de Vere didn't like the feeling.

"Take the thief to the castle and rid him of the hand that would have stolen a soldier's boots." Ignoring the thief's panicked pleas for mercy, de Vere turned to de Chesney. "They must be found. If they are indeed headed for Wales, they are likely in the woodland beyond. I want patrols out there now, looking under every bush if needs be."

From Oxford's multitude of abbeys and churches, the bells called the clergy to the midafternoon office of *none*. The earl of Oxford strode back to the castle, praying the Welshman was found before the archbishop arrived so he could personally slip a noose around Rhodri ap Dafydd's neck.

Nicole was out of breath, low on vigor, and devoid of patience when Rhodri finally allowed her to take what he warned would be a short rest.

She knew patrols would soon be searching the countryside, and Rhodri's decision to keep to the concealment of the forest was wise. Still, she wished for an easier path at a less hurried pace, knowing neither was possible.

Rhodri, blast his hide, wasn't short of wind or lacking fortitude, even though he'd covered the same rough ground. While she was grateful he allowed her to gather her vigor, she couldn't help her vexation that he showed no weakness of his own.

Nicole plopped down at the edge of the trickling stream and filled her scooped hands with cool water.

The first two scoops she drank to ease her thirst. The third scoop she splashed onto her hot, sweated face. Sweet mercy, she couldn't remember the last time she'd sweated from prolonged exertion. Years, surely. Likely since childhood.

"Better?" Rhodri asked.

"A bit," she admitted, noting his face wasn't red. Not one drop of sweat marred his brow.

"We need to put more distance between us and Oxford before nightfall."

She groaned inwardly, every muscle in her body protesting movement, no matter the urgent necessity to move on.

Rhodri must have sensed her body's unwillingness to budge. He extended a hand for her to grasp, a lending of the strength he possessed in abundance, which had been so evident and startling when he'd fought with the guards at the gate.

With a sure, warm grip, he pulled her up into an unsteady stance, the muscles in her legs twitching and her knees shaky.

Running again seemed impossible, but if she must then she would, or so she thought until a cramp in her calf nearly sent her back to her knees.

At her wince and sharp intake of breath, Rhodri showed not a dram of contrition for having pushed her to this pitiful condition.

"Legs sore?" he asked.

"I am unaccustomed to leaping over logs and pushing through underbrush!" she snapped at him, peevishly revealing the extent of her agony.

"By the time we reach Wales you will be able to leap logs with ease."

"You may be assured that after we reach Wales, I have no intention of ever again leaping a log!"

His mouth quirked in amusement as he released her hand, but he said nothing as his muscular legs bent gracefully without strain, allowing him to dip his hand into the stream for his own drink of water.

Droplets glistened on his rugged chin, caressing two

days' growth of dark facial hair, until he wiped the water away with the back of his long-fingered hands.

Forcing herself to look away from the devilishly handsome man she had every right to be wroth with, Nicole walked out the painful cramp. Concentrating on which spots on the forest floor she placed her feet upon so she wouldn't suffer the indignity of falling on her face, she didn't realize Rhodri had risen until she almost ran into him.

"Listen," he ordered, just above a whisper.

Nicole heard the bubbling water in the stream, the chirp of a bird in the breeze-rustled canopy of leaves overhead and, faintly at first, the unmistakable galloping beat of horses' hooves, coming from the east.

Apprehension coiled in her stomach.

"A patrol," she said in the same low voice Rhodri used.

"We must have come far enough west to now be near the road that leads to Bristol."

Nicole reasoned that if she couldn't see the road, then no one on the road could see her. Still, like hares hoping to go unnoticed by a circling hawk, they stood silently as the sound of hard-ridden horses became louder and more menacing, until at long last the thunder rumbled past them.

Now the patrol was ahead of them, and not behind, but no less a threat.

Not until she let out her held breath did she notice Rhodri's hand on the hilt of the sword that he'd tucked into his belt. That small action stressed the depth of their jeopardy, even more than the thundering of hooves. More than Rhodri's violent, bloody fight with the guards at Little Gate.

Nicole inwardly shivered at the remembrance of those few moments. She'd seen men fight before, in the practice yard at Camelen, but never when in earnest for their lives.

At Camelen, she'd observed soldiers spar with staves and swords, but had not seen them leave a victim sprawled on the ground, bleeding and senseless. Before today she hadn't realized how fast and far a man's head snapped backward when his jaw was struck with a solid, swift fist.

Truly, she didn't want to witness what damage Rhodri could do with a sword to someone he considered an enemy.

The violence had upset her, but she also admitted the proof of Rhodri's prowess was reassuring.

She might be possessed of some intelligence, and despite her current discomfort and petulant mood, she was neither delicate nor weak-willed. But neither was she foolish. A woman did *not* traverse the roads alone. Even Mother Abbess, her habit and reputation giving her some measure of protection on the road, always hired two or three of the village's most imposing-looking young men to act as escort, her favorite being the blacksmith's bulky and coarse son.

Mother Abbess would have loved a man such as Rhodri to serve as her escort. Not only was he wide shouldered and possessed of an intimidating scowl, he had a quick wit and magnificent voice.

Sweet mercy, had it been only yesterday they'd buried Mother Abbess?

Again following Rhodri, at a slower pace this time, Nicole tried not to allow her grief to well up again. But as the forest shadows deepened, from not far ahead came the clang of a bell, ringing *terse,* the early evening prayer.

At Bledloe Abbey the nuns would be gathering in the chapel to chant the office and then retire to the refectory for a light supper. It probably shouldn't be surprising that at the moment she longed for the quiet order of abbey life.

And her body fair screamed for a long rest and a bite of bread.

"There must be an abbey or church ahead," she told Rhodri. "We could beg a night's hospitality."

"We cannot chance it so close to Oxford. However, you are right about finding shelter soon. We also cannot risk lighting a campfire to keep away the wolves."

Nicole shivered at the thought of spending the night in the forest with the wolves, bears, boars, and other dangerous creatures. Just when she could barely see her way in the dark and began to shiver again, this time from the chill of the night air, they came across an unoccupied cottage.

Rhodri kicked at the latch until the lock gave way. The door opened into a large room too well-appointed to have been the home of a peasant farmer.

"Some lord's hunting lodge," Rhodri announced with a tone of both surprise and pleasure. "Let us see how well it is provisioned."

Rhodri found flint and stone on the mantel and used the twigs and split logs in the woodbox to start a small fire in the hearth. With light to see by, Nicole gave silent thanks to whatever lord was supplying unintended hospitality.

While Rhodri went out to the well to draw up a bucket of water, she searched for treasure—like food.

She ignored the bows, arrows, and spears leaning against the wall in favor of rummaging through the crates on the floor. From one she drew out a stout candle, which she lit and placed on the table along with tin cups, wooden bowls, and a small cauldron to hang on the hook in the hearth.

The only food to be found was a sack of oats, enough to provide them with gruel for their supper. 'Twould suffice. And afterward, she planned to curl up on one of the bearskins, toss a woolen blanket over her, and drift into an undisturbed, dreamless sleep.

Rhodri entered with the water bucket. While she set about making the gruel, which they would need to drink from the bowls because she'd found no spoons, he looked through the crates, too.

The more crates he rummaged through, the more it irked her. True, she'd done exactly the same thing not moments before. So why did it bother her that Rhodri did the same?

"What are you looking for?"

"Something we might find of use on the road."

"Such as?"

From his scrunched position in front of a crate, he turned on the balls of his feet, holding up a length of rope. "Rabbit snare."

Nicole placed the dipper in the cauldron and stirred the watery, unappealing gruel, doubting that adding bits of rabbit would make it less repulsive.

"'Tis a devilish long way to Wales. We will starve if we must depend upon snaring rabbits. I hope you have some notion of how to live off the land."

He took immediate offense at her lack of trust in his

ability to provide for them. "Believe me, had we been able to retrieve my horse and money pouch I would have done so. But I have had some experience in living off the land. We will not starve, princess."

"I do not expect this journey to be pleasurable, but I do expect to be fed." She lifted, then tilted, the dipper, allowing the gray gruel to drizzle back into the cauldron. The mixture smelled almost as repugnant as it looked. "If you manage to catch a rabbit with that snare, you had best know how to roast it, too, because I do not."

"You never learned to cook?" he asked, incredulous.

"I never needed to learn. The only time I went into the kitchen at Camelen was to pilfer sweets, and Mother Abbess was of the opinion that each of the abbey's residents should work according to her talents and interests. My interest was growing herbs, not adding them to stews."

"You have certainly led a most pampered life."

Pampered? Not hardly! But before she could refute the claim, he dismissed her, turning his back on her to again rummage through the crate. The wretch!

"Ow!" he said, shaking his hand.

"What?"

"Sliver. Damn crate."

She smiled. 'Twas as if the crate pricked him for his nasty comment.

He came over to the hearth and leaned toward the flame to better see the sliver embedded in the pad of his right thumb.

Nicole ceased stirring, her body infused with warmth she couldn't blame on the cooking fire. Now wasn't a good time to become aware of Rhodri's lean length. Or of how the fire's light flickered along the jut of his strong jaw, or of how his brow furrowed as he concentrated on the irritating sliver.

Nor should she be so aware they were completely alone in a cottage deep in the forest.

The stirring in her woman's places reminded her of the two superb kisses they'd shared today.

Rhodri had surprised her when he'd kissed her quickly in the tower, giving her no chance to feel more than light-headed surprise. The second kiss had lasted longer and still lingered on her lips.

His mouth had been warm, his lips supple and sure on her eager mouth, infusing her with arousing heat. And oh, how her thoughts were winding a wanton path to that most forbidden and so intriguing act of fornication, which the maids at Camelen had whispered about and the nuns at Bledloe Abbey had warned her against.

Rhodri let out an explicit curse that precisely reflected her unruly, unchaste thoughts, making her face hotter.

Except he wasn't looking at her lustfully. He studied the thumb he squeezed, then stuck in his mouth to remove the sliver with his teeth. Judging from his aggravation, he wasn't enjoying success.

"Still in there?" she asked, hoping her voice sounded calmer than she felt.

"All I managed to do was push it in deeper."

She should leave him be, let him care for his own wound. However, having spent so much time in the abbey's infirmary, Nicole had removed many a sliver. She could have it out in a trice.

"Would you like me to take it out?"

"I can do it."

Stubborn? Or merely so accustomed to being self-reliant

he foreswore assistance, even for so minor a thing as a sliver?

Deciding it wasn't her thumb that wanted tending, Nicole used the thick square of cloth that had been stored with the kettles to remove the cauldron from the hearth's hook.

All through their meager supper, which he ate without comment, he rudely pushed and scratched at the pesky sliver.

She forced down the gruel because it might well be the last thing she would get to eat for a while. Finished, she pushed the bowl aside and crossed her arms on the table.

"Rhodri, it needs cutting out."

"So it seems."

He reached down into his boot and drew out her dagger and began poking at his thumb. Nicole bit her bottom lip, withholding comment, her restraint not breaking until he drew a drop of blood.

She held out her hand, palm up. "Give me the dagger before you slice open your thumb."

He ignored her. "Almost had it that time."

"Rhodri!"

His eyebrow rose at the implicit command in her tone, which rather startled her, too. She was on the brink of begging his pardon for interfering in what was truly none of her concern when he placed the pommel of the dagger across her palm.

Now having begun, she must finish. The candle provided enough light to eat by, but she required more light so *she* didn't slice open his thumb.

"Come into the light by the hearth."

Nicole wrapped the thick cloth, with which she'd handled the cauldron, around the dagger's blade, then knelt before the hearth. After an aggrieved sigh, Rhodri followed and knelt on the hearthstones, facing her, his right hand raised.

She took hold of his thumb; his fingers curled around her wrist, warming her blood. Could he feel her pulse beat harder, faster?

Forcing herself to concentrate, the dagger a heavy, awkward weapon when held near the pointed, sharp tip, Nicole gingerly removed the offensive piece of wood without provoking further bloodshed.

Pleased, she looked up, intending to proclaim victory. The hearth's flames danced in Rhodri's brown eyes. Fascinated, she forgot to gloat.

"Nicely done," he said, nearly echoing the words uttered before each of their kisses today.

Dare she claim another kiss as reward for removing a sliver? Silly notion.

"I have had practice. At Bledloe, I spent the greater part of my day in the infirmary, treating ills and burns. Removing the occasional splinter."

"And you enjoyed it?"

She laughed lightly. "For the most part. 'Twas better than spending more time on my knees in the chapel."

He smiled, his expression a mix of confusion and wonder. "What manner of woman have you become, Nicole de Leon?"

"Not so different from any other."

"Does any other have the bearing of a Pendragon princess, with the body of a goddess? You possess uncommon hearing and a healer's touch." He tucked a stray strand of hair behind her ear, his fingers skimming her skin so tenderly she almost melted. "Yet you retain a touch of the hoyden's spirit. 'Tis a captivating combination."

She was inordinately flattered at the variety and sincerity of his compliments. But then, Rhodri was a bard. He'd trained for many years in the use of words, of poetry. Still, the hoyden he apparently admired was both aroused and curious.

"Even though I cannot cook?"

"The gruel was not so bad. Perhaps there is yet hope."

Nicole couldn't say who leaned forward first, and she didn't much care. Their lips met and eyes closed, and her presence of mind lasted only long enough to drop the dagger before flinging her arms over Rhodri's shoulders.

She savored the sweet, stunning force of his long, lingering kiss and rejoiced in the security and danger of his powerful arms enveloping her. She felt on the edge of a cliff, her footing precarious, and she was precisely where she wanted to be, knowing deep in her soul that Rhodri wouldn't allow her to fall.

He broke the kiss and promptly rose to his feet. Nicole sensed his urgent retreat and wanted to pull him back.

Rhodri towered over her, his eyes dark with the same desire that raged in her woman's places. "'Tis a long, hard walk to Glenvair," he said raggedly. "Best you get some sleep, princess."

Then he grabbed the bucket and walked out the door, leaving her achingly restless in the half-circle of firelight.

She wanted to be angry at him for not fulfilling her wishes, but she couldn't, realizing Rhodri had saved them from a tumble into an abyss. He'd done the honorable thing by her, and she should admire his restraint.

Still, as she curled up on the bearskin to attempt to sleep, Nicole fantasized about tumbling naked on the fur with Rhodri, in most unprincess-like abandon, at the moment quite willing to explore an abyss.

Come home, Nicole. Come home to Camelen.

Unmercifully wrenched from a beguiling fantasy, Nicole resisted the impelling urge to raise her defenses. This was the second time William had taken her by surprise. Again his voice was calm, the order given without his usual rancor.

'Twas the strangest feeling to *want* to talk to her brother.

You must give me a reason, William. I do not willingly follow your orders, as you should be well aware.

Silence.

He'd treated her this meanly and unfairly before, when he'd ordered her to leave the abbey. She disliked it as much now as she did then.

If you do not give me a reason, you cannot expect me to obey. Why should I go home?

Again William didn't answer. But then, she knew precisely what he wanted her to do, if not the reason for this second oddly given command.

I will not kill Alberic! I shall refuse every time. If you wish me to come home to help you move beyond this world, I shall try. Are you ready to move on?

He answered her question with silence.

Chapter Eight

I s it done yet?" Nicole asked.

Rhodri smiled at the longing in her voice, sharing her impatience. He gave the rabbit, speared on a stout stick, another turn over the small fire before glancing her way.

Nicole sat cross-legged on the brown woolen blanket taken from the hunting lodge. For the past three days, she'd used the blanket as a cloak during the day and then rolled up in it at night. Alone. As she would tonight, too. No matter how much he wished otherwise.

"Almost done," he said, hearing his stomach growl in earnest appreciation for victuals other than apples plucked from orchards they'd passed or berries picked from patches alongside the road. A road they were still avoiding, for the most part, because Rhodri wasn't yet confident he and Nicole were out of reach of the earl's patrols.

The damn patrols were persistent, and Rhodri wasn't sure whom the earl wanted to get his hands on more—him for having the audacity to kidnap Nicole, or Nicole, so he could hand her over to King Stephen's choice for her husband.

Nicole, most likely. A Pendragon princess would be the more valuable prize to an earl who wished to remain in his king's good graces.

Fortunately, they hadn't seen a patrol since yester noon, making this small fire somewhat safe, not only to roast the meat but to keep away the beasts of the forest. They'd been blessed so far to find shelter along the way, but tonight there was no lodge, barn, or cave in sight, so they must spend the night in the forest. He'd seen no sign of wolves or bears in the area, but that didn't mean the beasts didn't lurk nearby.

"How much longer?" she asked, still eyeing the roasting rabbit with a desirous look nearly as intense as she'd cast Rhodri's way a few nights ago.

He again turned the stick, trying not to remember Nicole's unveiled hunger and passionate kiss, or how he'd come within a hair's width of succumbing to her blatant invitation for a tumble on the hearthstones.

Or on the bearskin.

The tantalizing image of Nicole sprawled naked on a bearskin still stiffened his rod to aching readiness. 'Twas why he'd rarely come within an arm's length of her for three days and three long, cold, restless nights. As now. She sat within reach of the fire's warmth, so he'd scrunched down on the opposite side.

Determined to put out of mind the knowledge that Nicole might allow him full liberties with that sweet body of hers—because he damn well shouldn't be itching to run his hands all over her creamy skin, to suckle at her high, proud breasts, or to bury his aching cock within her heated female sheath—he forced his attention back to the roasting rabbit.

"Soon. Give me your dagger."

From her boot she pulled out her brother's dagger, which he'd given back to her before leaving the hunting lodge. With the innate grace of a princess, she rose from the blanket and came toward him, holding out the weapon. He took it, careful to avoid touching her hand.

After several pokes into the meat to check for a thorough roasting, he sliced off a chunk and dropped it into Nicole's outstretched palm. Laughing lightly, smiling hugely, she juggled the hot offering from palm to palm before lifting it with delicate fingertips to place the welcome fare between her eager lips.

Rhodri inwardly shivered at her mew of pleasure, knowing beyond doubt he could evoke that same cry of satisfaction from her in an entirely different way.

"Oh, Rhodri, that is utterly without compare. I daresay I have never had better."

Hell's bells, he had to cease comparing her every movement or utterance to coupling or he would go mad.

"More?" he asked.

"Certes," she said eagerly.

Damn, it was tempting to tease her, to make her suffer just a little for all the suffering she caused him. Make her hunger as he hungered.

But this was food, not sex. One did not tease with the nourishment they both needed to remain strong for the hard days of walking still ahead of them. So he cut off another chunk for her, then a chunk for himself.

Nicole had the right of it. The rabbit was flavorsome and might well be the last satisfying meal they would enjoy for several days.

With his knees beginning to feel the strain, Rhodri stood up, and side by side they greedily ate rabbit.

"I do not suppose," she said between bites, "'tis possible to snare a dove or two."

"Not likely, and a dovecote would be more risky to filch from than an apple orchard."

"A swan, or heron?"

"One nèeds a hawk or falcon to hunt the bigger birds, unless you are of a mind to wade into a pond and attempt to pounce on one."

She sighed. "That would depend upon how hungry I am."

He supposed she had the right of that, too. If desperate for food, a man, or woman, would go to great lengths to procure whatever morsel could be found, including poaching.

Having no idea whose land they camped on, Rhodri wasn't sure if he'd committed that grievous offense when snaring the rabbit. Norman lords were protective of their hunting grounds and had no qualms about hanging poachers.

But he and Nicole needed to eat and must forage for whatever they found available. Given the circumstances, Rhodri thought they'd done rather well.

"Do you tire of apples already?"

"Nay, but I cannot help wishing the next apple was sliced, mixed with sugar and cinnamon, and baked into a pastry. That may be the first thing I ask of Uncle Connor, to have his cook bake a huge pastry, filled with apples and almonds. And I intend to eat the *whole* of it while still warm!" She held up a hand to refuse another slice of rabbit. "You eat the rest."

Given her wish for an abundance of victuals, her refusal struck him as odd.

"You are sated?"

She shrugged a shoulder. "Not hardly, but I did notice you have been serving me the bigger slices. You are larger than I and must be strong enough to wield a sword in our defense if needs be. I will not usurp your share."

Rhodri hadn't thought she'd noticed, and damn, she shouldn't be in a position where she didn't know whence would come her next meal, or if she would eat at all. She shouldn't have to plow her way through underbrush or sleep on the hard ground with naught but a blanket for her pallet.

This wasn't the way he'd planned to take Nicole to Wales.

They should be on horseback, able to use the road without fear of a patrol overtaking them. She should have proper shelter at night, either in an abbey or inn, with a bowl of stew, hunk of bread, and goblet of wine provided as her supper. She should be wearing her own cloak for warmth, not a blanket.

To assuage a small portion of his guilt, he again held out a large slice of meat.

"One more piece," he insisted.

She folded her arms, adding to the strain of the snugly laced gown across her breasts, forcing him to wrestle with another shot of lust.

"I am content!" she adamantly declared.

Obstinate woman.

"Well, I am not content. If you grow faint with hunger, you will slow us down and make us easier prey for the earl's patrols."

Her brow furrowed with ire. "I have managed to keep up with you thus far, have I not?"

Rhodri decided not to remind Nicole of her less-than-out-standing efforts in leaping logs. "Your success thus far has naught to do with what might happen on the morrow. Eat."

She cast her gaze heavenward in an appeal for forbearance, exposing the length of her creamy white throat, before begrudgingly relenting. "I will make you a bargain. I shall eat one more piece, then the bones are yours to gnaw on."

"Agreed."

Nicole snatched up the meat and popped it into her mouth. She swallowed, then made him rue the impulse to force her to bend to his will.

She licked the juice from her fingertips, one at a time, swirling her pretty pink tongue in an erotic circular motion over each tip.

The tip of his cock fair begged for such exquisite treatment. Rhodri stifled a groan and gnawed hard on the bones.

⌁

Rolled up in a blanket on unyielding ground, Nicole woke to the soft, lilting sound of Rhodri's harp.

'Twas still dark, but from eight years of residing in an abbey, she sensed that bells throughout the kingdom would soon ring matins, calling the clergy to the first prayers of the day.

She smiled, thinking Mother Abbess would be delighted to know that something of clerical life still affected Nicole. Then she frowned, wondering if Rhodri had slept as yet.

She understood his need to sleep lightly, to stand guard. Her father had once boasted that his soldiers were so well trained they could sleep with their eyes open—surely a falsehood, but not far from the truth. She imagined Rhodri had slept lightly these past nights, an easier thing to do when in a lodge or cave, where he must guard only a single entrance.

He sat two paces away, the harp's sack and the sword he'd won away from the guard in Oxford between them.

Though the fire had burned low, it cast enough light for her to study the face of the man with whom she shared this adventure.

He'd scraped off his facial hair, allowing her to see him as she had when he'd arrived at the abbey. In profile, the jut of his rugged jaw was more pronounced. His full lips were pursed in concentration. His nose was well formed. And a hank of raven hair hung forward on his high brow.

Rhodri ap Dafydd was one of the most handsome men she'd ever set eyes on. And, God's truth, she'd discovered she was as weak willed as the lowliest of women whenever she peered too long into his entrancing eyes.

A craving for more than kisses burned low in her belly and made her squirm. He noticed that moment of discomfort and ceased playing.

"Beg pardon, Nicole. I did not mean to wake you."

"'Tis not all your doing. I was primed for waking. The bell for matins will ring soon. Truth to tell, I rather like waking to the harp over a bell."

"Ah."

She rose up on an elbow.

"You play beautifully, Rhodri. Your father would be proud of how you honor his harp."

He ran a hand along the frame's curve in both a loving and respectful fashion, much the way he would touch a woman—or so she imagined. Much the way she wanted him to touch *her*.

"I have another harp at Glenvair, the one awarded me when I finished my training. It has a wondrous voice, and I play it often. However, I seem able to fashion new songs more easily on this one."

"Is that what you are doing, fashioning a new song?"

"With me the music comes first, then the words. I know of others who insist the music must fit the poetry." He shrugged a shoulder of indifference. "Neither way is right nor wrong, merely an individual preference."

Fascinated, Nicole sat upright.

"Have you words to your song as yet?"

He shook his head. "The event has not yet happened that suits this melody. I will know when the event and time is right, then settle on the words."

Rhys, the bard at Camelen, always wrote his poetry first, then set the melody to fit the words. It had never occurred to her that composing could be done differently. But then, she'd never given thought to how bards did what they did, merely enjoyed the results of their labors.

Rhodri reached for the harp's soft, protective sack, which now carried several more items than his harp. Her circlet. The rope he'd used to great advantage yester noon as a rabbit snare. A hook and line that hadn't yet earned its space in the sack but might yet prove useful. Several apples they'd picked yester morn.

The thought of food prodded her stomach to once more protest its lack of regular meals.

"Why not go back to sleep?" he suggested. "There is time yet before daylight."

Nicole rose from elbow to hand, wishing she *could* go

back to sleep. "I am not an advocate of rising before the sun, but once my eyes are open they stubbornly remain open. What of you? Did you stand guard all night?"

"Not all."

"But most, I would wager." She sat up and rearranged the blanket to drape over her shoulders. "'Tis time you sleep, and I will keep watch."

He looked so horrified she almost laughed aloud.

"Heavens above, Rhodri, if you felt it safe enough to play your harp, then you have already determined we are not in immediate danger from either patrols or bears. The most noteworthy event likely to happen in the next few hours is sunrise."

He didn't hide his apprehension over her suggestion. "True, however—"

"I give you my oath I will wake you if a twig snaps or a leaf rustles. I will not be able to go back to sleep in any event, so you may as well do so if you can."

Which she knew most warriors could do, because they'd been trained to sleep when the opportunity arose when on the march. She and Rhodri might not be headed into battle, but their circumstances warranted similar tactics to survive this journey.

Silently, he reached into the sack, drew out an apple, and tossed it her way.

"Any sound, any movement, you scream," he ordered.

She couldn't help smile with delight that he would place this small trust in her.

"I can scream."

His answering smile was wry. "I remember."

She felt her cheeks grow warm. The only time he'd heard her scream was as a little girl at Glenvair.

Deciding not to comment, Nicole took a bite of apple while Rhodri stretched out on his back, his feet toward the fire, using one arm on which to rest his head. She would offer him the blanket to use as his pillow but knew he'd refuse, insisting she needed the blanket for warmth.

Not that she was cold. Too often since their kiss in the hunting lodge, she'd been tempted to lie down beside Rhodri and entice him into another kiss and a more intimate embrace. 'Twas wicked of her, but at the moment she had to force herself to remain where she was and not to offer herself as his blanket.

And 'struth, she had to admit she wasn't sure if he would accept or reject such a bold offer.

He wanted her, had conveyed as much in the hunting lodge. But he also possessed the fortitude to resist the passion she was so curious about and hungered for.

Nicole took another bite of the apple, which would have benefited from a few more days on the tree, the memory of his darkened eyes and blatant desire refusing to dim.

Oh, she knew he'd done the honorable thing in the lodge by denying them further intimacy, not allowing their lust to overcome them. Unfortunately, on this sixth morning since Rhodri reentered her life, she perversely wanted to know precisely why Sister Amelia so willingly spent nights with a certain visiting bishop, and she wanted Rhodri to satisfy that curiosity.

With a sigh, she tossed the apple core into the fire and looked around the small clearing, eager to find a distraction for wanton musings.

Two shining eyes peered back at her from the edge of the clearing, only a few paces off.

Fear shot through her. Could she have been wrong about the bears? Had the fire burned too low to hold a dangerous creature at bay?

She was about to scream when the fear abated somewhat. Those shining eyes didn't belong to a large animal. They were too small and too close to the ground for a bear or wolf on the prowl.

A rabbit? Oh, why hadn't Rhodri put out his snare? But no, this animal was larger.

Confident she and Rhodri were in no immediate danger of being mauled or eaten, Nicole sat statue still, watching their predawn visitor. The animal didn't move, not even when dim light and the first sounds of birdsong heralded the coming dawn.

When the sunlight was bright enough that the animal's eyes stopped shining, she continued to sit quietly and stare at the same spot until the sun's rays finally proclaimed the day.

A pig. Small and white, it couldn't be more than a few months old, likely out of a sow's second litter of the year.

Had it wandered off from its mother, and if from a village's herd of pigs, would a swineherd come looking for it? Or was it wild and therefore free for the taking?

Well, not free. She well knew that lords frowned upon anyone taking game from their forest lands, and most of them employed foresters to catch poachers. Rhodri had already snared a rabbit that some forester might consider his special charge, but still, Nicole's mouth watered at the thought of roasted pork.

Moving slowly, Nicole slid sideways until she could touch Rhodri's shoulder. His eyes instantly snapped open.

Oh, sweet mercy, she'd forgotten the captivating effect

of those eyes, the amber-flecked brown now all soft and liquid from sleep. 'Struth, she could sit here until dusk staring into those wondrous pools.

"Is aught amiss?" he asked, breaking her all-too-brief trance.

"How fast can you run?"

His eyes narrowed. "Need we?"

"Not we, you." Nicole pointed to where the pig still stood beside a stout oak. "Tonight's supper."

He rubbed a hand over his eyes. "You want me to catch a pig."

She didn't sense any enthusiasm for the venture. She glanced at the pig, who twitched an ear, as if waiting to hear her answer. She kept her voice low.

"'Tis small, and I see no tusks, so 'tis likely a sow. It has also been standing there for a long, long while, so I have to wonder if there is aught wrong with its legs."

"Or perhaps it smelled the apple you were eating and is waiting for us to leave so it can investigate the possibility of easy food. Nicole, have you ever tried to catch a pig?"

"I cannot say I have ever had reason."

"They may have short legs, but pigs can be wily and swift, nigh on impossible to catch."

Nicole warmed to the plan that was beginning to form. "I will entice it with an apple, and while it is looking at me, you can sneak up behind it."

He arched an eyebrow. "If you can entice the pig, then it is likely accustomed to people, and we will see a swineherd come hunting it soon. Otherwise it is wild, and we have already poached a rabbit. 'Twould not be wise to take two animals from the same lands."

She glanced longingly at several meals still on the hoof.

"So we let it go?"

He was quiet for a moment before he ordered, "Give me an apple and your dagger."

Encouraged, Nicole did as bid. Rhodri sat upright, sliced the apple into quarters, and tossed the pieces into the long grass between them and the pig, the last piece landing not far from the fire. He wiped the juice from the blade before, to her surprise, he slid the dagger into his own boot.

"If the pig takes all of the bait," he said, "and we hear no swineherd calling his charge before we are ready to leave, then we will see what we can do to catch the little bugger."

Making ready to leave wouldn't take much time at all. To Nicole's delight, by the time they'd both risen to their feet, the pig was already munching the first apple slice, giving her hope.

Since the day promised to be a fine one, Nicole folded up her blanket to carry over her arm while Rhodri began to scatter the last embers of the fire.

And the pig trotted over to devour the second apple slice.

The pig was taking the bait. All it needed was time to sniff out all the pieces.

Pleased, and most willing to give the pig a leisurely last meal, Nicole put the blanket atop the harp's sack and ambled off into the brush behind them for her morning bodily relief, taking care to remain within hailing distance and not taking overlong, so Rhodri wouldn't become concerned and come looking for her. Still, she didn't hurry the task, either.

By the time she came out of the thicket, Rhodri had

stomped out the last of the campfire's embers. Nicole halted, watching Rhodri bend down to retrieve the dagger as the dear little porker strolled toward the fourth piece of apple.

With graceful, sidelong strides, he took up a position he must consider advantageous—behind and to the right of the pig. Nicole crossed her arms tight against her midriff, her heart beating wildly in anticipation of the chase.

Rhodri took one long, slow step, then another, then broke into a run. The pig sensed the danger and sped off, nigh on flying on those little legs. Had the pig run straight, Rhodri might have made short work of the hunt, but the pig circled back, speeding toward the oak tree whence Nicole had first spotted it.

Rhodri spun in pursuit, gaining ground on his prey, not slowing even when the pig shot into the woodland. Several rapid heartbeats after she lost sight of hunter and prey, she heard a mighty warrior's cry, then winced at the alarming crash that followed.

Then there was silence. And the silence became ominous. Her excitement fading to concern, Nicole hiked up her skirts and ran to the spot where Rhodri had entered the woods.

Praying the silence meant he was merely slaughtering the pig, she called Rhodri's name.

His disgruntled "Here" didn't reassure her.

The trail of broken branches and trampled grass was easily followed.

Nicole found Rhodri sitting next to a log, his mouth and brow tight with a mix of anger and pain, his hands wrapped around his still-booted ankle.

Oh, this wasn't good. Not good at all.

Chapter Nine

The messenger's news was both astonishing and distressing, and Alberic, lord of Camelen, wished the earl of Oxford hadn't felt obligated to inform Gwendolyn and Emma of the details of Nicole's disappearance.

Alberic was worried about Nicole, but he was more concerned with the distress the news caused his wife.

Huge with their third child, and as beautiful as the day they'd met eight years past, Gwendolyn sat on a bench near the great hall's hearth with her elder sister, Emma. The two held hands, drawing comfort from each other.

Darian, Emma's husband, didn't like the misery on his wife's pale face, either. Of a height and warrior's build as Alberic, the former mercenary stood with his feet spread and arms crossed, frowning into the flames.

Likely the dire possibilities, both for Nicole's safety and the political repercussions, were flickering through Darian's mind, too.

Gwendolyn looked up at him with pleading, liquid doe-brown eyes. "What are we to do, Alberic? We cannot stand by and allow Rhodri to whisk Nicole off to Wales!"

He placed a hand on her shoulder, hoping his touch offered a measure of comfort.

"'Tis possible the earl's patrols have already captured them and Nicole is even now on her way back to Oxford."

Gwendolyn wiped away a tear and grunted indelicately. "Aubrey de Vere has much to answer for! Had he not taken Nicole and Rhodri into his custody and forced them to go to Oxford, this would not have happened!"

Emma squeezed Gwendolyn's hand. "Had Uncle Connor not sent Rhodri to Bledloe Abbey, the earl would not have had reason for his actions. Endeavoring to assign blame for Nicole's plight, beyond Rhodri's despicable use of her to escape Oxford, is a waste."

"Agreed," Alberic stated, glad to see Gwendolyn's emotions shift from devastated to angry. Her tears wrenched out his heart, but her anger he could deal with—mostly.

"But what are we to do?" his wife still wanted to know. "Nicole is not accustomed to being out in the wild, and the change of season is upon us. She could be cold, and hungry, and—sweet mercy, I cannot believe this of Rhodri! How dare he!"

The message from de Vere had been long and thorough, and Alberic wasn't sure what to believe. Had Connor ap Maelgwn sent Rhodri ap Dafydd to Bledloe Abbey merely to inquire of Nicole's health and contentment? Or had Connor planned for Rhodri to entice or kidnap Nicole from the abbey all along, as the earl believed?

If the former, the pair might well be headed for Camelen and not Wales. The journey from Oxford would take them several days afoot, especially if they stayed off the roads to avoid capture. If they were bound for Wales, the journey would take longer, and thus his wife would worry all the more.

Alberic rubbed at his chin, trying not to believe ill of his wife's Welsh uncle but not succeeding.

"The first thing I must do is send a messenger to Connor. I want to know precisely why he sent Rhodri to see Nicole." Not that the wily Connor wasn't above lying, but the attempt to learn the truth needs be made. "We must also send out our own patrols on the possibility the pair is headed here. If I send men Nicole might recognize, wearing Camelen's livery, she will know they can be approached without fear of harm."

Darian nodded in agreement. "'Twould be good for Rhodri to realize that, too. 'Struth, were I locked in a castle tower, I would employ whatever means I must to escape. Rhodri's misuse of Nicole may have been part of a ploy to gain freedom for them both, so he may not be deserving of punishment, at least not by us."

Emma arched an eyebrow. "You think Rhodri holding Nicole by the throat was part of a ploy, that she may have known what he was about?"

"'Tis possible."

Gwendolyn shook her head. "Then how do you explain her actions at Little Gate? The messenger said she ran to the guards and begged them for protection from Rhodri!"

"A diversion. Nicole may have sent most of the guards off to chase Rhodri, leaving him only two men at the gate to get past. Nicely done, if that was the case."

Alberic saw the sense in Darian's reasoning but couldn't approve of Rhodri's using a woman in such fashion. "Damn devious and dishonorable."

Darian smiled hugely. "Aye, astute and cunning, and

the scheme worked. They might not have been able to pass through the gate otherwise."

One of the oddities of having a brother-by-marriage who had once been a renowned mercenary was their sometimes differing attitudes toward what was acceptable behavior and what was not, with Darian being more lenient. Overly lenient, to Alberic's way of thinking.

Still, it wasn't Darian's character in question, but Rhodri ap Dafydd's.

He addressed Gwen and Emma. "What do you know of Rhodri? Whether he forced her out of Oxford or no, can he be trusted not to harm her?"

The sisters glanced at each other before Gwendolyn answered. "Neither of us had seen Rhodri for an age. What I know of him in recent years comes from Connor's letters, and Connor always mentioned Rhodri with pride in his accomplishments, first with a sword and bow, then with the harp."

Emma nodded. "Connor had reason for pride. Not every man who plays a harp and writes poetry becomes an honored bard. A man must have talent, but the study also takes years of hard work and perseverance."

"Which only speaks well of his skills and ambition," Alberic countered, "not of the man's honor."

Gwendolyn sighed heavily and put a hand on her huge stomach—which moved with the squirming of the babe—and Alberic once more berated Fate for sending upsetting news at such a time.

"I must believe Rhodri will take care of Nicole or worry myself into an agitation not good for the babe."

After a moment's hesitation, Emma leaned toward Gwendolyn and whispered, "Should I look?"

Alberic inwardly shivered.

He'd long ago accepted the existence of magic. The ring that wouldn't budge from his finger, binding him to Gwendolyn as joint guardians of an ancient spell, was a visible reminder of magic's existence. But he and Gwendolyn might never be called upon to recall King Arthur from the Isle of Avalon to come to Britain's aid—at least he hoped not—so Alberic tried not to dwell on magic's use, and for long periods of time he could put it out of mind.

However, Emma could peer into water and call forth a vision. Nicole could hear voices of the dead. Knowing the suffering those abilities had caused the sisters in the past, Alberic had to wonder if being a female in the line of Pendragon wasn't more a curse than a blessing.

And what turmoil that heritage could cause his own children, he didn't wish to contemplate.

"Oh, Emma, I hate to ask it of you, but knowing where they are would aid us greatly in deciding what must be done," Gwendolyn answered with a mix of true regret and a spark of hope.

Emma straightened and looked to her husband for guidance.

"The decision is yours, sweetling," Darian said, "but pray, do not put too much hope on the outcome."

Emma's visions always told true, but she didn't always receive the answers she hoped for.

She glanced around the hall, where servants bustled about to make the hall ready for nooning. "Not here."

Alberic could clear the hall with the wave of his hand, but that might cause idle speculation among the servants, and 'twas clear Emma wanted full privacy.

"Our bedchamber," he said.

In agreement, all four headed up the tightly winding stairway that led from the hall to the upper floor, Alberic's hand at Gwendolyn's back to keep her steady.

Children's laughter greeted them in the upper passageway, and Alberic wished he were heading instead for the nursery, where under the watchful eye of a trusted nurse, his son Hugh, named for Gwendolyn's father, and daughter Elena, named for his mother, were entertaining Emma and Darian's son Wyatt, who was barely old enough to toddle across the floor.

Within the lord's bedchamber, Gwendolyn fetched the silver pitcher and washbasin from the bedside stand and placed them on the round oak table in the center of the room.

While Emma eased into the armed chair, Gwendolyn poured water into the basin. When the water's surface was both smooth and clear, Emma leaned forward and for a long while stared at the water.

The room was silent, Emma's concentration complete.

Alberic let loose his held breath when Emma finally closed her eyes to break the lure of the water.

Darian strode over to stand behind his wife, placing his hands on her shoulders in a loving and protective gesture.

Emma reached up to touch Darian's hand. "I am fine, dearest, truly."

"Take whatever time you need," Darian said gently.

Alberic reined in his impatience, knowing if he tried to rush Emma he'd draw Darian's wrath. Truly, he liked and respected the man too much to risk a breach in their friendship.

"I saw them," Emma reported. "They are walking along a road, slowly. Rhodri appears to be using a walking stick, but whether from necessity or not I cannot say. I do not believe they are on their way to Camelen. Were they coming toward us, I might have seen their faces, but I did not."

"You are certain it was Nicole you saw, not some other woman?"

"I am certain the woman was Nicole, so I assume the man is Rhodri." Emma held out a hand, which Gwendolyn grasped hold of. "I sensed no fear on Nicole's part. Nor does she appear to have suffered any physical harm. I truly do not feel she is in any danger, at least not from Rhodri."

Tears again sprang to Gwendolyn's eyes, her emotions so easily swayed and visible these days. This time her tears were of happiness, for which Alberic was grateful.

She hugged Emma. "I know how much you dislike courting a vision. My thanks, dearest, for relieving my mind on Nicole's well-being."

Alberic wasn't as relieved as his wife. Nicole might not be in immediate danger of harm, but the little minx was likely headed toward Wales, precisely where she shouldn't be going. Surely by now Aubrey de Vere had also informed King Stephen of Nicole's disappearance, and the king would not be pleased that his ward was gone, and in the company of a Welshman.

Unhappy kings could cause problems for the family of errant subjects.

Darian's expression revealed that his thoughts were running along the same path.

Alberic hated leaving Gwendolyn so close to the

babe's birth, but better he try to retrieve Nicole before either the earl's patrols caught up with her or, worse, she crossed the border.

Surely he could do so in less than a fortnight.

"Think you we can find them before they enter Wales?" he asked Darian, whose talents would be most useful during such a venture.

"Perhaps." Darian shook his head. "There are only a few roads they can take west, and fewer places where they can cross the rivers. Were I Rhodri, I might make first for Gloucester. Or he might make for Bristol, where he could hire a boatman to take him and Nicole to the nearest Welsh port. Problem is, to which town are they headed?"

A problem, indeed, and one Alberic must solve quickly. And when he did, and Nicole was safely in hand, he had several pointed questions for Rhodri ap Dafydd, who had best have good answers.

❧

"I need to rest, Rhodri, just for a moment or two."

He cast her an irritated sidelong glance. "I know what you are about, and I order you to cease."

Nicole sighed and kept walking. The stubborn man was determined to put another full day's worth of leagues between them and Oxford, regardless that if he continued on this unwise course, she feared he might not be able to walk on the morrow.

Reckless, to her way of thinking.

"You are no good to me if you go lame!"

"My ankle is merely sore, not broken, and as long as I leave on my boot, I can walk on it."

"Not if you continue to abuse it! You only aggravate the injury. Come one morn soon, your ankle will refuse to hold your weight."

"So be it, just so long as when that morn comes, we are farther from Oxford."

And closer to Wales. The nearer to the border, the less chance of being captured by one of the earl's patrols. She knew that as well as Rhodri did.

She should probably be content that he'd agreed to use a walking stick, and she'd won the battle over whether or not to use the road. Walking was less strenuous on a rutted dirt road than through the forest's brambles and fallen logs.

They'd left the road only twice today to hide in the thicket. The rumbling cart that had come up behind them had scared her most but proved to be no more than a cloth merchant, probably on his way to Oxford. The second had been to allow a group of young men on horseback to ride by, headed in the direction of Bristol.

Neither had proved an immediate threat, but Rhodri didn't want anyone to see them who might eventually learn the identity of the man and woman they'd seen walking on the road and report the sighting.

Each time they left the road, Nicole worried over what else could go wrong on what might prove to be a very long journey afoot. And she felt horribly guilty for goading Rhodri into chasing the pig.

Because the thought of roasted pork made her hungry again, she turned her mind to other things, like the prospect of passing through Bristol.

She'd never seen Bristol, but her father and brother had told wonderful, colorful tales of their visits. The seat of Robert, the powerful earl of Gloucester, the town and castle had provided a haven and stronghold for the empress Maud, Robert's half sister, during much of the war with King Stephen.

Her father would be upset to know Earl Robert had died, ripping the heart out of the rebellion, and furious to learn that without the earl's leadership the rebel cause had floundered. Shortly afterward, Maud had returned to Normandy, to her Angevin husband. Their son, Henry, who'd since grown into his manhood, now took up the fight his mother had begun.

Nicole remembered her first days at Bledloe Abbey when, in her youth and despair, she'd plotted to escape and join the cause her father and brother had fought and died for, utterly sure Maud would welcome a child into her service at Bristol Castle. A silly notion.

Still, perhaps a measure of her rebelliousness had survived, because now she would pass through Bristol to reach an even more rebellious place. Wales.

"Tell me of Glenvair."

Rhodri shrugged a shoulder. "Not much to tell. The manor has not changed since you were last there."

"Connor has made no improvements?"

"It is the Norman way to construct large, imposing buildings and surround them with walls to protect them, not Welsh."

"Had Connor built a castle, I would surely have heard of it from Gwendolyn. Is there no new well, or a repair to the mill? A storeroom added?"

"No."

Irritated by his crusty answers, Nicole was almost ready to leave him to his black mood. Almost.

"Do butterflies still frequent the long grass near the stream?"

"I would not know. Likely."

"The children I played with—did most remain at Glenvair when grown?"

"Most."

Nicole surrendered. If the man insisted on being surly, he could damn well keep it to himself.

They walked in silence for at least another league before he surprised her by asking, "Do you remember Winnifred?"

The name sounded familiar.

"Not clearly."

"She has a scar over her left eyebrow."

His description jolted a memory of not only the girl, but the other children she'd asked about earlier.

"Winnifred served as a maid to my sisters and me, did she not?"

"I believe she did. Anyway, she married Beven, has two children of her own now."

Nicole realized he'd made a peace offering, of sorts, by speaking to her devoid of his earlier sharpness. So what could she ask of Winnifred to keep him talking?

"Is she happy in her marriage?"

"I should think so. Beven provides her with a snug cottage, does not beat her, and has given her children."

As if those things alone would make a woman happy in her marriage. But then, Nicole knew women could do worse in a husband than one with whom she found contentment.

"Why have you not married?"

The question brought no startled or indignant look

from Rhodri, for which she was grateful. Truly, it was a very personal question she shouldn't have asked, and she wouldn't be surprised or offended if he didn't answer.

"Have not found the right woman."

A man as well put together and talented as Rhodri ap Dafydd could have his choice of numerous eager women. That he was also a bard would have them swooning at his feet. And she would be willing to wager he'd sampled more than a few of the swooners. So must this *right* woman be an ideal of beauty and grace, or must she come with more than a lovely face and shapely body?

"The right woman, or a suitable dowry?"

"Both. Such a woman is hard to find."

"Perhaps you ask too much."

"I think not. She must come with land, of course, a *cantref* at the least, and a sack full of shiny gold coins. And ten horses, all brown with white socks."

Nicole's jaw dropped in astonished awe at his precise and rich requirements, but before she could comment, he continued.

"Naturally, she must also come with portables—a chest filled with embroidered table linens, bejeweled goblets, and pewter platters. Also spices. Sugar, salt, rosemary, and cinnamon. I am particularly fond of cinnamon. Two cows, six geese, a flock of doves, several bunches of turnips and onions, and a large cauldron—"

Nicole groaned loudly enough to halt his litany, finally realizing he teased.

She laughed lightly. "'Tis no wonder you have not married. So many turnips would be hard to come by."

"Aye, always the turnips prove a difficulty." He turned his head slightly, distracted. "Someone comes."

Nicole didn't need to be told to leave the road far enough so she couldn't be seen. Rhodri limped into the woods behind her but, with his lack of grace, didn't handle the suddenly steep slope of the forest floor as nimbly as she. He stumbled, lost his footing, and slid down the small hill.

She glanced behind her toward the road. They hadn't gone far enough for safety. Even if they pressed up against the hill, they could be seen by anyone who cared to take a close look.

And the only ones who might look closely would be members of the earl's patrols.

"Nicole, come down here," he ordered.

Rhodri would not be pleased with what she was about to do, but damn, the possibilities running through her head were simply too insistent to ignore. She stood up, wrapped the brown blanket around her to cloak the blue of her gown, and headed back toward the road.

Rhodri harshly whispered her name. She ignored the summons, crouching behind a leafy bush, straining to see what they'd heard. A cart came into view, pulled by two oxen.

No patrol, this!

She hurried back down to Rhodri, who fair glowered his displeasure. Nicole ignored his anger, caught up in her excitement.

"'Tis a farmer, his wife, and three children that I can see. The cart does not appear full. Rhodri, perhaps we can beg a ride, maybe even a night's lodging in their barn."

Rhodri shook his head emphatically. Nicole wanted to shake *him*.

"You *must* rest your ankle," she argued, "and I do *not* wish to spend the night in the open if we need not!"

He still shook his head.

The sounds from the road changed subtly, from the cart coming toward them to passing them by. Why would not the man see reason?

"If we ride, 'twill give us the day's distance you desired, in comfort. Rhodri, I beg you, allow me to ask their assistance."

He sighed. "We have no means to pay them."

"People have been known to extend hospitality out of the goodness of their hearts. We cannot know unless I try. I vow, I will do so with caution."

Rhodri stared at her a long time, the sound of plodding oxen and creaking cart wheels becoming fainter. "Tell them I will make the trouble worth their while."

Elated, Nicole didn't ponder how Rhodri intended to do so, just swiftly climbed the hill and ran up the road, hailing the farmer.

Chapter Ten

Rhodri's goal in life was to become a *pencerdd,* the duties of which included training future bards.

Right now, seated on the dirt floor of a one-room cottage, he taught a wee girl to pluck out a tune on his harp.

The girl's eyes shone with joy at her accomplishment, and the mother's gratitude for entertaining the girl while she and Nicole cleared away the remnants of the evening meal gladdened his heart and made him feel less a burden on people who could hardly afford the generosity of two added people at their supper table.

Damn, but the simple hot stew had tasted of heaven. The bread might have been made of coarse brown flour, but it satisfied in ways only poetry could describe.

On the morrow, he would make a spectacular recovery. Before he and Nicole left, he would help the farmer and the two young boys with morning chores. For now, he would sit here and play the invalid because it so pleased Nicole.

Earlier, she'd coated his ankle with moss, wrapped it in linen, and *ordered* him to stay put. She'd made such a fuss over taking care of him that he'd lost the heart to tell her, again, that his ankle didn't hurt as much as she believed.

She flashed him a smile as she passed by, hauling cleaned bowls to a crate in the corner. Earlier, she'd chopped cabbage to add to the stew, working alongside a peasant as if she weren't a noblewoman. As if she knew how to cook.

The farmer's wife knew the difference. She'd called Nicole "milady" from the first and given her the simplest of tasks.

While Rhodri enjoyed his meal from his place on the floor, Nicole had eaten at the table with the family, all smiles and good cheer, most agreeable to comparing remedies for various aches and ills with the farmer's wife.

Talk at the table had turned to news of the area, and Rhodri had a better notion of how far he and Nicole had come. This farm was a bit west of Swindon, the small market town he and Nicole had skirted around this morn, where the farmer had traded eggs to a blacksmith for mending a kettle.

'Twas also where Nicole had slowed when, at the end of town, they'd come upon a church and its graveyard. Whether a spirit had called out to her, or if she answered, she hadn't said. Nor had he asked her, too wary of the strange ability she claimed to possess to want to know more.

In his head, Rhodri knew that henceforth he must guard against surrendering to Nicole's whims. Had he not chased the damn pig because Nicole craved roasted pork, his ankle wouldn't be sore, and she wouldn't be overly pampering him. But then, had he not recognized her desperate need for a roof over their heads tonight, they wouldn't have enjoyed so good a supper.

Resisting Nicole's pleas proved almost futile. Each time she cast her doe-brown eyes his way, his insides reacted foolishly. Betimes he softened to dangerous weakness, and at others he felt able to slay the dragons of old. And always he wanted her, his desire becoming an uncomfortably familiar ache in his loins.

He shifted slightly to resettle the little girl on his lap so she wouldn't feel his body's response to the lusty thoughts he shouldn't be allowing.

The girl's mother saw him move and clapped her hands. "Come, minx. The harper's legs will be going numb if ye do not get off them. 'Tis time for ye to ready for the night, anyway."

The girl rose reluctantly and went straightaway to her mother, who scooped her up and climbed the ladder to the loft.

Nicole sat down beside him. "You do well with children," she said quietly, referring to his entertaining the little ones at the abbey.

"'Tis the harp they are drawn to, not me."

"As you say," she commented, not truly taking him at his word. "How does your ankle? Does the wrapping ease the pain?"

The memory of Nicole's hands patting the moss around his ankle, her gentle fingers causing tingles to creep up his leg, made other parts of him beg all the more for attention. He refused to burst her current contentment by telling her the coddling hadn't been necessary.

"Why the moss?" he asked, truly curious.

She shrugged a shoulder. "Sister Enid believed it eased

aches. I imagine that even if the moss does not aid healing, it cannot do harm. A full night's rest is sure to do the injury good, moss or no."

True enough.

"I feel rather useless sitting here, rather like a two-legged stool."

She drew up her knees and wrapped her arms around them. "Play your harp. That is how you thought to reward the family for their trouble, is it not?"

It was, so he played, gay tunes at first. After the boys clambered up into the loft for bed, Rhodri chose lilting melodies. The fire in the hearth had burned low and eyelids drooped before the mistress of the house declared it time for sleep.

"Milady, we would be honored if the two of ye would accept the use of our pallet."

Jolted from the calm he'd effected with his music, Rhodri glanced at the drapery hanging in the corner. Knowing what was behind it, his now unruly parts urged Nicole to accept.

She held up a hand, palm outward. "You have been kindness itself to take us into your home and feed us. I thank you for your generous offer but will not deprive you of your bed and proper rest. We are content where we are."

Rhodri forced an agreeing smile.

The wife looked unhappy but resigned. "Another blanket, then?"

Nicole agreed to the offer, and after a round of good wishes for a pleasant night, the farmer followed his wife into their snug little nest behind the drapery.

As she had for several nights, Nicole wrapped up in her blanket, but unlike other nights, she now stretched out beside him, well within arm's length. In the quiet, he could hear her breathe.

Too close, his common sense warned. *Not close enough,* his base self countered. Not even if he rolled onto his side to face the wall could his body ignore her nearness. So he remained on his back, successfully keeping his hands from reaching out to pull Nicole closer.

She squirmed, then rose up on an elbow. "Why is it I have slept on the ground all this while without trouble but tonight cannot find comfort?"

He knew why *he* couldn't find comfort. Was Nicole's reason the same? Best if he didn't know.

"Not tired?"

"Not tired enough to sleep, apparently."

"Try anyway. We must put a few leagues behind us on the morrow. 'Tis too dangerous to remain here, both for us and for our hosts. I should hate for this family to come to harm for sheltering us."

She glanced at the drapery. "I agree. How much farther must we travel until we are out of the earl's reach?"

They wouldn't be entirely safe until they crossed the Welsh border. He didn't like adding the days he must allow because he didn't know this part of England very well. He'd taken a more direct, northerly route on his way from Glenvair to Bledloe Abbey to fetch Nicole.

"A sennight, perhaps more, depending upon how much trouble we have crossing rivers. Let us hope there are bridges aplenty and no toll is required for the crossing."

Her eyes narrowed. "If there are no bridges?"

"Then we ford the rivers."

She chewed on her bottom lip. "I know not how to swim."

"We will find a way to cross, never fear."

Except Nicole did fear, despite his assurance, and the woman certainly had reason for concern. "Perhaps we can find a boatman to take us across."

"Ferries cost coin, and we have none."

Too true.

The more difficult she made the journey sound, the more obstacles she tossed in his way, the more resolute he was to overcome them.

He rolled to his side and rose up on an elbow to face her.

"I give you my oath, we will cross the rivers without mishap. Nicole, why do you expect the worst?"

"I do not . . . I." She closed her mouth, her shoulders slumping. "These days, I do not know what to expect. At the abbey, I knew from the moment of rising how the hours of my day would progress. Prayer, meals, sleep— all were done in order, by the bell. I have lost the pattern of my days, and I find that disconcerting."

He brushed back a lock of reddish-brown hair that had come loose from her waist-length braid. "'Tis merely a new pattern."

"An ungainly pattern."

Rhodri wasn't sure who leaned toward the other first, but when his lips touched Nicole's, he didn't care. When their mouths melded, he couldn't think beyond enjoying the taste of Nicole and noticing how perfectly his hand fitted the curve of her waist.

Nothing was so natural as lowering her to the floor, and nothing so grand as her soft body beneath him. Unless it was the splendor of her arms wrapping around his neck, her fingers twining into his hair, holding him firmly in place.

Nothing would have stopped him from raising her skirt and lowering his breeches except the knowledge that he might hurt her. Oh, he would love to be the first to sink into her virgin's depths, but breaking a maidenhead took time and care and betimes caused enough pain for a woman to cry out.

If Nicole cried out, she would alert the household. Besides, her first coupling should be done properly, in a comfortable bed with privacy ensured. Not on the dirt floor of a farmer's cottage.

"This is new to me, too," she whispered.

If Nicole had been fully raised in a castle, and not in a nunnery, some lad would have surely found a way to kiss Nicole. Rhodri was suddenly perversely glad she'd been sent, at a young age, to reside among the nuns.

"Do my kisses frighten you?"

"A bit, but not as much as the thought of fording a river."

"Once we cross the Avon, we will be in territory still very loyal to the rebellion, where the earl's royalist patrols dare not roam too freely. There we should be able to find an inn or two where I can earn some coin to make the rest of our journey less difficult."

Her fingers slid along his whisker-laden jaw in what he was sure was an innocent exploration, making him wonder which of them would be more familiar with the other when they were finally able to couple.

"Innkeepers allow you to play your harp in the taproom. That is how you earned your way from Wales to Bledloe Abbey, is it not?"

"Patrons can be generous, and if business is good, sometimes the innkeeper allows me free board."

And bed, which could be shared and put to vigorous use.

Rhodri indulged in one more kiss before he forced himself to roll off Nicole and onto his back. With every fiber of his being aware of the woman beside him, he looked forward to the oblivion of sleep.

Except the woman didn't accept his abandonment. Nicole brazenly snuggled up to his side, tossed an arm over his chest, and laid her head on his shoulder.

He breathed in her scent, felt the rise and fall of her bosom, noted the graceful, possessive weight of her arm across his chest, knowing he should be content with having earned her trust.

Hellfire. He wasn't a callow youth with scant control over his lust, but it was damn hard to resist such enticement to unleash the demon, even if the woman who so naively lay in his arms didn't know precisely what havoc she invited.

Using every dram of his resolve, Rhodri managed to lie still while he fought the demon, not winning until the wee hours of the morn.

❦

Three days later, Nicole was nearly ready to walk back to Oxford and throw herself on the earl's mercy.

From a position of concealment among the trees along the road, she observed the men who stood between her and easy passage over the Avon. Two soldiers, garbed in the earl's livery, shared a jest with the man who collected the toll to cross the lovely wooden bridge. She also saw the soldiers' horses—beautiful brown, strong-legged animals.

Possession of just one horse would make this journey so much easier.

They'd pressed hard since leaving the farm, through the forest because Rhodri shunned the road. They'd not yet eaten today, and it was well past nooning. Tired, hungry, her gown filthy, her hair a mass of tangles, Nicole fought the despondency that threatened to overwhelm her.

She tried to think of this new disheartening obstacle as merely one more difficulty to overcome along a journey fraught with hardship. But God's truth, she wanted to scream out her frustration or sit down and have a good cry. Except she didn't dare utter a sound and alert the soldiers to her presence.

Nor dare she say a word about attempting to relieve the soldiers of their horses. Rhodri would outright reject any such suggestion, not only because 'twould be nigh impossible to do, but merely because she'd suggested it.

Since leaving the farm, no matter what she thought a good plan, he thought it a bad one. His caution was becoming irksome. Especially at night, when she wanted to sleep closer to him and he did *not*.

She glanced at Rhodri, standing next to her, leaning on the walking stick he didn't need anymore, carried only to humor her. His gaze narrowed in on the horses, his wish to possess them likely as fierce as hers.

With a sharp jerk of his head, he told her to follow him away from the horses, and the solid bridge, and the earl's patrol.

Nicole knew she should be more upset over coming so close to a patrol, but damn, right now what scared her more was wading through the Avon.

The sound of flowing water should be soothing, not

terrifying. There was no hope but to go through the river if they didn't wish to travel leagues out of their way.

But she didn't know how to swim. If she lost her footing and became caught in the current—Nicole shivered, not wishing to contemplate disaster. She followed Rhodri along a narrow path for what seemed a long way, before he paused to inspect what could be a place to ford.

"I wager others have crossed here," he said, pointing to where the path sloped down to the bank.

"Successfully, I hope."

His hand swept out to draw her attention to what would be a beautiful view of the river and surrounding greenery were she able to appreciate it. "See you any bones lying about?"

How could he jest! "You are not amusing."

"After we cross, you will wonder why you worried so. Leave on your boots, but hike up your skirts."

Nicole's nose wrinkled with distaste, not liking wetting her leather boots. They'd be uncomfortable to walk in afterward. However, she supposed it made sense to wear them. The soles would protect her feet against rocks.

At this moment, Nicole wanted nothing more than to point her nose north and go home to Camelen. Aware that wasn't wise for several reasons, she held out her hand.

"Might I have the rope, please?"

Rhodri dug into the sack and pulled out the length of rope he used as a rabbit snare. With the rope securely belted around her waist, she grabbed hold of the gown's back hem and pulled it up and forward between her legs, as she'd seen peasant women do when laundering clothes in a stream near Camelen. She tucked the back hem under the knot, securing the skirt and baring her calves.

How odd to feel early autumn's cool breeze whisper against her legs, a sensation she'd not enjoyed since outgrowing girlish short tunics. A pleasure she would be most willing to forego if not for the necessity.

Rhodri had bared his legs, too, his breeches rolled up to just under his knees. Nicole couldn't help but admire those sculpted limbs, the muscles of his hair-sprinkled calves clearly defined.

He also inspected her legs. She might have been discomfited by his intense stare, if not for his obvious approval and the flicker of desire that had gone lacking since their night at the farm.

Sleeping in Rhodri's arms had been both wonderful and disturbing. She'd wanted more than those few stirring kisses, more than cuddling against his hard body, but hadn't been bold enough to entice him to further endeavors.

Since then, he'd kept his distance, especially at night, going so far as to bed down on the opposite side of the small fires he built. Deep down Nicole knew Rhodri was being noble, but his rejection still hurt.

Perhaps tonight he wouldn't be so reticent. Maybe she could muster the courage to make a bold advance on his defenses.

But first they must cross the river.

Be bold, be brave. Rhodri was right. Others had used this ford across the Avon. No bones were scattered about.

Except any old bones would have washed downstream.

Nicole swallowed hard and draped her blanket around her shoulders as a mantle, tightening the knot over her breasts.

Rhodri smiled at her preparations. "The river is passable,

Nicole. I doubt the water is very deep here, nor is the river wide. Why, I could throw a rock and hit the opposite bank!"

"Maybe *you* could," she grumbled.

He picked up his walking stick and slung the harp's sack over his shoulder. "Just walk where I do, mind your footing, and stay close."

She already had a plan for doing so. Rhodri no more than turned around when Nicole grabbed a fistful of his tunic. He glanced over his shoulder and smiled but said nothing as they entered the river.

Using his stick, he measured the water's depth before taking steps. When not far from the bank, she felt the tug of flowing water, then the water itself when it flowed over her boots' tops. Sweet mercy, the water was cold, chilling her clear through.

She glanced south toward the bridge, glad to see they'd come far enough along the path and around a bend so they couldn't be seen by the soldiers. Still, she could hear the men's voices carry up the river, though she couldn't understand what they said.

"Careful here," Rhodri quietly ordered.

Indeed, the rocks were smooth and slippery, and the closer to the middle of the river, the deeper the water, the louder the rushing sound, the harder her heart pounded.

Rhodri's breeches were getting wet, as were her skirts that hung just above her knees. Nicole diligently strode forward, her eyes on the opposite bank. Not until the water reached her thighs did she begin to pray.

Her foot slipped on a rock, abruptly unsettling her balance. Only her hold on Rhodri's tunic and his solid footing saved her from a tumble.

He halted, standing sturdy and strong as if rooted in

the riverbed. "The worst is behind us," he whispered. "Only a few more steps."

She tried to smile and tell him she no longer feared for her life—a lie—but smiles and speech were both beyond her. 'Twas all she could manage to slog through the too-cold and swiftly flowing river.

Within four more steps the riverbed began to rise; the water became more shallow. The closer to the bank, the easier each step. The less treacherous the rocks, the more she took comfort in having survived the crossing.

With the water now below her knees, finally confident she wouldn't drown today, Nicole released Rhodri's tunic to gather up the sodden, sagging skirts coming loose from her rope belt.

Rhodri reached the bank first, his longer stride giving him the advantage.

Bemoaning her discomfort, she flung the soaked skirt over her arm. The shift of weight upset her balance. Her foot slid sideways. Nicole dropped her skirts and, with arms reeling, fell backward, hitting the water with an inelegant splash. She shrieked her outrage at her ill fortune before she landed hard on her bottom, her fear of drowning welling up again before she managed to put her hands down to keep from tumbling over.

She felt the veriest fool, sitting in water up to her bosom. If she weren't so angry, she might cry.

Rhodri put down the harp's sack and waded back into the water, trying not to laugh at the humorous sight she presented.

"It appears you let loose of me too soon," he said, planting his feet and extending a hand.

She grasped his hand—and heard a shout. The bend

in the river had put them out of view of the bridge, until now. She could see the very end of the bridge. One of the earl's soldiers stood there, pointing.

Sweet mercy, the soldier must have heard her shriek!

Rhodri pulled her upright. "Hurry," he said curtly.

"Halt!" came the cry from the bridge. "In the name of the earl of Oxford, I order you to halt!"

Nicole scrambled up onto the bank, her heart in her throat, her hand firmly clasped in Rhodri's. Without pausing, he scooped up the harp's sack and turned upriver.

Behind her, she could hear horses' hooves pound across the wooden bridge.

Rhodri steered her to a clump of bushes. He tossed the harp's sack and walking stick in amongst them. "Give me your blanket."

Nicole untied her cumbersome brown shawl, thinking Rhodri intended to lightly hide their belongings and relieve them of extra weight until he added, "Crawl in there. I will cover you so you cannot easily be seen."

Myriad questions begged answers as she settled into the thicket, but only one was important enough to voice. "What do you plan to do?"

"I intend to relieve one of the soldiers of his horse. I will return in a trice."

He tossed the blanket over her, leaving her in the dark to sit and await his return.

She didn't like this at all.

Rhodri intended to take on two soldiers and two battle-trained horses and come away with a horse. True, she'd watched him thrash two guards in Oxford, without a proper weapon. He might now possess a sword, but Nicole well knew the value of a trained horse.

Rhodri could get stomped on! His head split open. His bones broken. He might not come back for her!

Alarmed, Nicole pushed aside the blanket far enough to take a peek toward the bridge. The thicket obscured most of her view, but she could see Rhodri hurrying toward a large oak tree, his sword drawn. He wasn't limping, but certes, if he made one misstep and again injured his ankle, he'd go down and the patrol would have him.

She heard the horses coming toward them, faintly yet, but most definitely headed their way.

Biting down on her bottom lip, she debated over how to help Rhodri, vainly wishing she had a sword and some knowledge of how to use it. Her dagger was in her boot, but the short blade was no match for a sword.

But then, she didn't need a weapon to be of help. She'd assisted Rhodri once before to their benefit.

Rhodri took up position behind the oak tree, taking a moment to push down the legs of his wet breeches before settling into a stance.

Nicole watched the path along the river, awaiting the opportunity to give Rhodri a better advantage.

Chapter Eleven

After a glance behind him to ensure Nicole was huddled securely beneath the blanket, Rhodri settled his stance behind the oak tree.

He'd never been one to shun a fight when it was necessary, as this one had become. True, he would have preferred to slip unnoticed past the men on the bridge. Nicole's fall had rendered that plan nil.

And now they were both wet, Nicole's garments nearly soaked through. Swiftly getting her to an inn or someplace of the like where she could warm up and dry out would be easier accomplished on horseback.

The patrol's horses would do nicely.

The horses were coming at a hard, fast pace, causing the earth to tremble. Rhodri took slow, steady breaths, as he did before entering any battle, to remain calm and concentrate.

Then the horses slowed, their riders likely looking for the spot where he and Nicole had come out of the river.

Rhodri dared a glance around the tree. Indeed, both soldiers studied the riverbank.

The soldiers quickly discerned where the prey they sought had come out of the river. He waited impatiently for the lead soldier to believe Rhodri and Nicole were still running upriver and spur his horse to give chase.

Instead, to Rhodri's chagrin, both soldiers reined in.

"Appears this is where they came out," one said.

"Aye. Do you think they might have gone back to the other side?" the other wanted to know.

Nay, you dolts! Do you not see how trampled and wet the grass is?

"I believe they are still on this side of the river. But where?"

When the lead soldier turned to look around, Rhodri ducked back behind the tree.

"'Ere now, what is this?"

The creak of leather and jingle of tack indicated that at least one of the soldiers dismounted. If both dismounted, then he could rush them without fear of them using the horses to run him down.

"Looks like they went upriver."

Rhodri ventured another peek. Both soldiers had dismounted and were looking north. 'Twas as fine a time as any to attack. With both hands gripping the sword's pummel, a warrior's cry gathering in his lungs, Rhodri heard a voice that jolted him to his soul.

"'Tis about time you found me!"

Nicole!

Rhodri swung around to see her striding toward the soldiers. Confident the soldiers were under the earl's implicit orders not to harm Lady Nicole, Rhodri didn't worry for her safety, only her capture.

But what the devil was she about?

"Lady Nicole?" a soldier asked, and Rhodri couldn't blame the man for questioning the identity of the woman rushing toward him.

Nicole looked like a bedazzling hoyden, not a princess. Her hair was an impossible mass of tangles, several long strands having come undone from the thick braid hanging limp and wet between her breasts. She clutched her dripping, dragging skirts. Her boots squished with each step.

Yet her shoulders were squared, her chin tilted forward, her entire demeanor demanding deference.

"If you hurry," she said with urgency, "one of you should be able to capture the wretched *beast* who has held me captive! Last I saw he was limping his way upriver."

Rhodri slumped against the tree, realizing Nicole was repeating the plan they'd used at Little Gate. He nearly groaned aloud. He realized she wanted to be of help, but he had no need of her aid this time and wished she'd stayed put. He didn't want her to again be in a dangerous position. Had she no confidence in him at all?

He dared another look at the soldiers, who still stared wide-eyed at Nicole. Neither soldier seemed in a hurry to chase after the *wretched beast.*

Nicole placed her fists on her hips. "Surely one of you is brave enough to capture a crippled man!"

Crippled? Hell's bells, he hadn't limped since leaving the farm!

"The Welshman is crippled?" the first soldier asked.

"He can barely walk. While you fetch him, your companion can aid me with my belongings." She turned to the second soldier. "Have you a blanket? I am wet and cold and do not wish to sicken and die before you can return me to the earl."

Reminded of her importance to the earl of Oxford, the second soldier took down the bedroll tied behind his saddle.

Nicole turned back to the first. "Why are you not gone?"

Her tone of arrogant nobility, expecting immediate obedience, this time urged her victim to mount his horse and spur it upriver.

Once more she'd played the princess that she was, and Rhodri wished the devil he knew how to make a princess obey a direct command. True, she'd split the enemy for him, but he would have preferred she'd stayed hidden and out of harm's way.

With his original plan in tatters, with no choice but to allow Nicole's scheme to play out, Rhodri watched Nicole wrap the soldier's dry blanket around her shoulders.

"Oh, how wonderfully warm," she sighed, the sentiment not at all feigned. Then her lashes fluttered at the hapless soldier. "I cannot tell you of how I have suffered in that . . . whoreson's company, or of how grateful I am for your timely rescue."

Whoreson. Rhodri rolled his eyes at her inventive description of him.

The soldier puffed up with unwarranted pride. "The earl will be most pleased to have ye back, milady."

"As I will be most pleased to return to Oxford. But pray, how shall we manage a hasty return with four people and only two horses?"

"Ye can ride with me, milady. As for the Welshman, we will tie him to a lead rope and let him keep up as best he may. The earl will not mind if we drag the whoreson a bit, as long as we take him back alive enough to hang."

Nicole nodded as if the arrangement suited her. "Then let us fetch my belongings so we might leave as soon as your fellow soldier returns."

The soldier turned away for a moment to grab hold of his horse's reins. Nicole turned fully, and only then did she glance around, likely wondering where he was and why he hadn't yet dispatched the soldier.

He was tempted to make her wait a while longer, allow her to worry just a little about his coming to her rescue.

But he couldn't. Nor did he want to take the chance that Nicole might be hurt, so he tucked the sword back into his belt, deciding he didn't have to kill or badly injure the soldier, just knock him out.

Rhodri waited until he was sure he wouldn't be noticed before leaving the protection of the tree. Quietly, he sneaked up behind the guard, grabbed hold of his shoulder, and spun him around. The soldier's eyes went wide, but he didn't have time to bring his hands up or shout a warning before Rhodri planted a solid fist to his chin. The man spun backward and went down in a heap, and stayed there.

Rhodri grabbed hold of the horse's reins before scolding Nicole. "Did I not tell you to remain hidden?"

She didn't look the least remorseful for her disobedience. "I was merely trying to be of help." She glanced down at the unheeding soldier. "Will he be all right, do you think?"

Rhodri didn't much care about the health of the soldier, so he ignored her concern. "I did not require your help and will thank you not to interfere next time."

A storm gathered in her eyes. "I worried you might be trampled by a horse!"

He knew why she worried. Without him to guide her, she'd be alone in unfamiliar lands. Without him to grab hold of, she might have fallen in the middle of the river and drowned. Without his protection, she might now be on her way back to Oxford.

And she didn't fully trust him to protect her, and that stung.

"Shall we depart before either this soldier awakes or the other returns?"

They hurried over to where she'd left their belongings. Nicole snatched up the wet blanket and began to fold it. Rhodri let go of the horse's reins to pick up the harp's sack, planning to tie it to the back of the saddle.

Nicole gave the blanket a shake and, when it didn't straighten as she wished, shook it harder. The flap startled the horse; the resultant snap sent the frightened animal galloping back toward the bridge.

Nicole groaned and hid her face in the blanket. Rhodri could only stare at the escaping horse and blurt out a sharp curse.

How could she have been so careless!

He had every right to upbraid her, but when she uncovered her face, 'twas so full of woe and remorse he didn't have the heart to utter a reprimand.

After a glance at the soldier, who hadn't yet moved, he hefted the sack over his shoulder and headed west, Nicole walking silently sullen at his side.

∽

In a circular clearing about five long paces across, Nicole stood close to the larger-than-usual fire Rhodri had built, not surprised he'd decided to make camp even though the day wasn't yet close to ending.

They both needed to warm up and dry out. Though from the look of the darkening sky, she would wager that about the time her gown started to dry, the rain would fall and soak her through again.

Apparently of the same opinion, Rhodri hurriedly built a shelter of cleverly entwined branches and wide-leafed ferns. She'd offered to help; he'd insisted she stay by the fire.

She didn't press because he hadn't yet forgiven her for her last attempt to lend aid. Still, she'd done what she could to help him make camp without getting in his way.

Both blankets were spread over nearby bushes, with her and Rhodri's short hose spread atop the dry blanket she'd been given by the soldier. Their boots stood side by side close to the fire, roasting nicely, and she carefully watched over them.

Rhodri had already placed the harp's sack and her dagger in the shelter.

He used his sword as a scythe to mow down the ferns, adding several more to the roof before he stepped back to inspect his handiwork.

Nicole glanced down at his bare ankle, which he didn't seem to favor overly and which was no longer swollen. The injury appeared to have healed enough to allow him full use of his ankle.

He'd left the walking stick behind at the river. Chagrined, Nicole admitted she might have misjudged the extent of his injury, misinterpreting the amount of pain. She excused her understandable mistake. She was accustomed to treating the ills and injuries of nuns, not of warriors—a tougher breed.

He tucked the sword back into his belt, apparently satisfied he'd piled enough ferns on the roof to keep out the rain. From the sack, he fetched their last two apples.

As he handed over her combined late nooning and early supper, Nicole wished they were back at the farm, safe and dry, cuddled up on the floor. Before her dunking in the river. Before she'd startled the horse. Before Rhodri couldn't bring himself to speak to her for making such a dim-witted error.

She also wished he would just shout at her, berate her for her error and be done. 'Twould be far more tolerable punishment than his sullen silence.

Nicole swallowed her pride along with a bite of apple. "I am sorry, Rhodri. I truly do know better than to wave a blanket in a horse's face."

He stared into the fire, eating his apple, making no comment. The wretch wasn't about to make her admission of stupidity and the necessary apology easy for her.

"I should have done as you told me and stayed hidden."

"Aye, you should have."

Having finally gained a bit of ground, Nicole yearned for more. "The next time you give me an order, I vow I will obey."

His sharp, humorless burst of laughter didn't bode well. "'Tis not in your nature to obey orders, Nicole. Best not to make vows you cannot keep."

That rankled. "I do not give my word lightly."

"I do not doubt you mean every word you say, or that you will not try to adhere to the vow."

Vexed, she crossed her arms. "Yet you disbelieve me."

"You follow only those orders you find agreeable. The others you dismiss as mere suggestions."

She frowned. Did she? Perhaps so.

Nicole knew Rhodri had her best interests at heart. He was her protector on this journey, and though it chafed to fully admit her shortcomings, she knew his knowledge of surviving in the wild and of how to avoid capture was superior to hers.

"Henceforth, I shall do whatever you say I must do."

He finally looked her way, his expression doubtful. "Will you?"

Resolute, she nodded.

"Wonderful."

He lobbed his apple core into the flames, slid the sword from his belt, undid the buckle, and set both down at his feet. Then he began to undo the laces at his tunic's throat.

Nicole swallowed hard when he pulled the tunic over his head to reveal his muscular, hair-sprinkled chest, the like of which she hadn't seen since watching her father's soldiers in the practice yard at Camelen. The comparison wasn't a good one. Nay, not a one of those soldiers had looked so splendid when bare-chested.

Every muscle in Rhodri's upper arms and chest was startlingly defined. His dark hair didn't soften the hard planes or serve as a shield against her fascination.

Her woman's places flared, the heat spreading throughout her body, her fingers itching to skim over his chest, and lower, where the hair arrowed down over his flat stomach to disappear beneath his breeches.

He held out his brown woolen tunic. "Put this on. It may not be as warm as your gown, but it is drier."

Nicole took the last bite of her apple and tossed the core into the fire, deciding what to do. Was this an offer or an order? Did he test her vow?

True, she'd worn her wet garments too long for health's sake, but he shouldn't sacrifice his own health for hers.

"If I accept your tunic, then you will be cold. The fire is hot, and my gown will soon—"

"Nicole, *change*."

Ruing the vow she'd obviously made too hastily, she snatched the tunic and headed for the thick brush behind the shelter.

When certain Rhodri couldn't see her, she held the tunic to her nose and breathed in the heady, dusky scent of its male owner. Still warm from Rhodri's body, the tunic would soon warm hers.

She hung the tunic over a tree branch and untied the side laces on the gown she'd put on so very many days ago. With a bit of twisting and tugging, she managed to pull both gown and chemise over her head.

Her skin broke out in little bumps. Her nipples puckered in protest against exposure to the chill air. Swiftly, she donned Rhodri's tunic, and just as swiftly her whole body sighed with pleasure.

The sleeves hung down past her fingertips. The tunic's hem, still damp, fluttered at her knees. She gathered the rough wool around her, hugging it to her, basking in Rhodri's heat and scent.

Arousal returned full force. Her nipples again puckered, whether from the rasp of rough wool or from want of Rhodri's touch, she couldn't say. Either way, Nicole relished the sensation.

She rolled up the sleeves, becoming ever more aware

that tonight they would share the shelter and blankets and, 'twas to be hoped, their bodies.

Unless Rhodri was still too angry over the loss of the horse, or bent on being noble.

Then what was she supposed to do to relieve the delicious ache in her nether regions if Rhodri refused to assuage it for her?

She gathered up her garments and slowly padded back to the clearing, the breeze again whispering around the bare legs and feet Rhodri had already seen. Did he wonder about how the rest of her looked, as she wondered about the rest of him?

She had her answer upon entering the clearing.

He looked relieved that she'd finally returned, and then his eyes burned with the desire she hadn't seen from him since they'd left the farm.

"Warmer?" he asked.

So warm she might melt. "Some."

He nodded toward the shelter. "I put a blanket in there for your use. Go on in. I will spread out your garments to dry."

Nicole decided her best course was to obey his order this time, too. Perhaps when he was done testing her vow, he would be more willing to act on his desire.

He'd spread the blanket on the ground of the shelter, the blanket being larger than the space it covered. With them both and all their belongings tucked inside, it would indeed be a cozy place to spend the rest of the afternoon and the long night.

She ducked inside and sat cross-legged in the corner near the harp's sack to watch Rhodri separate her chemise from her gown and spread them over a bush. He took his time at the task. Feeling her warmth? Catching a whiff of her scent?

She wanted to invite him into the nest he'd built but knew that at the moment he'd refuse. He guarded the boots still near the fire, and her garments and their hose, and would likely do so until everything was dry or the rain began to fall.

With a short stick, he poked at the fire, resettling the wood. The day wasn't over, but clouds the color of thick smoke blocked the sun, the fire's flames a beacon on a gray day.

"You are not worried about the patrol finding us again," she commented.

"Unless the man I struck makes a fast recovery, and he manages to find his horse in timely manner, they will not likely begin their search until morn." He looked up at the foreboding sky. "Let us hope they are blessed with enough foresight to ware the weather the same as we."

He'd been right before, so she had to trust his judgment, something she was learning to do.

But now that she'd broken free of the restraints of clerical life, enjoying a freedom she'd never experienced, it was damn hard to place her fate in another's hands, even Rhodri's large, strong, capable ones.

Again he stirred the fire. The firelight caressed his chest and broad shoulders, tingeing his skin with a golden glow.

Her fingers itched to touch every inch of that expanse of bare skin. To keep her restless hands busy, she tore the travel-weary length of leather from the end of her braid, intending to pull apart the worst of the tangles.

Lock by lock she unwound the braid and, with a shake, sent the waist-long tresses tumbling down her back and over her shoulders. Bemoaning the loss of the comb she'd left behind in Oxford, she had no choice but to settle for the imperfect grooming of separating the strands with her fingers.

The rake of nails against scalp felt wonderful. A wash would feel better still. If she could collect rainwater—but she had no bucket or even mug to collect it in. 'Twas amazing how many ordinary things one didn't miss until one had to get by without them, and how annoyed one could become by the deprivation.

Complaining would do her no good. Rhodri couldn't provide a means to collect water. But he'd said after they crossed the Avon the risk of capture would lessen, so they might risk staying at an inn soon. Which meant she might bathe, and wash her hair, and borrow a comb.

That pleasant possibility in mind, she again shook her head hard and slid spread fingers through her unruly, damp mane. It would dry faster if she stood by the fire, if Rhodri would allow her to come out of the shelter.

She looked up, intending to make the request. His expression stopped her.

He'd been watching her tend her hair, and her womanly instincts understood his preference that she should continue.

Mon dieu, could a man be seduced by so simple an action? Nicole had no notion, having never before made the attempt.

So she again ran her fingers through her long locks, from scalp to tips, spreading her arms wide to reach the ends, holding him enthralled, as if she were a woodland sprite, silently beckoning him to join her in a lusty pagan ritual.

A low rumble of thunder snapped the delicious fantasy and spurred Rhodri into a frenzy of gathering boots, garments, and the other blanket.

He ducked low to enter the shelter and dumped the blanket and garments into her lap while he arranged their hose-stuffed boots in the far corner. Miffed by nature's intrusion, disgruntled by the sharp return to reality, Nicole swept her hair to the side and began folding the garments.

The linen chemise was nearly dry. She should probably put it on and give Rhodri's tunic back to him. But unwilling to give up the tunic's warmth and Rhodri's scent, she placed the chemise atop the sack, followed by her not-quite-as-dry gown.

He bumped her shoulder twice while settling his large body across the back of the shelter, his knees bent because he couldn't stretch out fully, his bare feet behind her rump.

The rain began to fall, hissing into the fire's flames, pattering softly on the ferns.

Rhodri rolled his shoulders, setting muscles to rippling and her insides to fluttering. "Good time to catch up on our sleep," he muttered before closing his eyes.

She didn't want to sleep and suspected Rhodri didn't truly want to, either. Confident the bulge in his breeches bespoke his true yearnings, Nicole laid aside the blanket and, still cross-legged, scooted around to face him.

Rhodri's eyes remained closed, but he was awake and surely as aware of her as she of him. His glorious body tempted her beyond endurance. The memory of his kisses urged her to solicit another kiss—and more.

And the man was being obstinate. She wanted to shake

him into taking the lead, have him kiss her senseless so she wouldn't be pestered by all the righteous, sensible reasons she should leave him alone.

Aye, there might be penalties aplenty for losing her virginity in this woodland shelter, but for desire of Rhodri, every one of those reasons seemed trifling or endurable.

Audaciously, she placed a hand on his stomach, and to her delight, his muscles twitched beneath her touch and his breath hitched. The response delighted her, but she couldn't voice her spiraling need outright.

"Your breeches are still damp. You should take them off."

His eyes opened, narrowly. "That would not be wise."

Probably not, but she couldn't allow wisdom to intrude.

"You considered it wise for me to change out of my wet gown. The same should hold true for you."

He was silent for a moment before saying, "For your first time, you deserve better than a tumble—" he glanced around at the shelter "—here."

In the sturdy, cozy shelter he'd built, both of them already half naked, and no one about to disturb them— Nicole could think of no better place or time.

"Better in here than out there in the mud."

The corner of his mouth twitched with amusement, and his long-fingered hand, rough with the calluses of a warrior, gently caressed her cheek, eliciting another wave of passion to surge through her.

"Better than in the mud, but not as nice as a thick mattress."

Nicole leaned into his touch, so welcome and thrilling against her skin. Right now, if he ordered her outside into the mud, she'd comply.

Near breathless with need, she suggested, "Perhaps next time."

With an agility and speed Nicole didn't question, Rhodri swept her up to lie angled atop him. He hadn't removed his breeches, or she his tunic, but as Rhodri claimed her mouth in a most gratifying kiss, Nicole didn't doubt that soon they'd be skin to skin, male to female.

At long last, Rhodri would become her lover.

Chapter Twelve

With Nicole's lips pressed against his, her persuasive body seeking better purchase against his chest, Rhodri knew resistance was futile. His good intentions couldn't compete against his own desire for Nicole and the woman's inexperienced but effective seduction.

And sweet mercy, he admired her for far more than her delectable body.

Her earthy sense of humor charmed and amused him, more now that she was grown.

Any other noblewoman would have long ago foresworn this ill-favored journey, despairing of the hardships. Not Nicole, who'd forged through the brambles, climbed over logs, even forded a river though frightened to her core.

And her nature was to think things through before acting—when hailing down the farmer for a ride in his cart, or even when creating a diversion for him at the river.

Nicole's placing a hand on his stomach and reaching out for him hadn't been a whim. She knew she might suffer consequences if they became lovers but had decided

the price wasn't high enough to deny them the pleasure
they both craved.

Rhodri indulged his earlier wish to play with a lock
of her unbound hair. Had Nicole known, when she'd unwound the braid and shook her head, setting the glorious
tresses loose to tumble around her in a sensual veil, how
much she'd tempted him? Aroused him? Perhaps, but
likely not.

The gift of her virginity wasn't to be taken lightly, and
he would honor her boldness and bravery with passionate
gentleness and ensure she reached ecstasy.

With that worthy and admittedly selfish goal in mind,
Rhodri aided her effort to fully sprawl atop him, her
weight welcome, his tunic an irritating barrier between
her skin and his. His hands slid down her sleek sides and
grabbed fistfuls of tunic, pulling it up until his palms
cupped the cheeks of her tight, enticingly curved buttocks, eliciting a startled but not fearful gasp.

Gently, slowly.

The reminder of her inexperience kept him from
squeezing her backside too hard, until Nicole's eyes went
dark with intense passion and she kissed him fiercely,
firing his loins, damn near obliterating all thought but
one—of burying his cock deep within Nicole and never
retreating.

Thunder rumbled in the distance. What remained of
those senses tuned toward their survival noted that the
worst of the storm would pass far to the north, that he
need not be concerned that either wind or rain would
wreak havoc with their meager shelter.

A good thing, because Nicole was wreaking havoc
within.

Her thighs now straddled his right leg. He wished to heaven he'd removed his breeches, eager for skin to rub against skin. But then, anticipation was one of the delights of coupling with a woman, and with this woman he intended to prolong the enjoyment to fullest measure.

And ensure Nicole enjoyed their coupling to full measure, too, giving her no reason for complaint afterward.

So, for now, his breeches must stay on, but by the saints, his damn tunic did not. He pushed the rough fabric upward, over the dip of her trim waist. His thumbs grazed along the lowest of her ribs, and with no prodding at all, Nicole braced on his shoulders and eased upward a few inches, allowing him to grasp her breasts.

The soft but firm mounds filled his hands, the nubs hard against his palms. She moaned low in her throat, a sultry approval of his sensual petting and of the particular attention he paid to the sensitive tips no other man had been granted the esteemed privilege to touch.

The honor both humbled him and urged him onward, the wish to see as well as feel now an overpowering need.

"Sit up," he commanded in a feral growl that Nicole obeyed immediately.

She leaned back against his upraised knee, her own knee pressing in hard against his balls. He hissed at the splendid intimacy, swept the offensive tunic over her head, and beheld Nicole in her naked glory.

Skin the hue of cream. High, proud breasts, the tips a dark rose. The thatch of curls at the juncture of her thighs matched the red-tinged brown of her lovely tresses.

"Magnificent," he whispered.

She blushed, coloring not only her cheeks but her throat and upper chest, as well. Though self-conscious of her bared body, she neither argued with his praise nor sought to shield herself from his view.

Nor was she willing to sit quietly and allow him to admire her beauty overlong. She hooked a finger under the waist of his breeches, knuckling his navel.

"You next," she ordered.

He didn't dare remove his breeches yet. "Soon, after you are prepared to receive me."

She tilted her head, her confusion sincere. "What more is there than the joining?"

Apparently Nicole knew no more about coupling with a man than what transpired at the end. He could unleash his cock, pierce her maidenhead, take his pleasure, and she'd be none the wiser.

"Much more. Kissing. Touching. Fondling. All make the joining easier and more memorable."

She smiled at that. "I enjoyed the kissing part."

"Then come down here for another."

Flesh pressed to flesh. Her mouth tasted of apple dipped in honey. He collected kiss after kiss, until her lips swelled from his tender abuse. Until her soft moans demanded he further prove his statement.

Rhodri eased them onto their sides, their legs entwined thigh to thigh, and worshiped her breasts with reverent caresses and primitive suckling. Nicole squirmed when he lavished attention on both, licking at one and petting the other.

"I believe I . . . like that . . . too. Are we not yet . . . done preparing?"

Her thready breaths thrilled him. The rapid beat of her heart echoed his own. Her ardor was nearly his undoing, but he couldn't yet allow his passion free rein.

"Nearly." He abandoned those sweet breasts to glide a hand along her silken skin, down over the curve of her hip, and up her sensitive inner thighs before ruffling the curls at her entrance.

Her lower body arched at the intrusion of a single finger into her hot, wet sheath. He stroked her slowly, mimicking the coupling soon to come.

She writhed and thrashed. He was losing any sense of control while marveling at Nicole's uninhibited response, aware that when she reached ecstasy, she would pulse hard—and he wanted to be within her, to feel her inner muscles grasp and release his cock when she came undone.

Rhodri rose up to his knees and pulled loose his breeches' lacing. Nicole's eyes were wide with anticipation of his unveiling, staring at his crotch so intently it gave him pause.

He hadn't disappointed a woman yet, had been told often enough that his cock and balls were huge, and well formed, and never failed to please. So why, with Nicole, did he spare a moment's worry over her reaction to his male parts?

She'd never coupled with a man before, likely never seen a male fully naked, much less in a state of arousal. What if she found his parts repulsive and recoiled?

His ridiculous hesitation gave Nicole time to rise up on an elbow and place a hand along the bulge in his breeches.

"What must I do to prepare you?"

He was too damn prepared already—not a normal state for him. He usually enjoyed a woman's attentions, with both hand and mouth, particularly if a woman knew how to effectively use her tongue.

An image of Nicole taking a long, slow lick along his shaft was nearly his undoing. If he didn't enter her soon, he might well go mad.

"I am prepared," he stated, shoving down the rough cloth to reveal his absolute readiness.

Her doe-brown eyes widened further. To his relief he saw no fear, only curiosity. 'Twas hell to remain unmoving under her inspection, worse still to endure the touch of a single finger to his tip. His cock twitched in answer, drawing forth an odd smile from the woman it craved to satisfy.

"Magnificent," Nicole declared, and Rhodri could stand the waiting no more.

After a few deft movements, he knelt between her spread legs, her knees raised. Poised to slide within her depths, he wished he'd built the shelter a bit longer so he could properly stretch out atop her. Instead, he placed his hands beneath her buttocks and raised her up to meet him.

Watching him, surely realizing what he was about to do to her, Nicole's fists clutched the blanket she lie upon.

And knowing what he was about to do to her, Rhodri again ran a thumb through her moist heat, the last of his preparations. Her response was immediate and most gratifying.

Sure that Nicole was on the verge of a woman's bliss, he slid inside that tight, hot place where he'd yearned to be, sorry he must be the one to hurt her, not sorry at all he was her first. Her inner muscles clamped around him in an arousing caress. When his penetration was halted by a barrier, he struggled for control.

"Some women feel pain when the maidenhead breaks; some do not. Either way, 'twill be over in a trice, and then all will be pleasure."

The warning and promise given, Rhodri thrust swiftly to breach the maidenhead, then plummeted deep to fill her, claiming Nicole as his lover.

She cried out, her head tilted back—and then she relaxed, and smiled.

"Not so bad," she said softly.

Grinning like a fool for an accomplishment he truly couldn't take credit for, with solid, bold strokes Rhodri strove to keep his promise. With each thrust and withdrawal, his smile faded a bit more, as did Nicole's.

Sweat beaded on his upper lip. Nicole's eyes closed, her lips parted and breath ragged. His grip on his control began to slip away, the agony an ecstasy all its own.

With a shudder and hiss, Nicole bucked upward. The pulse of her bliss washed over him, permitting the rapture of his own release. Tremors shook him to his core, deeply, violently, with pleasure too intense to describe.

Nicole went limp, staring up at him in awe. "Oh, Rhodri," she whispered and reached for him.

To answer Nicole's invitation to embrace, he reluctantly slipped from inside her and, with a bit of rearranging of limbs, joined her on the blanket. The only way for them to both lie down in the small space available was on their sides, her back pressed to his front, their knees raised.

Her tight, firm bottom squirmed, and parts of him that should be satisfied and silent began to anticipate activities he shouldn't be able to perform as yet. Hellfire, how could he become randy again so soon?

Perhaps it was the scent of her hair, so close to his nose the stray hairs moved with his outward breath. Or because he could feel the silken skin of her breasts on the arm he'd wrapped around her.

Or maybe he'd simply been without a woman for too long.

Rhodri scoffed at the inept attempt to explain away the incomparable experience of coupling with Nicole. No woman had come close to pleasing him half so much, and Nicole had not done much physically at all. Sweet mercy, even when he was old and gray and withered, he would remember this night in a fern-covered shelter with unrivaled fondness.

She sighed. "Do you think the rain might fall for a day or two? And if it does, must we venture out in it?"

Her wistful questions gave him pause and, for a moment, he entertained the idea of halting their journey and staying curled up in the shelter—naked—for another day.

"The earl's patrol is out there somewhere, and I suspect Connor is beginning to watch for us. Rain or not, we must move on."

And Connor wasn't going to be happy if he learned Nicole was no longer a virgin. She wasn't meant for the likes of him, but for a prince, as a means to unify a country, and to bear fruit on the Welsh branch of Pendragon.

Rhodri tried to upbraid himself for taking advantage of the foul weather, and Nicole's state of undress, and the overwhelming temptation he hadn't been able to resist—and couldn't.

Perhaps at some later time he'd feel the need for contrition or atonement. But for tonight, and for several nights yet to come, Nicole was his, and for that Rhodri couldn't summon a wisp of sorrow or regret.

He pushed away the hair from her shoulder and placed a string of kisses along her bare skin, paying particular heed to the curve of her neck.

"Mmmm."

He smiled at her approval. "You like that."

"Oh, aye."

So he continued, his hand moving slightly to cup the swell of her breast, his thumb finding and grazing the nub at the tip.

She laughed lightly. "Now I know why Sister Amelia was always so joyful when Bishop Edward came to visit."

He didn't have to ask why and was rather pleased that Nicole considered their coupling enjoyable.

The notion of a nun servicing a bishop didn't shock Rhodri. He knew of many men of the Church who kept a mistress or a housekeeper. Sons of bishops could be assured of high positions within the Church, and their daughters of good marriages.

"Odd for a bishop to keep his mistress in a nunnery."

"The arrangement suited them. Mother Abbess did not approve, but short of locking Amelia in a cellar, there was naught she could do to keep the lovers apart." She was quiet for a moment before softly asking, "Do you have a mistress?"

The question was fraught with danger if he wasn't careful in answering. But Nicole needed assurance that, for the present, she was his only lover.

"No mistress."

"But you have had other lovers." Before he could form a suitable comment, she continued, "Naturally, you have, or you would not have known so precisely what to do. I suppose I should be grateful that one of us had some knowledge of coupling, because I knew naught."

Rhodri wasn't sure which irked her more—his having

had previous lovers, or her lack of knowledge of carnal matters. He could do nothing about his former experience with women, except use his knowledge to add to hers, selfish beast that he was.

"You now know somewhat of the pleasure a man and woman can share, and I would be pleased to teach you all I know."

"Tonight?"

"Not *all* tonight, but enough so you do not feel so unskilled next time. And truly, Nicole, most of making love to a partner is merely doing what makes the other feel good. Like this."

Rhodri applied himself to the delightful lesson of showing Nicole which parts of her body were most sensitive to his touch, petting and kissing until she again moaned with need.

"This seems unfair," she said. "Surely I should be taking a more active part, pleasuring you, too."

This time she could. This time he would be slower to rouse and better able to maintain control over a cock again readying to do its duty and be blissfully compensated for its efforts.

"Come up atop me," he said and was rewarded with near instant obedience.

On his back, with Nicole half lying, half sitting across his body, he cursed the space constraints that limited their movements, didn't allow them the freedom to enjoy each other to full measure. But there was always tomorrow night, and that would be another new experience.

Nicole's doe-brown eyes were wide and full of the curiosity and eagerness of a new student wanting to know which harp strings to pluck, in which order, to play a pleasant melody. Best to allow her to explore the instrument first.

He placed his hands behind his head. She gave him a questioning look, then smiled in a way he thought a bit too knowledgeable and cunning for a novice.

"I am to touch you as you touched me, am I not?"

It wasn't truly a question, and she didn't wait for an answer before testing her assumption. Lightly, at first, she explored his upper chest, fingers fluttering over his collarbone, palms massaging his breasts. She used her thumbs as he had, teasing his nipples to hard nubs, a normally sweet stimulation that he enjoyed but didn't usually respond to overmuch—until now, when it was Nicole's thumbs grazing his nipples.

Next she found the jagged scar over his lower ribs and frowned at the result of an old wound. "Dagger?"

"Sword."

"Practice?"

"Battle."

"Did you allow the wretch to live?" she asked fiercely.

He smiled at her ire that someone should dare mark him and not pay the penalty. "No."

"Good!" she declared, then bent down to gently, reverently kiss the scar from end to end, as if to ease any lingering pain.

The brush of her lips sent tendrils of heat straight to his loins, but the veneration of her actions tugged at his heart and brought a lump to his throat. But before he could sort out his peculiar combination of reactions, Nicole discovered that if she raked fingernails across his stomach she could make the muscles twitch.

He sucked in hard, tightening that area too vulnerable to tickling, refusing to double over in laughter under her effort to torment him. She gave up tormenting him quickly enough, only to try her hand at exquisite torture.

A touch so light, so innocent, shouldn't stiffen him to steel so fast. All she'd done was circle the tip before lightly stroking the shaft, and already his cock appreciated the attention as if it had been expertly handled.

This wasn't right. He'd obtained release only a few minutes ago, should be able to withstand hours of lustful fondling without fear of erupting in a woman's hand or worrying about his stamina when it became important to his partner's pleasure.

He feared. He worried.

Rhodri pulled Nicole up for a kiss before she could further damage his threadbare control over his desire to toss her on her back and rut like a wild beast.

Except her kisses fueled the flames, his sanity slipping away with the smoke. From somewhere in the haze he heard his name on her sweet lips.

"Hmmm?"

"So as a man can take a woman, so can a woman take a man."

Oh, blessed be, if only she would just *do* it.

And then she did. Straddling him, she found the source of his need and slid down, down, down until she fully entrapped him in her slick heat.

He shuddered at her possession, questioning the wisdom of allowing Nicole to become the aggressor and he her willing victim. More fool he, he'd meant to teach and ended up learning.

But he *was* a bard, and he knew that while a melody

played with single notes could be entrancing, the song was always enriched with harmony.

Her hands pressed to the blanket on either side of his head, Nicole hovered over him like a victorious goddess, splendid in her nudity and unbound tresses. And it would be his pleasure to haul the goddess back to this earthly realm.

With deft movements, he latched on to a dark rose nipple and suckled hard, using teeth and tongue to nip and soothe. She remained still, her eyes closing, her breath soon breaking into passionate little pants. Her hips began to move, imitating the stroking rhythm she'd learned when he'd taken her.

Almost, he let her have her way, but for harmony her body must thrum with his. Reluctantly, he released her breast and pushed her upward, pulling her knees forward so she sat upright.

Never had he been so deep within a woman, but while his cock cried for release, he slid a finger between them and played insistently within her moist folds.

She arched and shattered first, with her head thrown back and a moan in her throat. For the second time on a rainy afternoon, Rhodri enjoyed the bliss of a successful sensual encounter.

The goddess fell, limp and sated, onto his chest. "Sweet heaven above, never tell me there is more to learn."

He chuckled. "No more lessons tonight," he said, wondering which of them would, next time, be the teacher.

∽

Alone in the shelter, wrapped in the blanket which now bore a small dried bloodstain, staring out at the night's rain turned to morning mist, Nicole marveled at how very alive she felt, and how very tired and sore.

And at how very willing she was to endure another lesson if Rhodri would only allow it.

He would not, however. Even now he was fully dressed and out "taking bearings," or so he'd said. He'd left her here to also dress and begin preparing for a walk in the English mist, and she hadn't yet brought herself to budge.

She shook her head at her foolishness, sitting here like a petulant child, wondering what the devil was wrong with her.

Last night had been a magnificent revelation, and during their lovemaking she'd taken great pleasure in the sensations of touching and being touched. The stirring kisses. The blissful, astounding completion.

Afterward she'd slept the sleep of the innocent, warm and safe in Rhodri's arms, beneath the blanket he'd covered them with when insisting their coupling was over for the night and they should sleep.

Truly, she didn't regret having lain with Rhodri, allowing him liberties and taking several of her own. She'd come into her full womanhood willingly, joyfully. The signs of her lost innocence were all there, from the soreness of chafed nipples, to the niggling sensation in her nether regions of having been stretched to accommodate Rhodri's size, to the bloodstain on the blanket they'd frolicked on and then slept in.

So why did she feel somehow incomplete this morn, as if she'd missed something important in Rhodri's lessons last eve?

If she were now fully a woman, shouldn't she feel

more than the physical effects of the coupling? Shouldn't she feel older, perhaps wiser and more worldly?

Why the discontent this morn when she'd been utterly content throughout the night?

Would Rhodri know?

Again she shook her head, sure that she wouldn't ask Rhodri about her probably foolish, useless musings. Perhaps all women experienced an emotional bloodletting on the morning after their first coupling, even if the coupling had been a splendid affair. To have him realize she hadn't even known *that* about coupling wasn't to be borne.

And oh, how she wished to share a private moment with either Gwendolyn or Emma! One of them would surely have an answer to soothe her upset. But her sisters were beyond her current reach, and she wouldn't see them anytime soon, so she would simply have to work this out for herself.

Resolute, she flung off the blanket, yanked on her clothing, and prepared to make ready to leave. From outside she heard a rustle in the brush and, believing Rhodri purposely alerted her to his return, thought nothing of it.

Until a male voice softly called her name, and she froze.

Not Rhodri. Not a spirit.

Her heart beating wildly, she recognized the voice of the beloved mercenary who'd married her sister Emma.

Somehow, he'd found her.

How? *Why?*

Having no answers, but praying her sister Emma might not be so far away after all, Nicole burst out of the shelter and flew into the arms of Darian of Bruges.

Chapter Thirteen

Rhodri crouched out of sight, sword in his sweating hand, his heart pounding against his ribs.

Somehow, a tall, well-hewn man garbed all in black had slipped past his guard and entered the camp. Nicole must know the man, or she wouldn't be hugging him, smiling. A smile also softened the intruder's otherwise rugged face.

Rhodri's grip on the sword tightened, ready to run the man through for doing no more than embracing Nicole and making her smile. But more, he wanted to punish the man for having entered the camp unseen and unheard, posing a new danger Rhodri didn't know how to deal with as yet.

And he heartily disliked not knowing.

Nicole backed away far enough to look up at the man but not leave his embrace.

"'Tis good to see you, Darian! Is Emma with you?"

"Nay, little one. Emma is at Camelen, with Gwendolyn. Both of your sisters are most concerned for your welfare. You chose a bad time for an adventure, Nicole, with Gwendolyn so close to her babe's birth."

Nicole accepted the scold without rancor. "I did not mean to worry my sisters. 'Tis one of the reasons I have stayed away from Camelen, so not to cause Gwendolyn any hardship. How does she fare?"

"Last I saw, she paced the hall, fretting."

Rhodri saw Nicole's heartrending regret even as he figured out the man's identity. Darian of Bruges, a Flemish mercenary, once a king's trusted assassin, now Emma's husband and pledged to serve Gwendolyn's husband, Alberic.

Damn! He couldn't slice off the hands that dared hold fast to Nicole's upper arms. She would be most wroth with him for injuring a man whom she obviously held in affection.

But 'twas certainly time to interrupt, before Darian convinced Nicole that returning to the bosom of her family was her only course.

Rhodri slid the sword beneath his belt and stepped into the small clearing, making enough noise to alert Darian and Nicole to his presence. Both turned to look at him, Nicole misty-eyed, Darian with a cold, evaluating stare.

Nicole finally stepped away from her brother-by-marriage. "Rhodri ap Dafydd, this is Darian of Bruges, my sister Emma's husband. He means us no harm."

Rhodri inwardly scoffed. Not physical harm, perhaps, but this was no chance meeting. Darian had come seeking Nicole, likely intending to take her home, which Rhodri couldn't allow.

And Darian was currently taking Rhodri's measure, just as he'd taken Darian's, deciding on the best way to vanquish a foe if necessary.

Nicole was a precious gem coveted by two greedy men, though the reasons for the men's greed were different.

Nicole stood between them, not more than an arm's

span away from both men, physically showing no preference to either.

Rhodri longed to grab hold of Nicole and push her behind him but didn't dare. Darian would be on him in a gnat's breath. The man didn't carry a sword, but from what Rhodri knew of Darian's reputation, the mercenary didn't need a sword to either put up a defense or send a man to his grave.

"You two have caused quite a stir," Darian commented.

Looking a bit sheepish, Nicole tossed a dismissive hand in the air. "Not all is as it may seem, Darian, or as you may have heard."

"The messenger sent to Camelen was most thorough when relating the details of your leaving the abbey and your escape from Oxford. So, too, were the two soldiers who drank overmuch in the inn last eve. Since you are not begging *me* to save you from this whoreson, I shall assume my original conjecture correct, that you aided Rhodri's escape from Oxford, just as you helped him escape the earl's patrol yester noon."

Nicole's mouth twisted with chagrin. "We have tried to maintain the ruse that Rhodri forced me to go with him. If you discerned the truth, then others might, too."

"But others will not know for certain, as I was not sure, unless they see you together in an unguarded moment."

While Rhodri gave the man his due for a correct conjecture, he was more concerned with Darian's revelation. "I gather the inn is on the road ahead. Are the soldiers still there?"

"They were when I left. Last eve, we overheard them planning to begin a search this morn, so I departed the inn well before they were up and about."

"We?" Nicole asked.

Darian's smile for Nicole was soft. Sympathetic?

"Alberic is here, too. We decided it best that I come find you and bring you to the inn, so you would have time to prepare to see him."

Nicole's expression said she would rather not see Alberic. Why would she need to prepare? Did bad feelings still exist between the two for her childhood attempt to stab him with a dagger, or because Alberic had then sent Nicole away from Camelen to reside at Bledloe Abbey? Perhaps both, but it didn't matter. If he had his way, they'd not be going to the inn.

Rhodri stepped closer to Nicole, into a better position to push her behind him if he must.

Darian arched an eyebrow, a small sign he understood the shift in stance.

"We cannot risk the inn if the earl's patrol is there. You can tell Alberic, and Nicole's sisters, they need not worry over her well-being. I will see her safely to Wales and her uncle Connor."

Darian crossed his arms. "Aye, well, that is one of the questions for which Alberic would like an answer—for what reason you were at Bledloe Abbey to begin with."

Rhodri opened his mouth to tell the false tale he'd given everyone else; Darian held up a hand to forestall the explanation.

"No sense explaining twice. Besides, the decision over what to do with Nicole is Alberic's, not mine." Darian's eyes narrowed to dangerous slits. "I *will* take Nicole to Alberic. 'Tis your decision to come with us or no, *alive* or no."

Rhodri grabbed hold of the sword's hilt. Nicole placed

a hand atop his, her fear and anger so apparent he could almost smell it.

"Cease! Both of you! I will not have you two fighting. Rhodri, pray you, I must see Alberic. He is lord of Camelen and so is now patriarch of my family. He and Darian have come all this way to find me and should be granted the courtesy of an explanation. Once done, we can go on."

She was doing it again, turning plea-filled eyes on him, determined to have her way, battering at his resolve.

Her respect for Alberic and Darian was commendable and reasonable—but damn—he didn't want to be reasonable! If they went into that inn, he might not be able to get her back out.

And would that be so bad?

Yes, his heart shouted. *Perhaps not,* a less selfish part of him contradicted.

Had he only Nicole's best interests at heart, then allowing her to go home to Camelen with Alberic, giving up the task Connor had set him to, letting her go to possibly never see her again, might be best for her.

Failing Connor didn't sit well but could be explained. Letting go of Nicole fair twisted his gut, especially when she'd made it clear she wished to see Alberic only before going on to Wales. With him.

But once Alberic had Nicole within his grasp, would the baron allow her out? Going to the inn was sheer folly!

"If you are so anxious to see Alberic, then why does it bother you so much that you must prepare?"

"'Tis not Alberic I must prepare for, but William. My brother's spirit still wishes me to avenge his death and so rants at me to kill Alberic whenever we are together, which of late has been whenever Alberic brought Gwendolyn to the abbey for a visit. I have no doubt that the moment I set eyes on Alberic, William will know and again order me to do murder."

Stunned, Rhodri struggled with this new twist. Aye, she'd told him she could hear spirits, had told him of the first time she'd heard William. But she'd also said she must be near where the person either had died or was buried. They were nowhere near either of the places of her brother's death or burial, so she shouldn't be able to hear William's voice.

Except she was so certain that she would, as must be Darian and Alberic to have made allowances for it. Both men must have known of Nicole's ability to hear spirits, and in particular of William's ranting, for some time.

Truly, this was madness.

"How is it you are able to hear William's spirit when we are leagues upon leagues away from the places of his death and burial?"

"I know not. He is the only spirit who can reach me wherever I seem to be. I fear he would be only the stronger if I were home. 'Twas another reason I did not press you harder to take me to Camelen."

He'd wondered why she'd given in so easily, thinking his powers of persuasion had ruled. Instead, she'd been rather averse to the idea of going home all along, because of William.

Hellfire, if William's spirit had the power to reach Nicole wherever she might be, the spirit would be stronger and harder to resist at Camelen, the place of William's burial!

He glanced at Darian, who didn't seem surprised at any of this and was still willing to take her into Alberic's presence. Damn cruel, he thought.

"If you do not see Alberic, then you need not deal with William. Best we simply be on our way and let Darian assure your family—"

She placed a finger to his lips, her smile returning. "As I said, I see Alberic once a year, at Easter, when he brings Gwen to the abbey for a visit. I have quieted William before and can do so again. I refuse to avoid any of my family because of a dead brother's refusal to listen to reason."

Nicole's finger slid from his lips to place her palm on his chest, over his heart. "I need to talk to Alberic, Rhodri, if only to assure him that I have come to no harm."

She was set on this course, and there was no way to prevent it short of besting Darian and forcing Nicole to go with him.

At one time, he'd suffered nary a qualm over kidnapping Nicole. But no longer. Especially after last night.

Calling himself all kinds of a fool, he tore his gaze away from those doe-brown eyes he couldn't seem to find the willpower to resist. He looked to Darian, who hadn't said a word since threatening his life.

"What of the earl's soldiers?"

"Leave them to me."

Then Darian gave a sharp whistle, and from out of the woods came a splendid, obviously well-trained horse. "Your mount awaits, my lady."

Which earned Darian another smile and hug from Nicole, leaving Rhodri with his arms empty, his heart aching, and getting a bad feeling about meeting Alberic of Chester, lord of Camelen.

❧

From her high perch atop the horse, Nicole called down to a still-disgruntled Rhodri. "If it eases your mind, Darian must consider you an honorable man, or he would not entrust you with me or his horse."

Indeed, Darian had surprised her a few moments ago when, after announcing that the inn was less than a league ahead, he'd handed over the reins to Rhodri before sprinting silently into the woods to check on the whereabouts of the earl's soldiers.

"We should take the horse and ride hard," Rhodri grumbled, not bothering to look up at her, walking along at a steady pace to a meeting he most certainly did not wish to attend.

"But we will not."

"If I did not believe Darian would hunt me down and slit my throat for stealing both his sister-by-marriage and his horse, I would give flight consideration."

Long ago she'd accepted the mercenary her sister married, a man who could coldly, secretly take another man's life when necessary. Darian was quite capable of disposing of anyone he judged a threat.

Alberic would do the same, only without secrecy. He would simply challenge his enemy and then cut him down.

Such were the men her sisters had married—ruthless when they must be, and yet the most devoted of husbands and loving of fathers.

And she cherished them both.

As she was coming to cherish Rhodri, too.

In some ways he was much like her brothers-by-marriage—a warrior when he must be, yet gentle with innocent children. Would he also be a devoted husband?

He was most certainly an excellent lover.

She bit her bottom lip, well aware this line of thought wasn't wise, but she couldn't help but wonder what it would be like to be Rhodri's wife. To lie with him every night, live in the court of a Welsh prince as the honored mate of a *pencerdd*.

Useless musings, to be sure. They might have become lovers, but they would not become mates.

Nicole had never balked at having her husband chosen for her by her father or brother or, after their deaths, by her royal guardian. Rarely were women afforded the luxury of choosing their mates. Truth to tell, neither did men of a certain rank choose their wives. Marriage wasn't a personal affair, but one of political alliance, or to otherwise benefit the involved families, or as a benevolent overlord's reward to a favored underling.

She couldn't marry Rhodri ap Dafydd, but she wished to marry someone like him. Solid and sure. Possessing the power of a warrior and heart of a poet.

Rhodri ap Dafydd was a rare man.

The inn came into view. In the yard, Darian stood near the stables in plain sight—the agreed-upon signal that the earl's soldiers were gone, or that Darian had ensured the soldiers' absence.

Rhodri glanced over his shoulder to look up at her. "Are you prepared?"

She smiled down at him. "More ready than you are, I suspect. I can assure you that Alberic is not so much a royalist that he would give you up to the earl."

"Aye, well, Alberic was enough of a royalist to obey

the king's order to send you to Bledloe Abbey, and you are still Stephen's ward. Are you not at all concerned that he feels compelled to hand you back into the king's care?"

As they'd walked along the road this morn, Darian had related the tale of how he and Alberic had come to look for her, and Nicole was glad the reasons were more personal than political. And while she was sorry she'd caused her sisters to worry, she also took their concern as a sign she was loved.

"At the moment, Alberic is more concerned with easing Gwendolyn's mind over my well-being than aught else."

"To do that he must take you back to Camelen. What then, Nicole? Into whose care will his king demand he hand you over to next?"

She wanted to say that times were different, that Alberic was no longer so beholden to King Stephen. But she couldn't truly know Alberic's mind on the matter. Then she didn't have time to think at all.

Alberic stepped out of the inn.

Kill him! Kill the whoreson who cut short my life and is the cause of all of your woes!

Her brother's enraged words hit her like a blow, nearly unseating her. She lurched forward and clung to the horse's mane.

She'd been prepared to hear the familiar order, and again she must refuse to heed her brother's demand for revenge.

I will not kill Alberic. Go to your peace, William.
Release me to my peace, Nicole. Kill him! Kill him now!
Never. Never!

Remember how you loved me! Remember your grief at my death! Avenge me, dearest!

Oh, how well she remembered. Her young heart had inconsolably ached for her golden, beloved brother, dead on his bier, so dear and so cold. Her heart still ached, but not because of grief.

During the years since the one time she'd tried to obey her brother's demands, had come so close to stabbing Alberic, she'd anguished over William's inability to give up his anger and hatred, to see beyond his narrow-sighted, selfish, and unwarranted need for revenge.

Why couldn't she find the proper words to force him to realize his folly?

Alberic killed you in defense of his own life! You attacked him in honorable battle. You unreasonably blame Alberic for being the victor in a fight he did not seek!

See him, Nicole! He wears no chain mail or sword! He is vulnerable! Kill him!

William wasn't listening, not truly responding to her pleas for reason. He *never* did.

The hopelessness of his spirit being bound to the earthly realm, and her frustration over her failure to reach him, brought a lump to her throat and tears to her eyes.

Someone grabbed hold of her leg. Rhodri.

His mouth was tight, his eyes narrowed. "Are you in pain?"

Her physical reaction to William's voice must have alerted Rhodri to her inner struggle, and while his touch and voice soothed her, nothing could make William's malevolence less difficult to bear.

"Only heartsore," she answered. "William rants at me to kill Alberic and refuses to listen to reason. I desperately want to help him move on, but I know not how to convince him."

Kill Alberic! Use the dagger, Nicole. One swift strike to his villainous heart and I will be avenged!

Alberic is no villain. Have you no notion of how wonderfully he treats our sister Gwendolyn, or how fairly and prosperously he rules Camelen? Give over, William. I pray you. I beg of you!

Rhodri pulled her down from the horse. She clung to his tunic, shedding tears against his chest, grateful for those strong arms supporting her.

So easy to end our suffering, Nicole. Do it, do it now!

I cannot. I cannot.

Knowing she must silence her brother or suffer further, hating that she'd failed William this time, too, Nicole closed her eyes. In her head formed a stone wall, becoming higher and thicker, separating her from William.

Nay, Nicole! I will not be silenced! By the love you bear me, do not—

William continued to batter her defenses, as he would until she was once again well away from Alberic. Keeping the wall from crumbling would be an exhausting endeavor, one she willingly endured in order to have a few moments with Alberic.

From within the circle of Rhodri's arms, she glanced at the two men who stood together in the inn's yard. Darian made some comment to Alberic, who nodded in response.

Sweet mercy, if Darian had harbored any notions of how she and Rhodri had spent last night, he must now be sure of his conjecture. Had he told Alberic? Would he be angry, treat her differently now?

But then, however Alberic or Darian felt about her taking Rhodri as her lover wasn't important. For the nonce, her body was her own, as was the decision of to whom she would yield its use. Until she must marry and was forced to bed a husband—and she didn't much care whether that unknown and undesired husband objected to the loss of her virginity or not—she would do with her body as she pleased.

She pleased to allow Rhodri whatever liberties he wished to take, whenever he wished to take them.

Disinclined to give up Rhodri's comforting embrace, but knowing she must, Nicole pushed at his chest. "We can go on now."

Rhodri didn't move, or release her. "Your brother does not talk to you, he attacks you. How do you bear it?"

Today's attack had been particularly savage, more so than the last time he'd known Alberic within her reach.

On a humorless burst of laughter, she admitted, "Sometimes better than others."

His gaze strayed over to the inn's yard. "Alberic knew you would suffer and yet insisted he see you. The man is cruel."

"Never that. You will see for yourself when you get to know him. Please, Rhodri, I have silenced William for the nonce but cannot hold him at bay forever."

He let go of her then.

"We should just ride on past the inn," he grumbled, but he tugged on the reins to lead the horse into the yard.

The nearer she came to the man William hated above all others, the more he pounded against the wall. Resolved to hold out against her brother, to not let him interfere with her reunion with Alberic, she stepped into Alberic's open arms.

Alberic's embrace was quick but heartfelt.

"You gave us a fright, little one," he said gently.

"So Darian said, and he has already given me a lecture so you need not."

"Aye, so he told me. Come into the inn. We need to talk."

Talk. Which meant Alberic wasn't yet set on the course he meant to take. If he'd already decided to take her to Camelen, he would have horses and provisions at the ready.

Nicole began to hold hope that they could all converse amiably, until Alberic pointed angrily, accusingly at Rhodri.

"And you, master bard, had best have a damn good reason for putting our Nicole in danger, or the next tune you strum will be to entertain the angels!"

Chapter Fourteen

Rhodri's doubts over Nicole's ability to hear the dead had vanished, cast out by the attack that had doubled her over and brought her to tears.

In the inn's dim, stale, otherwise unoccupied taproom, he stood off to the side and sipped watery ale while Nicole and her brothers-by-marriage sat at a table and spoke of family matters—at Nicole's insistence. Her foremost interest was in news of her sisters' children, which the proud fathers were most willing to provide.

She smiled, but the lack of sparkle in her eyes and the fleeting appearance of furrows on her brow revealed how hard she fought to hold her brother's voice at bay.

"And Gwen will give birth any moment now," Nicole commented. "Truly, Alberic, you should not have left her."

Unflustered by the scold, Alberic crossed his arms on the table and leaned forward. "Nay, I should not have, but Gwendolyn and Emma will have no peace until they know you are safe."

Alberic hadn't spoken harshly, so Nicole's wince made no sense until he realized what must be happening.

William had broken through her defenses and was no longer silent.

Before he could move toward her, Darian rose from the bench and held out his hand. "Come, Nicole. We have rooms upstairs. Best you rest for a time."

Tears again welled in her eyes. She nodded agreement at Darian, then reached across the narrow table and placed a hand on Alberic's arm.

"I am so sorry, Alberic." She took a deep breath, her mouth tight, as if in pain. "You know I love you and would never harm you."

Alberic didn't move a muscle, purposely holding himself very still and quiet.

"I know, little one. I love you, too," he said with a tenderness that, to Rhodri, didn't seem possible for a man of his rank and reputation. "Go with Darian."

She rose, and Rhodri fought to remain where he was, wrestling with the impulse to sweep Nicole out of the inn, steal a horse, and ride away.

But they would never make it out the door.

Nicole cast moist eyes his way and tried to smile. "You should play your harp while you talk to Alberic. Music always sweetens his mood."

Her attempt to jest when in distress hit him in the heart and tightened his grip on the tankard. "I will keep your suggestion in mind."

Without further word, she grasped Darian's hand and allowed him to lead her up the stairs.

The thought crossed his mind that he might never see her again. Alberic intended to take Nicole back to Camelen, Rhodri was sure, unless he or Nicole could convince the baron otherwise.

Since Nicole was in no condition to argue the case, that task was left to him. Unwilling to feel the underling, Rhodri took the seat on the bench Nicole had vacated and faced Alberic squarely.

Where to start? What did Alberic most want to know?

"Nicole has come to no harm, I assure you, even though naught has gone as planned since I arrived at Bledloe Abbey."

Alberic moved then, but merely to pick up his own tankard and take a healthy swallow of ale.

"Did we not believe Nicole willingly left Oxford with you, or that she suffered nary so much as a bruise, Darian would have slit your throat and left you where he found you this morn."

Rhodri had no cause to disbelieve. The mercenary might well have succeeded, given the circumstances. Both of Nicole's brothers-by-marriage were dangerous men, though Rhodri didn't consider himself their inferior.

Still, he decided not to mention how he'd used Nicole to escape the tower cell, even though Alberic had probably learned of it from the earl's messenger.

"Nicole came willingly enough. She was displeased with the earl for removing her from Bledloe Abbey and was most unhappy that the king planned to negotiate her marriage to a Welsh prince without consulting either her or you."

"Nicole is the king's ward. He has the right to negotiate her marriage."

A slight tightening around Alberic's mouth said he didn't like it, either.

Darian slid onto the bench next to Alberic. Damn!

How had he not heard the man come down the stairs or cross the floor? Rhodri knew how to move quietly, but Darian seemed to slip through air like a wraith.

Then Darian smiled and seemed human again. "Nicole fell onto the bed like she had never seen anything so grand before. She will try to sleep for a time and then join us for nooning, which she says she is greatly looking forward to."

Rhodri managed to keep his stomach from growling at the thought of food, of meat—and at the memory of a certain pig he would dearly have loved to roast.

"Is it possible the innkeeper can provide pork?"

Alberic raised an eyebrow. "One would think you would not be particular in the victuals available."

He wasn't, and neither would be Nicole. However, the pork would surely jar her memory of the pig, perhaps make her smile.

"I ask only because Nicole has had a yearning for pork for several days. It would be a small thing to please her."

Alberic nodded, and Rhodri didn't doubt Nicole would have pork for her nooning if Alberic had to hunt down a pig and slaughter it himself.

"Why did Connor send you to Bledloe?"

Rhodri opened his mouth to tell the same tale he'd told everyone, even Nicole, then took a sip of ale instead, chagrined that he couldn't bring himself to lie anymore.

His respect for both men had risen with each protective gesture and kindness shown to Nicole. Though the three were related only through marriage, she loved these men, and they loved her in return. They were her family, and far and above everyone else involved, they truly had Nicole's best interests at heart. Even above her Welsh uncle.

Even above himself.

And both of these men were suspicious of him. One or the other would know the tale for an untruth. If he had any chance of convincing them to allow Nicole to go to Wales, then a true and full accounting might serve him well.

"When Connor received Gwendolyn's letter, he realized what effect Prince Eustace's death would have on your King Stephen and the war with Duke Henry. More personally, he berated himself for what he sees as neglect of his nieces when their father died. He expressed the wish that he had gone to fetch them immediately to save them from the king's machinations in their lives."

Neither man reacted unfavorably, even though neither would be married to Nicole's sisters, the wives they now cherished, had the king not ordered those marriages.

Rhodri continued. "So Connor believes it is his duty to do right by Nicole, and he thought the best chance of success was to send me to fetch her."

Alberic gave a short burst of humorless laughter. "I have had dealings with Connor. There is more to this than a sudden wish to play the good uncle to Nicole!"

"Certes, there is. Connor is also mindful of her Pendragon heritage. According to him, the line can remain strong only if there is a Welsh branch. He knows the king means to marry her to a Welsh noble but fears which one the king might choose."

Alberic again leaned forward. "So it is as I guessed. Connor wishes to use Nicole for his own selfish reasons."

Rhodri fought to keep his sudden ire under control. "Did not your king intend to do the same, without consideration to either you or Nicole? If Connor chooses

Nicole's husband, then at the least, the decision will be made in an effort to unite Wales and further the cause of peace! The same cannot be said of Stephen."

"Or the marriage may give Connor's choice of her husband ill-founded notions of greatness and cause more jealousy and strife than already exists. Has Connor a man in mind?"

Probably, though Connor hadn't said who that might be.

"Not that he confided to me," Rhodri admitted, wishing he knew so he could put Alberic's concerns to rest.

All this talk of giving Nicole to another man, no matter who that man might be, soured Rhodri's stomach. No matter how much it saddened and sickened him that she was but a pawn in political affairs, there was naught he could do to stop it. He would be forced to deal with his personal distaste for her arranged marriage when the time came.

For now, all he could do was convince Alberic not to take Nicole into his custody, and the best reason had naught to do with England or Wales, king or princes, war or peace.

"My lords, I realize neither of you approves of Connor's scheme. I have my own reasons for not liking it, either. But we have come too far for Nicole to go back. The earl of Oxford will not allow her to return to Bledloe Abbey. Should she fall into his grasp, in the guise of protecting her, he will lock Nicole away at either Oxford or Headingham."

Anticipating Alberic's counterargument, Rhodri continued. "I grant you, the king might allow you to keep her in your custody. 'Tis known you are loyal to Stephen where other magnates are not, and Camelen is a well-fortified, ably garrisoned fortress. A safe place for Nicole to reside. But you cannot, in good conscience, ask that of her. 'Twould be the cruelest of tortures."

The baron's countenance turned stormy. "Torture? To be reunited with her sisters? To live among those who care for her? How so?"

Alberic couldn't be that unfeeling or dull-witted! Or perhaps he didn't realize how severely Nicole suffered.

Rhodri flung a hand in the direction of the stairway. "Did you not just send her away from you? To see you is to suffer. William batters at her defenses even now! How much stronger will his ranting be at the place of his burial? How long can Nicole hold out against him before he drives her to insanity and she picks up a dagger and aims it at your heart? Whether she aims true or no, she will hate herself for the rest of her days!"

His fervor overflowing on Nicole's behalf, Rhodri's fist hit the table. "You cannot do that to her, Alberic! By the saints, you cannot subject her to constant suffering and still profess to hold her in affection! I will not permit it!"

Rhodri knew he'd gone too far, his sensible argument had turned too passionate, his tongue had run on too long.

Alberic backed away, not in retreat, but in preparation for battle, with the assuredly single-minded goal of lopping off Rhodri's head—until Darian clamped a staying hand on Alberic's shoulder.

The mercenary asked, "Rhodri, when did Nicole tell you of her ability to hear spirits, of William in particular?"

Grateful for the man's interference, still wary of Alberic's next move, Rhodri answered, "She told me in Oxford.

We damn near got caught because some spirit asked for Nicole's aid and she gave it. When she explained why she had wasted so much of our time, she also told me about William, and how he'd goaded her into trying to kill Alberic. I did not realize until this morning how horrific her brother's attacks on her could be."

Darian nodded, as if satisfied on some point. He cupped a hand to the ear of a still-angry Alberic and whispered urgently, leaving Rhodri to wonder if he'd saved his skin or sounded his death knell by revealing what he knew of Nicole's unusual abilities.

Alberic didn't like what he was hearing, but slowly he relaxed. When Darian backed away, Rhodri began to believe he might live to see sunset.

"You are sure?" Alberic asked Darian.

Darian tossed his hands in the air, a gesture of exasperation. "Were I not, would I have said so?"

With an aggrieved sigh, Alberic crossed his arms. "Hellfire! Then I must allow Nicole to go to Wales. Gwendolyn and Emma will *not* be pleased, Darian. You *will* own up to your part in this."

"I like it no better than you, but aye, Nicole must be allowed to go with Rhodri."

What the devil had Darian said to convince Alberic? Stunned, thoroughly confused, Rhodri could only gape at the baron, who placed his palms on the table to push himself off the bench.

"There is a horse in the stable that we brought for Nicole's use. Take it." Alberic reached for a string around his neck and pulled a small leather pouch from under his tunic. The pouch landed on the table in front of Rhodri, the sound of jingling coins unmistakable. "Use it wisely."

Alberic's eyes narrowed, and he wagged a threatening forefinger. "Tell Connor that Nicole is not to marry without her free, wholehearted consent. If I find out—and I *will* find out—that she was denied approval, I will consider the deed an act of betrayal and invade Wales myself, with the sole purpose of cutting out Connor ap Maelgwn's black heart!"

Then he stormed off, to inform the innkeeper that there would be pork on the nooning trenchers or he would tear the inn down with his own hands, no doubt.

Darian's smile wasn't comforting. "Time to play your harp, Rhodri, or Alberic's foul mood will spoil our meal."

"What the hell did you tell him?"

The disconcerting smile widened. "I feel that you and I are fated to meet again. If you have not guessed by then, ask me and I will tell you. For now, best you play and sweeten his mood lest Alberic changes his mind."

Nicole woke to a light hand on her shoulder.

The bright face of a girl barely past childhood, and most likely the innkeeper's daughter, peered down at her.

"Beg pardon, milady, but 'tis nearly time for nooning. The baron said I should come help you get ready."

"My thanks," Nicole said, still a bit sleepy but oddly clear minded.

She swung her legs over the edge of the bed, amazed she'd slept so long, so peacefully. Quieting William the second time today had been harder than the first, and she'd feared that as soon as she fell asleep he would wake her with his demands.

He hadn't. Her defenses had held while she slept.

Suspicious of her success, she looked inward, at the barrier at which William should be pounding with both fists, making it hard for her to think. Not a sound could be heard, not a ripple of hatred felt.

How odd, and how very welcome!

Nicole didn't understand why her brother had granted this unexpected reprieve, was just grateful. Not that she intended to lower her defenses to test their strength. No sense inviting William to rant at her, which he would surely do if given the opportunity.

On the other side of the room, the girl was pulling a brown woolen gown from out of a leather satchel that looked familiar.

"From where came this?"

"The baron, milady. He said the things in here are yours."

Not hers. But then Nicole smiled, realizing the gown the girl held up was one of Gwendolyn's, who must have sent it with Alberic. Delighted, Nicole rummaged through the satchel to find a heavy winter cloak, a fine-linen shift, a bar of lavender-scented soap, a handful of colorful ribbons, and a comb.

Thank heaven for thoughtful sisters!

And for a thoughtful brother-by-marriage who'd sent up the girl, along with a pitcher of warm water for the basin.

"Oh, the bard plays again," the girl said, her delight clear in both voice and expression.

Indeed, from the taproom below came the dulcet strains of the harp, making Nicole smile, too.

"How long has Rhodri played?"

"Not long enough, to my mind. Father hopes the bard plays right on through supper. 'Twould be good for business!"

'Twould be good for her and Rhodri, too, if he could earn a bit of coin to make this journey easier.

Eager to hear what Alberic, Darian, and Rhodri had talked about while she'd enjoyed a refreshing sleep, Nicole stripped out of the highly soiled blue gown and shift to take advantage of Gwendolyn's largesse. All through changing, washing, and braiding of hair, Nicole considered what options were open to her, if any.

Surely Alberic planned to take her back to Camelen. Then what? Would Alberic feel obligated to alert King Stephen to her whereabouts? Possibly. Hard to say where she might then be sent.

Another nunnery? The thought did not appeal. Worse, the king might demand she reside at his court. After the shunning and trials Emma had suffered while in the king's custody, Nicole cringed at having to endure the same.

Or Stephen might allow her to remain at Camelen. While the prospect of going home and seeing her sisters appealed, William would surely cause her no end of grief about Alberic.

William was quiet now, but as soon as she went downstairs he would again sense Alberic's nearness and surely begin another assault on her defenses. He'd broken through once today, and she was resolved not to allow him to do so again. For a day or so she could do battle and come away merely bruised. If she went home, she wasn't sure she could survive constant attacks.

William had also ordered her to go home, and following her brother's order couldn't be wise. She'd inadvertently done so when she'd left the abbey but wouldn't willingly follow another!

Nicole slipped on her boots. The innkeeper's daughter opened the door. Music floated in uninhibited, forcing Nicole to admit to one of her foremost inducements for going on to Wales.

Rhodri. She wanted to stay with Rhodri ap Dafydd for as long as she could.

Their becoming lovers might be overly swaying her common sense, but sweet mercy, she simply didn't want to give him up as yet. Even knowing the day would come that he would leave Glenvair to pursue his goal of becoming a *pencerdd,* or that she would someday be forced to marry for the sake of family or country, didn't alter her feelings.

If she were to have him for only a short time, then she desperately wanted these next few days when they could be alone, free to be together whenever they wished.

She walked out the door to the rhythm of Rhodri's song, the scent of lavender soap giving way to the mouth-watering aroma of roasted pork, fair pulling her quickly down the stairs.

Rhodri sat on a bench near the hearth, fingers plucking at the strings, his whole being centered in the music. He, too, had washed. Someone had given his tunic and breeches a hardy brushing, and no mud marred his boots.

His raven hair flowed down in waves to brush his wide shoulders, and she fought the urge to run her fingers through those now shiny locks. Perhaps tonight—but they might not be together tonight. Might not ever have another night of passion if Alberic insisted she go to Camelen with him.

Alberic and Darian sat a table, ale in their tankards, chunks of roasted pork and yellow cheese on their trenchers of brown bread, listening to Rhodri play. On the table sat a similar trencher, likely meant for her. She headed toward it, passing by the balding innkeeper, who smiled broadly, as well he should. Several patrons sat at tables or on benches placed along the walls, enjoying both victuals and music.

And still William remained silent, even when she sat on a bench across from Alberic, and the why of it was becoming bothersome. Had she, at long last, convinced him to move on? Oh, that would be a blessed day! But she doubted that day had come yet.

Then what was different? Had she somehow become stronger, or had William weakened?

Were William alive, she would blame his seemingly contented state on Rhodri. Certes, everyone else in the inn happily relished the harp's music.

Sweet mercy, could music have a calming effect on spirits, too?

"Charming," Alberic said, the compliment interrupting her ponderings on William's strange behavior.

She slid onto the bench. "You have no notion how wonderful are clean garments and the use of a comb. Gwen's doing?"

"Aye. Had I known you would not be coming to Camelen, I would have brought more. No matter. Rhodri now has enough coin to purchase whatever you may require."

A piece of warm pork in her fingers, her hand stopped halfway to her mouth, almost afraid to believe what Alberic inferred.

"You allow me to go to Wales?"

"Is that not your wish?"

"Aye, but—"

"You will be leaving soon after you finish your meal. Is the pork to your taste?"

She plopped the chunk into her mouth and nearly sighed with delight. "The pork is lovely! I have craved it for days, ever since Rhodri tried to capture a pig for me." The memory of that event, with no lasting harm done to Rhodri's ankle, brought back her smile. "He missed but gave good effort. Did he tell you the tale?"

Alberic and Darian exchanged a look she didn't understand.

Darian answered. "He did not, but he informed us of your wish for pork. He has taken good care of you thus far, and we are assured he will continue to do so, otherwise we would not let you go."

Alberic pushed aside his empty trencher. "You will write to Gwendolyn as soon as you reach Glenvair. She and Emma will not be pleased that Darian and I return without you. A letter from you will go far to ease their concerns."

An easy enough request to grant, all considered. "I will, but I do not understand how this came about. I was prepared to give argument."

Alberic folded his arms on the table. "Make no mistake, I do not like this, but after talking to Rhodri, Darian and I agree that allowing you to continue on to Wales is the best course. Rhodri has much to explain to you, and I have his oath that he will, later. For now, 'tis best you eat and leave before William causes you pain again."

There was her answer. Reminded of how much pain William caused her, Alberic had decided not to take her back to where her brother's power over her would be strongest.

"Aubrey de Vere will not be pleased. Will he cause you trouble?"

"Should he try, I will simply remind him of his error in removing you from the abbey. Damn earl should have tended his own concerns, not meddled in others'."

And now that the time for parting was near, why was she loath to leave her brothers-by-marriage behind? Damn. She wanted to go, but she didn't. Oh, she was going to cry when they said fare-thee-wells, she just knew it. But for the course of a meal, she could enjoy their company.

"William is quiet for the nonce," she said, which greatly pleased Alberic. "I do not understand why, but he is."

"And you have a serene look about you that I have never had the privilege to observe. I am glad, little one, but let us not rely on your brother's unaccountable courtesy. Eat."

So she did. To the accompaniment of harp music, they again spoke of her sisters, of the children, of Camelen, carefully avoiding, she noticed, any mention of kings or princes, of the state of the war, or even her looming departure.

As if her final quaff of ale were a signal, Rhodri ended his song with a distinctive flourish and rose to join them at the table.

Kill him! Kill—

Angry that she'd allowed her guard to slip, Nicole swiftly shut out William's ranting. Again he pounded at her defenses, demanding attention she refused to give him.

All three men noticed her struggle, their concern apparent.

Rhodri placed a comforting hand on her shoulder. "Time to leave, Nicole."

She placed a hand over his, not yet ready. "One more song, Rhodri, I pray you."

"But William—"

"One more. Please."

Rhodri sat next to her on the bench, and again music filled the air.

To her amazement, the assault on her defenses faded, leaving only blessed, magnificent silence. Dare she believe William vulnerable to the music? To just Rhodri's harp, or to any music?

With joy, she realized she might be able to go home one day. Rhys, Camelen's bard, would certainly play his harp whenever she wished, giving her relief from William's ranting.

She felt almost vile about withholding the suspicion from Alberic, who felt terrible that William's desire for revenge had kept Nicole from seeing Gwendolyn more often.

But she dare not say a word until she was sure of her conjecture. Surely, before they reached Glenvair, she and Rhodri would pass a graveyard and she could test the effects of a harp on spirit voices.

If his music calmed one spirit, it would surely calm others. Would it not?

Chapter Fifteen

Nicole sat near the evening fire, huddled in her sister's hooded cloak, not in need of either for warmth, because fury boiled her blood.

At the moment, she didn't care if Rhodri's harp could soothe spirits, or that just hours ago she'd yearned to be alone with him tonight and for many nights to come. Alberic had told her that Rhodri had a tale to tell but hadn't said the truth might hurt so much she might never speak to Rhodri—or Uncle Connor—ever again.

And how very foolish of her not to realize Connor's true motive in offering refuge before now.

"So Connor's offer of refuge was but a ruse," she complained, still suffering the sting of the revelation and the upset over of her lack of foresight. "All along he planned to use me for his own purposes!"

Having retreated to the opposite side of the fire, Rhodri poked at the embers with a stick, unforgivably unapologetic. "You are a Pendragon princess, destined to marry a high-ranking Welsh noble. Is it not better the choice of your husband be made by someone who holds you in affection than a man who knows you not at all?"

That might be so, if the depth of Connor's affection were not now suspect. She hadn't seen Connor since she was five and had always thought of him as her kindly Welsh uncle. He might still be a kind man, but now, as head of her mother's family, he also wanted something from his youngest niece. That shouldn't come as such a shock. That it did caused her further distress.

"What difference, pray tell?" She waved a dismissive hand. "Oh, I know the politics of it. King Stephen negotiates my marriage with a Welshman who is apparently inclined to become his ally. Connor wishes me to marry a man who will not be swayed to allegiance with an English king. Either way, I am a means to their selfish ends, and I am *not* pleased! Why did you not tell me all of this before?"

"Would it have mattered?"

The dolt! Of course his deception mattered!

"Aye! Had you told me of Connor's intentions in the receiving chamber of Bledloe Abbey, I would have insisted you leave."

"Would you? I believe you might have asked me to play for Mother Abbess, no matter our differences."

Nicole couldn't quite be sorry she'd done so. Rhodri's music had made Mother Abbess happy in those last few hours of her life. And, to be honest, she hadn't truly thought of only the nun when she'd asked Rhodri to play at the deathbed.

"You spoke of refuge, and I wanted time to decide if I had the right or desire to accept the offer. Had you not lied, no decision needed to be made, and therefore I would not have asked you to play for Mother Abbess, so you would not have been in the chapel when Aubrey de Vere arrived and, to my mind, abused the power of his earldom."

"I told you no lies, Nicole, and think you I would have abandoned my quest so quickly?"

Not lied? Perhaps not by word, but certainly by deed!

"Certes, you did not tell me the whole truth! Sweet mercy, I should have allowed Sister Claire to toss you out the gate. That would have ended your quest."

He shook his head in emphatic disagreement. "Connor gave me the task of bringing you to Wales. If you did not agree to come willingly, I would have found a way to kidnap you."

"Cur! Think you I would not have clawed your eyes out had you made such a dishonorable, loathsome attempt? You allowed me to believe you acted in my best interests when all you sought was to take me from one place of captivity to another. Blessed be, I should have let you rot in the tower!"

His tolerance began to fray. "Better Wales than England. Better Connor than Stephen. Even Alberic agrees, or he would not have allowed you out of his sight. Damnation, woman! Alberic goes so far as to insist you have the right to agree wholeheartedly to any marriage Connor might arrange! Under threat of retribution, no less. Surely you must believe Alberic serves your interests!"

Oh, now, there was one more male she would dearly love to take to task. After he'd learned how Rhodri had deceived her, how could Alberic have agreed to let Rhodri take her to Wales? True, he'd given the order that she wasn't to be forced into marriage, but what good the order of a Norman baron to a Welsh chieftain when the chieftain owed no allegiance to the baron?

Alberic couldn't possibly believe kin ties would bind Connor. Kin strife ran further amok in Wales than in England, giving the Welsh a reputation as savages. The uncle who'd bounced her on his knee had shown her every kindness during her only visit to Glenvair, but she didn't doubt he could be as ruthless as the rest of his countrymen.

"Do you truly believe Alberic would risk invading Wales? Nonsense! He has no power over Connor, so he cannot enforce his order."

Rhodri waved the stick, the glowing tip making oddly shaped circles in the air. "Nay, he would not invade Wales, but do not take Alberic or Darian too lightly. Norman barons and Flemish mercenaries are dangerous men, and these two would surely make Connor suffer, I have no doubt."

Aye, her brothers-by-marriage could also be ruthless when provoked, but by the time they learned of her plight, 'twould be far too late for them to save her.

"No doubt, but by the time they hunt down Connor, I shall be wed, the deed done, my life . . . destroyed."

Rhodri tossed the stick in the fire. "I will not allow that to happen. Connor will abide by Alberic's wishes, my word on it."

"You will forgive me if I am reluctant to trust your word!"

His ire rose, his mouth tightening and nostrils flaring before he brought his temper under control.

"Believe as you will, but my word is good. After you have thought this through, you will acknowledge the wisdom of it for all concerned, even you."

Then he got up and strode toward the gelding Alberic had given him for their use, which would make the journey to Glenvair shorter and less strenuous. But her adventure now lay in shattered ruins, the pleasure of it fading away in the light of a harsh truth.

Dispirited, and deprived of a close target at which to fling barbs, Nicole silently brooded over her plight.

The wretch! She'd trusted Rhodri and he'd betrayed her. He'd spoken of refuge, which she'd apparently mistaken for sanctuary. Damnation, she should have realized Connor had sent Rhodri to fetch her for a reason other than for the love of a niece he hadn't seen in ten and three years.

What a dolt she'd been!

Both King Stephen and Connor wanted her to marry a Welshman. They just had different sorts of men in mind. Nicole wanted no part of either man's plans but didn't see how she could avoid becoming embroiled, especially since Connor now had Alberic's blessing to find her a husband.

She stared into the fire, the flames low now with sunset coming on, knowing she had little choice but to go on. Oh, she could probably steal the horse and make for Camelen, but she was wise enough to know that a woman traveling alone was vulnerable to more hazards than she cared to contemplate.

Besides, as much as she now wanted to be rid of Rhodri, she truly didn't want to face Alberic anytime soon. Were she seething angry at Alberic, she might not be able to hold William's spirit at bay, and she wasn't about to risk the possibility of her brother gaining a dram of power over her.

Hellfire, but she detested the authority men had over women, to decide their fates and expect docile obedience.

But that was the way of the world. And while she was neither meek nor fearful of speaking her mind, hadn't she always known that someday some man would decide her fate? 'Twas only a matter of which man.

Harp music wafted across the campsite, and Nicole cast an irritated glance in the direction of the source, to no avail, because Rhodri paid her no heed.

Heaven forefend, if the wretched bard thought a lilting song or two would soothe her, he was mistaken!

She refused to be comforted by either the harp's song or Rhodri's oath to ensure Connor didn't marry her off without her wholehearted consent. She dared not trust Rhodri's word or risk suffering heartbreak once more.

She dared not consider how she'd misjudged him, seeing too many of his good qualities and ignoring his faults. She'd allowed a skilled bard's tongue to mislead her into believing him an honorable man. But worse, she'd allowed a handsome face and smoldering lust to blind her common sense.

Well, now her eyes were open, and she vowed there'd be no more coupling! No more nights cuddled beside Rhodri's heated body after vigorous lovemaking.

She pulled up her knees and wrapped her arms tight around them, resolved to hold on to her anger. To let it loose was to invite a weakening she couldn't afford.

If she softened, she might contemplate the delights Rhodri had shown her while generously ushering her into her full womanhood. To remember his stirring kisses, gentle touches, and the splendor of his possession would be imprudent.

To admit that during last night's tumble in the shelter, she feared she'd surrendered not only her body but also her heart wouldn't be wise. Unwittingly giving one's heart to a man who didn't want it was the most foolish thing a woman could do, and Rhodri's rebuff was simply more than she could bear without falling apart.

Resolute, Nicole stared into the dying fire, refusing to shatter. From somewhere within, she would find the strength to wrest back her heart and the courage to face whatever awaited her at Glenvair.

She just wished she knew where that somewhere was.

They'd passed through Bristol, giving Nicole a chance to see the town and mighty castle from which Robert, earl of Gloucester, had directed Empress Maud's rebel army and which her father had so highly praised. They'd crossed the river Severn on a ferry, without incident, landing at Cas Gwent.

They were so very close to Wales, but not yet there.

Rhodri had surprised her when he announced he wished to visit a friend at Tintern Abbey, explaining that if there was news to be had of important recent events in either England or Wales, the monks of Tintern would surely have knowledge of it.

So they'd cautiously passed under the shadow of Chepstow Castle, one of the most imposing of England's strongholds in the marches, and made their way up the steep-sided valley of the Wye River.

Within Tintern Abbey's sparsely furnished but neat guest house, Nicole nervously paced while waiting for one of the white-robed Cistercian monks to fetch Rhodri's friend Kian.

"Troublesome spirits?" Rhodri asked.

Since her brother's attack on her senses at the inn, Rhodri had asked her the same question whenever they'd passed a graveyard. She hadn't seen a graveyard on their arrival at Tintern, but surely there must be one on the abbey grounds.

"Nay, the monks rest in peace."

"Then why so restless?"

'Struth, she should feel peaceful within the walls of the remote religious house surrounded by hills and woodland. And while she missed Mother Abbess and one or two of the nuns, she realized she hadn't missed Bledloe Abbey overmuch in many a day. She no longer missed the security of the cloister or the strict regulation of her life.

To think, she'd once been disconcerted because of the disruption to the pattern of her days. No longer.

Freedom had its challenges, but also its delights, and she mourned that she would likely lose her freedom again all too soon. Perhaps not immediately upon reaching Glenvair, but surely—later.

"Tintern brings to mind Bledloe. By the saints, one would think both abbeys were built from the same master builder's pattern. 'Tis disconcerting. Do you intend to beg hospitality for the night?"

"Abbot Henry might grant hospitality, but he feels the same about having a woman under his roof as Sister Claire felt about sheltering a man under hers. Best we move on, methinks. I should like to cease looking over my shoulder for patrols and cannot do so until we are on Welsh soil."

And perhaps that disturbed her more than the peculiar, disquieting familiarity of the abbey. She, too, was eager to reach Glenvair, if for reasons different than Rhodri's.

Foremost she wished to confront Connor, tell him of her displeasure at his scheming, and ensure Rhodri informed her uncle of Alberic's wishes.

Too, despite the delight of certain freedoms when she and Rhodri were on the road, she certainly wouldn't mind a soft pallet, regular meals, and a roof under which to shelter from the rain.

Perhaps at Glenvair she would also have better fortune in convincing her heart not to yearn for Rhodri's love.

The two of them had ridden intimately on horseback, her clutching his tunic for balance and trying not to bump into his too-stiff back. Once at Glenvair, she would no longer be forced to suffer his solitary, constant, too-intimate company.

At Glenvair, she could begin to push him out of her thoughts and heart. He certainly had no qualms about giving her over to another man, didn't object to her taking someone other than him as her husband. And why should he? Rhodri had other plans for his life that didn't include her.

The door opened to admit a tall, white-robed monk with dark hair and a brilliant smile. Nicole stood aside as Rhodri and Kian exchanged greetings, wondering why a man so handsome and charming would forswear the life of a bard to become a monk. Rhodri had said he and Kian had studied their craft under the same master but Kian had decided to heed a higher calling.

'Twas also odd to find a Welshman in a Norman chapterhouse on English soil. But then, if Kian had been attracted to the Cistercian order, then Tintern was one of the few abbeys in all of Britain he could enter.

With greetings over and introductions made—a slightly

raised eyebrow the only sign that the monk recognized her family name and so her Pendragon heritage—Kian's smile faded.

"I worried for you," he told Rhodri, "and prayed daily for your well-being. I am most pleased to see you alive and whole, my friend."

Rhodri's brow furrowed. "What caused your concern?"

Kian was ominously quiet a moment, making Nicole's skin prickle. The man had news, and it couldn't be good.

"I gather you were not at Glenvair when it was attacked."

Nicole gasped.

Rhodri's questions came fast and hot. "Attacked? When? Who would dare?"

"We received word three days ago. The raiders were said to hail from Gwynedd. Whether they acted with Prince Owain's knowledge or no is not known to us."

Rhodri cursed, expressing Nicole's precise thoughts. "How bad?" he asked.

"Burning, looting, a few deaths. Connor survived uninjured, praise be to God, but many cattle were taken and the grain barn is lost. I fear there may be much suffering at Glenvair over the winter months." Kian put a hand on Rhodri's shoulder. "I know this news comes hard, but Rhodri, there is other news. My friend, you should truly be on your way to Arwystli. In less than a sennight, Prince Hywel holds a contest for a new *pencerdd*. Indeed, when I heard of what happened at Glenvair, I had hoped you were already on your way to compete."

For a moment, Rhodri's eyes flared with excitement, and Nicole understood only too well.

This was Rhodri's opportunity to compete against the other bards of Wales for the grand prize of earning his chair and becoming the highly honored *pencerdd* in a princely court.

This had been his dream since childhood, his ambition as a grown man. Here was the opportunity for which he'd served a long, difficult apprenticeship. Practiced endless hours. Waited patiently for a *pencerdd* either to die or to relinquish a lifelong appointment to one of only ten positions in the entire kingdom. If Rhodri didn't compete, many years might pass before the chance came again.

As if in physical torment, Rhodri rubbed at the back of his neck. "I have been in England too long. I knew nothing of the contest." His short burst of laughter contained no humor. "I decided to come to Tintern because I wanted news of worldly events to relate to Connor. I did not expect Glenvair to be the topic of the news, or to learn of a contest. Truly, Kian, could you not have imparted a happier tale?"

Kian sighed. "I do have other news, but I am not of a mind to say it is happier. The archbishop of Canterbury is said to be in Nottingham to confer with Duke Henry on behalf of King Stephen. A settlement may be at hand, praise the Lord, for it will end the English war. 'Twill mean peace in England, but how England's peace might affect Wales is unknown."

Rhodri's frown deepened. "I wish to heaven I knew, but that is for future contemplation. For now, I must take Lady Nicole to Connor."

And wasn't that the decision she'd known all along that he would make? Rhodri would see to his duty before reaching out for his heart's desire. His loyalty to her uncle was commendable. But at what price to Rhodri?

She knew damn well she had no right to interfere but could no longer hold her peace.

"Rhodri, perhaps one of the monks would be willing to escort me to Glenvair. Then you could go to Arwystli." He began to shake his head, so she pressed on. "You have waited years for this chance to earn your chair. If you allow it to pass by, you might needs wait several more years."

He didn't answer immediately, and before he said a word, Nicole knew from the set of his jaw she hadn't changed his mind.

"Nay, this is my task to complete. We will see how things are at Glenvair. Perhaps, after . . ." He shrugged a shoulder, then turned away, his decision made. "Kian, since you heard naught of my journey to England, might I also gather you have heard naught of Nicole's disappearance from either Bledloe Abbey or Oxford Castle?"

"Not a whisper." Kian's eyebrow arched. "I assume you had somewhat to do with the lady's liberation. Are you being hunted?"

Rhodri shook his head. "If you have heard no whisper, then the earl of Oxford's patrols did not venture this close to the border. I believe we are safe enough and will be assuredly better off after crossing the Wye, which we should do sooner than late. Would you do me the great favor of sending word to Glenvair should you hear any whispers?"

With a sharp nod, Kian agreed. "Ferry or ford?"

"Ford, unless the course of the river has changed near Forden."

Kian smiled. "Nay, the only thing that has changed near Forden is Iorwerth ap Rhun's surety over the blessed state of his soul. He made a pilgrimage to St. David's and, while in Deueubarth, did a kindness for Rhys, Prince

Maredudd's *edling*. Now he feels the prince of Deueu-barth is in his debt, and the good deed absolves sins of the both the past and to come."

While the men shared another humorous jest over this Iorwerth's beliefs, Nicole shook off the last crumb of guilt over his decision, said a short prayer that they would find Glenvair in better condition than Kian implied, and strove to remember where St. David's might be. On the far southern coast of Wales, she thought. In Deueubarth, where Maredudd was the prince and his younger brother, Rhys, was apparently the heir.

A chill chased down Nicole's spine, becoming very aware of how little she knew about Wales.

Oh, she knew somewhat of Deueubarth, Gwynedd, and Powys, the three largest of the Welsh kingdoms, and knew the names of their princes—Maredudd ap Gruf-fydd, Owain Gwynedd, and Madog ap Maredudd. But there were other dynasties, like Arwystli and Cedewain, which were apparently ruled by a man named Hywel.

Of Hywel she knew not a crumb.

Nicole crossed her arms over her midriff to calm a heart beginning to beat too rapidly.

She was about to cross into a foreign land—a land most people in England considered a wilderness and its people savage—of which she truly knew of only a small piece. Glenvair.

And she knew near to nothing of the princes' *edlings,* those brothers, sons, or nephews who'd been designated the heir.

Even while she'd always been aware she might one day be called upon to marry into one Welsh dynasty or another, she'd always thought of the nobles in a hazy sort of way. Far away. As part of her future, not her present. Now they were becoming real, with names, flesh and blood and bone, and frightening.

With one of those men she would one day share a marriage bed.

'Twas well known the bards were required to be able to recite the lineage of the Welsh dynastic families and were often called upon to share that knowledge to settle disputes over the rights of inheritance.

Rhodri would know all the names. He was also likely familiar with the songs attached to each reigning prince and would know something of the *edlings*.

It irked her that she considered asking the man who held her heart to help her choose the man she might marry! While still a bit angry over his lie, she had to admit that but for the one lapse, he'd been trustworthy.

And, by the saints, if Rhodri didn't want her, then she may as well set her mind to choosing a man who might cherish her even if she might never love him.

During the three days Rhodri had said it would take them to arrive at Glenvair, she would have time aplenty to question Rhodri on the Welsh dynastic families. Then when the time came for her to make her dreaded decision, at the least the decision would be an informed one.

For all he'd disrupted her life, Rhodri owed her a few enlightening answers.

Chapter Sixteen

Wales. Home.

In less than an hour they would reach Glenvair, and while Rhodri wished he could urge the horse to greater speed, he didn't dare. 'Twasn't wise to gallop through the deeply rolling hills with Nicole mounted behind him.

She clutched his tunic at the waist, still trying to hold away from him, as she'd done since leaving Tintern Abbey. He might prefer to have her snug against him, her breasts pressed against his back, but so far he'd managed to convince himself that the less they touched, the better.

Hellfire, how he wanted to touch her! Wrap Nicole in his arms, lower her down into the long, sweet grass, and once more claim her as his own.

Unwise, surely. Foolish, absolutely. Yet his desire refused to abate, especially after all the questions he'd answered about unmarried male Welsh nobles.

He'd tried to be honest, but God's truth, when considering the princes and *edlings* from whom Nicole would choose her husband, many of whom he truly admired, he couldn't help finding some flaw with each one.

Too stout, too frail. Too tall, too short. Too given to bouts of rage, too much a quiet recluse.

Not a one of them was worthy of Lady Nicole de Leon.

"Will you be able to arrive in Arwystli in time to compete in the contest?" she asked, spinning his thoughts back to the competition, a most welcome change from the questions she'd asked earlier.

"Depends on how bad things are at Glenvair. If the only damage is to the grain barn, then there is naught to detain me. If more severe, then I will have to judge."

Rhodri was dearly hoping he wouldn't be obliged to stay, and not only because he yearned to take part in the contest.

Glenvair had been his home for many a year, and he would hate to see Connor or his people suffer overmuch. Too, the shorter time he must spend with Nicole, the better chance he stood of breaking away from her and getting on with the life he'd planned.

Before he left Glenvair, he'd have Connor's oath to heed Alberic's wishes with regard to Nicole's marriage. Connor would keep his word, if only because Rhodri intended to make clear that if the oath were broken, he'd write a song damning Connor's perfidy and sing it in every hall and at every campfire across Wales.

"Will Connor retaliate for the raid?" she wanted to know.

"He might if he is sure from where the raiders hail, and if the reason for the raid is known."

"Do you say Connor gave someone reason to raid Glenvair?"

He almost laughed at her tone of disbelief that Connor could do such a thing but refrained. "Connor has both allies and enemies. Any perceived slight or injury could have brought on a raid."

He also refrained from voicing the disturbing suspicion that had pricked at him since hearing of the attack on Glenvair.

While no word of Nicole's leaving Bledloe Abbey had reached Kian at Tintern Abbey, that didn't mean the news hadn't reached other, possibly princely, ears. 'Twas also possible someone had heard of his journey into England, guessed the two events were linked, and sent a raiding party to Glenvair to kidnap Nicole.

He'd been taken to task once for keeping secrets from her, and he was tempted to warn her of the possible danger. But damnation, he didn't wish to worry her over a mere suspicion! Best to wait until after he spoke with Connor and learned more of the who and why of the attack.

Within half a league of Glenvair, Nicole asked, "Is not the stream where I played nearby?"

Though anxious to see Connor, Rhodri saw no harm in a slight diversion. He nudged the horse off the road and down a slope, his memory filled with a bright summer day and a barefooted little minx of a girl. At the stream he swung a leg over the horse's head to dismount, then extended his arms to catch Nicole as she slid off.

'Twas nothing they hadn't done before. Her hands on his shoulders; his hands around her slim waist. But he could see in her eyes that she, too, knew this might be the last time he would perform this small service in private.

When his hands lingered overlong, she didn't protest.

'Struth, she didn't move at all, just peered up at him with those wide, doe-brown eyes that enchanted him beyond reason.

His beautiful Pendragon princess, who would shortly no longer be his. The day would come when he would have no occasion to span her waist with his hands. Or lose his senses in the depths of her eyes. Or breathe in the scent of roses that always seemed to be with her.

"No butterflies," she whispered, as if he should have arranged for them to flutter in the grass to greet her.

He wished he could have, just for her, to brighten her day.

"The butterflies refused to stay when they felt the chill in the air. The best I could do was order the trees to turn gold in honor of your return to Glenvair."

She smiled, warming his heart. "Then the trees obeyed with splendid grace. They are beautiful."

"You are beautiful. And brave and stalwart. I am honored to have served as your escort and companion, my lady."

Her smile waned. "There were moments when I thought you ready to send me back to Oxford."

"No more than the times you wished me to the devil. The journey was harder than I thought it would be, yet you persevered like a soldier on the march. Not many women could have endured all the hardships with so little complaint."

"You are being kind. I remember some rather pointed and loud complaints. Aye, there were times I wished you to the devil, but there were also times I was overjoyed for your company."

He didn't doubt which time was the most joyous. In a

small shelter fashioned of tree branches and wide ferns, they'd spent the night naked in each other's arms and enjoyed several bouts of mind-bending bliss.

His hands tightened on her waist; her hands clutched his shoulders.

He hadn't planned to kiss Nicole, but no force on earth could have stopped him from bending down for a last taste of her sweet lips, so lush and warm and willing.

Lust flooded through him, like a stream overflowing its banks, unstoppable. And it hurt. His loins were on fire. Worse, his heart ached so much he wondered if cutting it out and placing it in Nicole's keeping wouldn't hurt less.

But then, he realized, his heart was already in Nicole's keeping. He'd given it to her days ago.

He deepened the kiss and cursed Connor for sending him to England to fetch Nicole. He railed at the earl's patrols for allowing him to evade them. He even damned Alberic and Darian for not seizing Nicole when they'd had the chance.

But mostly he upbraided himself for being so thoroughly seduced by Nicole de Leon that he hadn't been aware of the danger until becoming ensnared.

He'd fallen in love with Nicole. Deeply. Futilely.

Her arms slid around his neck, her breath ragged, her mouth melding firm and perfect against his. She returned his kiss with all the passion of a woman in the arms of a cherished lover, sparking unwarranted hope.

Was his love for her truly hopeless? He might not be in line for a throne, but he was of good birth. He might be no more worthy of Nicole than any of the princes or their *edlings*, but at least he could assure her that he would love her until the end of their days.

He broke the kiss but didn't let go, wrapping Nicole into a protective, possessive embrace, delighting in the sweet scent of her hair.

What would Connor say if approached with a marriage bargain? What could he offer for Nicole to compensate for his lack of land and wealth? He would have neither until he became a *pencerdd,* which made competing for the position in Arwystli all the more urgent.

What of Nicole? She was to have her wholehearted choice of husbands. Would she accept him if he offered for her? She'd eagerly given her body to him with nary a qualm. She certainly wasn't struggling to get away from him now.

Whose consent did he need first, Connor's or Nicole's?

Connor's, he decided. A matter of honor.

"Ready?" he asked.

She nodded, a soft caress against his chest, then she slipped away.

The horse's reins in one hand, Nicole's hand tucked firmly in the other, Rhodri followed the path that led up the hill toward the manor.

The closer to the manor, the more distinct the stench of smoke. They crested the hill to look upon what remained of Glenvair.

The grain barn—gone. Several of the tenants' cottages—gone, many others blackened. The manor house had suffered the ravages of fire, too, the north end of it burned off. His shock at the destruction was so great he could barely voice his dismay.

"Ye gods. I had so hoped for better. The raiders did a damn thorough job of it."

Nary a soul was in sight, the place eerily devoid of

movement or sound. Not even a goose waddled among the ruins or a chicken pecked in the dirt. Where had everyone gone? Why was no one dragging away the burned timbers and beginning to rebuild?

Nicole squeezed his hand and halted. "Abandoned?" she asked, her confusion mirroring his own.

He struggled to make sense of it. "With winter coming on, perhaps Connor thought it wise to take everyone to—somewhere."

"Oh, Rhodri, look at the graveyard."

Her distress turned his head toward the small church used only when a wandering priest happened by. The number of fresh graves clenched his jaw in rage.

This was no ordinary raid. The villains had been after a greater prize than a few cattle, bolstering his suspicion the raiders had come for Nicole. Not finding her, the raiders had spent their rage on innocents.

Nicole slipped her hand from his and placed her palms against her temples, as if to keep her head from splintering apart. Her eyes squeezed closed, her lips pressed tightly together.

Attack! Except this time he suspected the spirit who tormented Nicole wasn't her brother, William.

"They suffered so!" she said, tears beginning to stream down her cheeks.

"Shut them away, Nicole." He again engulfed her in his embrace, never feeling more helpless in his life. "Shut them away. Heed them not."

"They are too many, too angry. And the child, she screams and screams for her mother. I need to reach the child, but her elders—play your harp, Rhodri. Pray, a soothing song."

He didn't question her request. If she wanted music, she would have it. He untied the sack from the back of the horse, pulled out his harp, and strummed a melody warranted to put a babe to sleep.

Her face melted into its normal softness, her hands came away from her head, and Rhodri marveled when she opened her eyes and gave him one of her enchanting smiles.

"It worked. I swear, Rhodri, you have the power of the wizards of old."

He could barely believe it. "You no longer hear them?"

"Oh, they are there, but I am better able to control them. In the inn, when I went up to try to sleep, you played your harp in the taproom the entire time, did you not? Nay, do not stop playing! Just tell me."

He obeyed. "I did."

"I thought so. Your music was the reason I was able to sleep. William battered at me until you started to play and did not try to rant at me again until you stopped. There is magic in your harp, Rhodri, and I thank you for it."

He could silence spirits? Lord have mercy! Was the talent his alone, or could any bard do it, too? He didn't have time to contemplate the amazing revelation.

Nicole grabbed hold of the horse's reins and headed down the hill. He hurried to follow. 'Twasn't easy to play a harp while walking down a hill, but he managed.

"Nicole, where are you going?" he asked, though he feared he knew.

"To the graveyard. You continue to play—"

"Better we leave and go far enough away so the spirits cannot reach you."

She glanced over her shoulder. "The spirits suffer and

will continue to suffer unless someone convinces them to move on to the afterlife."

Nicole was intent in her purpose, and he didn't dare cease playing long enough to give good argument or the spirits would batter her again. But he saw a flaw in her plan.

"You cannot hear a spirit if I continue to play." And he still thought it an amazing feat. "If you cannot hear them, how do you intend to give aid?"

She tied the horse to a post in front of the church. "I am not sure if my plan will work, but if it does, I shall hear them one at a time."

By some as yet untried method, she was resolved to do whatever good she could do, and 'twas hard to find fault with her for embarking on a noble, merciful quest. He glanced over the dozen or so graves, aware that each marked the resting place of someone he knew and would mourn.

They all, every one of them, deserved mercy.

"Will you know the names of all you speak with?"

"They all want me to know who they are, how they died, and what can be done to give them peace."

As in Oxford, when Thomas had informed Nicole he required forgiveness from the cobbler's family. As William forcefully demanded that Nicole murder Alberic. Spirits were a selfish lot. Some unmercifully so. And the only human who could help them move on to the afterlife was running toward the smallest of the fresh graves.

Nicole placed her hand on the mound of fleshly turned dirt. Tears welled in her eyes. She swallowed hard, then bent her head, no doubt striving to calm a child's terrified screams.

Rhodri's gut clenched with agony, both for Nicole's distress and for the dead child.

"Mererid, Beven and Winnifred's youngest," Nicole announced, stabbing Rhodri in the heart. "The raiders did not mean to kill her, I think. The last thing she remembers is being in the path of a horse when the raiders entered the yard and screaming for her mother. Mererid has gone on now. She recognized the tune you play and asked me to thank you."

He almost choked on the lump that swelled in his throat, so he merely nodded and continued to play.

Nicole rose from Mererid's grave and came toward him. "She did not know who the men were or why they were here. I would be willing to wager one of the men might know."

"I saw your anguish when you spoke to the girl. I hesitate to allow you to go through that again."

Her smile was a blessing. "I have never spoken to a child's spirit before. I admit it distressed me, but I was able to talk her into passing on, and for that I am glad."

"The others might not be so easily convinced."

"Likely not. But I have discovered that as long as you play your harp, I can call to each spirit, one at a time. There are four more, all men. Their deaths were recent, violent, and they are not yet willing to let go of their anger. I am hoping to convince them that they do the living no good by remaining in the earthly realm. Perhaps while I urge them to move on to their reward, I can also learn what happened here, and where Connor is."

She made sense, and still he was reluctant. But he also admired her courage, respected her determination to see this grisly task through. And, heaven help him, he *did* want to know more about the attack and of Connor's whereabouts.

Still, he should be doing more. "So I am supposed to stand here and play the harp while you do the difficult work."

"'Tis because you play the harp I am able to deal with the spirits one at a time. Without your music, they would overwhelm me and I would be forced to leave them to their misery. That would be cruel."

And these were all men who'd died defending Glenvair. To leave them in misery would be inhuman.

"All right, then, but perhaps I can be of greater help. Should any man refuse to move on, tell him Rhodri ap Dafydd, *bardd teulu* of Glenvair, commands him to go to his rest."

With a smile of approval, Nicole moved on to kneel beside a grave and place her hand on the dirt.

"Cyan ap Llewellyn," she said.

Again Rhodri grieved, this time for Glenvair's blacksmith. With his bulk and brawn, Cyan would have been a hard man to bring down. He would have died fighting to his last breath.

Nicole spoke to Cyan for but a short time before she rose. "He believes the men were of Gwynedd but knows not why they raided. Since he died without issue, his greatest fear is that his name will be forgotten, his life lived without his putting a mark on this earth. I promised him that one day, a lovely marker will stand at his head."

Rhodri nodded, already knowing that someday, when he knew more of the battle, those who'd died defending Glenvair would be immortalized in song.

Then she went to the next grave, and then the next, the burden of his grief becoming heavier with each fallen man she named. Even as he mourned, Rhodri noticed that Nicole's task of sending men to claim their heavenly reward seemed to become less arduous. Both men confirmed the raiders were men of Gwynedd, but neither knew why they'd chosen to raid Glenvair.

At the last grave, Nicole closed her eyes for just a moment before opening them again.

"Morgan pen Carwn. He fought beside Connor."

Where I would have fought had I been here!

He envisioned the gnarled elder as he stood side by side with his chieftain, loyal to the very end. Rhodri kept silent while Nicole spoke with Morgan. Dealing with the old man's spirit wasn't easy, judging from the variety of emotions flickering across Nicole's face. Then she went so still and quiet that Rhodri began to wonder if he'd allowed her to speak to the spirits for too long.

"Shut him away, Nicole. Come back to yourself for a time."

She shook her head. "Morgan requires an oath from you, Rhodri."

That shook him. "From me?"

"He says you must swear on your harp that you will allow no man of Gwynedd to have me, so his death will not be in vain."

Rhodri didn't hesitate. "He has my oath."

And his thanks. Now Rhodri knew for certain the raiders had come for Nicole. She wasn't safe as yet. The refuge he'd promised her lay in ashes. The raiders could still be in the area.

Nicole rose and came toward him, exhausted from

dealing with the spirits, and likely heartsore over the reason of the raid. For the first time ever, he was glad to set aside his harp.

She slipped into his open arms, in desperate need of whatever solace he could give her.

"All quiet now?" he asked.

She nodded, then gave him the names of the rest of those who'd died. By now he was so numb with grief he knew he'd have to mourn them all properly later. In song.

"Morgan lay wounded for a time before he died," she said, "long enough for him to hear Connor give the order for everyone to gather up what they could and make ready to go to Mathrafal."

Rhodri saw the sense in the order. "Mathrafal is the seat of the prince of Powys. Connor has gone to ask Prince Madog for aid for his people, and possibly to demand revenge against Gwynedd."

He sighed inwardly, so weary he wanted nothing more than to rest. Nicole's slumped against him in fatigue, barely able to stand. But they couldn't stay here, may have lingered too long already. He wanted to be far and away before the raiders learned that the object of their quest had passed through Glenvair.

"If we hurry, we can be in Mathrafal by sunset. Within the prince's castle, you will be safe."

"Rhodri, the contest—"

"You are not to worry over it now. With haste, I yet have time to make Arwystli before the contest ends."

Tears welled in her eyes. "This is my fault. A child and eleven good men died because of me."

He grasped her shoulders. "Nay, Nicole. These

people died because Owain Gwynedd is a greedy, selfish bastard."

She nodded an acknowledgment, but Rhodri highly doubted she believed him. Well, he'd just have to make her see reason, but not until she was safely behind the thick, stone castle walls at Mathrafal.

Chapter Seventeen

They arrived in Mathrafal just before the gates closed for the night, and Nicole was sorry for it.

Even as Rhodri tossed the horse's reins to a stable lad and pulled down the harp's sack, she wished the two of them could have one more night alone.

Her anger over his deception had fled somewhere on the road between Tintern Abbey and Glenvair. His kiss at the stream, beneath leaves of gold, had led her to hope Rhodri might feel more for her than she'd dared to believe.

Together, with his music and her words, they'd sped five spirits on the path to a glorious afterlife. A remarkable feat, to her way of thinking. But while the spirits were now at peace, she was not. She couldn't hear the voices anymore, but the tale the spirits told of the fight where they'd lost their lives had left her stomach unsettled and her heart sore.

Rhodri's intimate touch would help her forget the tales of bloodshed and smell of fear. His mind-numbing caresses would clear her mind of screams and death cries. Their shared bliss might bind him to her, make Rhodri realize he loved her. Forever and ever. 'Til death did them part.

"You look half dead," he commented.

Not precisely a lover's compliment, but at least he was honest. She likely looked a fright.

"I admit to fatigue. I have never at one time dealt with so many troubled spirits so freshly in their graves, and we did push hard to Mathrafal."

"With good reason."

Because he wanted to ensconce her in a place where he was sure Owain Gwynedd couldn't reach her. That a prince would sanction the near destruction of Connor's manor to capture *her* yet preyed on her mind.

Aye, she knew her worth as a Pendragon princess. Her children would be of lineage of King Arthur, continue his bloodline. But sweet mercy, to kill innocents for the privilege of siring those children was foully dishonorable.

At least she didn't needs worry about having to marry a man of Gwynedd. Not only had Rhodri given Morgan an oath against that event, but surely Connor wouldn't consider a man of Gwynedd's dynastic family as her husband.

In Rhodri's wake, Nicole crossed a muddy bailey crowded with tents and cook fires. Chickens, geese, cows, and pigs shared small plots with their human owners.

Glenvair's tenants, she realized. A lump threatened to close her throat, her heart aching for these people who'd been forced to leave their snug cottages for the squalor of a castle's bailey.

Only a few men were about, the women and children likely tucked into their blankets for the night. Rhodri greeted those men he passed but kept walking toward the castle stairway.

Apparently forewarned of their arrival by a guard from the castle gate, a man of elder years and middling height met them just inside the hall's doorway, holding a tankard of ale, a mightily pleased smile on his lips.

"Ah, at long last!" He extended an arm, inviting a hug into which Nicole stepped, having recognized Connor by his voice. "How tall you have grown, and how beautiful you have become! 'Tis glad I am to see you, my dear."

This was the uncle she remembered. Deeper lines creased Connor's brow, and his hair had gone from gray to white. But he was still boisterous, solicitous—and drunk. His sloppy, sour-smelling kiss on her cheek turned her stomach.

She supposed she could forgive him the inebriation. The man had left behind a severely damaged manor where he'd lost several of his people in a vicious raid. That must sit hard on him.

Torn between sincere relief that he'd not been injured in the raid on Glenvair, and wanting to ball her hand into a fist and punch him in the jaw, she backed out of his loose embrace.

Her energy sorely depleted from dealing with Glenvair's spirits and the subsequent punishing ride to Mathrafal, Nicole wanted nothing more than to fall onto a pallet and sleep for two days. However, her outrage at Connor demanded voice.

"I am glad you survived the raid, Uncle, but heaven have mercy, I am *not* pleased to be here! Do you realize how much hardship and misery you have caused with this scheme of yours?"

He blinked, taken aback. "Now, Nicole—"

She flung a hand in the air. "You nearly got Rhodri hanged! Did you know he was made prisoner of the earl of Oxford, and that we barely escaped with our lives?"

"I heard, but—"

"Then we were forced to *walk* across most of England while being hunted by the earl's patrols. We survived by snaring rabbits and pilfering apples. I spent too many nights shivering on the cold, hard ground, leaped too many fallen logs, and even forded a river!"

Connor's dark eyes narrowed and sharpened, reminding her she spoke uncommonly discourteously to a Welsh chieftain. "You look no worse for the hardship, my dear. Indeed, the experience may even have been good for you."

Aghast, she brushed aside a suspicion Connor might be right about that. Had someone once told her such a journey would make her stronger and more self-assured, she would have dismissed such a statement as nonsense. But that wasn't the point.

"Because you decided that 'twas within your right to choose a husband for me, you put me through hell. You nearly got Rhodri killed! Glenvair is in rubble!" And while a little girl's spirit was now at peace, Nicole knew she'd never forget the child's screams of torment. In a shaky voice she added, "Too many of your people died, and the rest are living in squalor. 'Tis too high a price to pay for this whim of yours, if you ask me."

Connor wasn't so far gone with drink that her barbs didn't sting. She'd drawn blood as surely as if she'd stabbed a dagger in his heart. He went pale and looked over her shoulder at where Rhodri stood behind her.

"You saw Glenvair?" Connor asked, suddenly seeming old and powerless.

"We did," Rhodri answered in a sympathetic tone.

In the ensuing silence, Nicole noticed the other people

in the hall. Men lounged on the floor and played at dice, or sat at trestle tables and drank ale. The only females in the room were the serving wenches, keeping the mugs full and ready to perform other services for the males for a coin or two. Such was the nightly ritual of most castles in England, and apparently in Wales, too.

Her arrival had interrupted both games and talk. Every eye in the hall was aimed at her and Rhodri, witness to her tirade. With the bubble of her anger burst, Nicole almost felt sorry for the uncle whose hand tightened on his mug, the color returning to his cheeks.

"Owain Gwynedd has much to answer for," he stated. "Come sit. I wish to hear more of your journey."

Her emotions wrung out, Nicole followed him across the hall and eased onto the bench. Connor sat down beside her and waved his mug at the man sitting on the other side of the table, who slid sideways on his bench to make room for Rhodri.

"Cynddelw, I ask you, is my niece not all I told you she would be? Lady Nicole de Leon will make for the most fair, most compassionate princess in all of Wales! Do you not agree?"

Nicole immediately recognized the name. Cynddelw Brydydd Mawr was the *pencerdd* of Powys, with whom Rhodri had studied the bardic craft.

With an indulgent nod, Cynddelw agreed to her uncle's overstated compliments, and Rhodri bit back a smile.

Connor placed his tankard on the table before saying, "Prince Madog agrees that something must be done about Gwynedd, and he will lend me the funds to begin rebuilding—Glenvair."

The hitch in his voice revealed his truly deep sorrow

over the damage to his manor and the loss of good people who'd died in the manor's defense.

'Twas good of Prince Madog to lend the funds. She looked about the hall but spotted no princely figure, so she assumed the high nobleman and his wife had already gone up the stairs to their bedchamber.

And now that she'd had her say—or most of what she had to say, because there was still the issue of her marriage to deal with—Nicole placed a hand on Connor's forearm. "I am truly sorry for your loss, Uncle."

"'Tis sweet of you to say so, my dear." He turned to Rhodri. "How did you know where to find me?"

Startled by the question she should have anticipated Connor would ask, all she could do was think, *Sweet mercy, Rhodri, lie!* She did *not* want to explain her burdensome gift to her uncle tonight, if ever.

"I assumed you had taken the people somewhere safe," Rhodri answered, "and Mathrafal seemed the most likely place. Given the destruction at Glenvair, I would have brought Nicole here, regardless. Best the lady reside behind the protection of thick stone walls."

Nicole didn't like the sound of what Rhodri considered best for her, reminded too much of how she'd felt about Oxford's thick stone walls. However, she was most grateful he'd seemed to hear her plea to withhold the truth from Connor. Only five living beings knew of her ability to hear the restless dead—her sisters and their husbands, and Rhodri. For now, she preferred to keep the knowledge from spreading further.

"Well done, Rhodri," Connor said. "Many good men died—and little Mererid." His fist hit the table, rattling the tankards. "I will never forgive Gwynedd for Mererid!"

"Nor will Wales forget," Rhodri promised. "Once I have heard the whole tale, I will put it to song. All shall learn of Gwynedd's treachery and dishonor."

"Certes you will," Cynddelw stated. "You must also put to song the tale of your bringing the last of the Pendragon princesses back home to Wales."

"Aye, but I believe I shall wait until that tale has a proper ending."

But before she could ponder over what Rhodri would deem a proper ending, she caught a disconcerting gleam in his eye she didn't quite understand.

Cynddelw laughed lightly. "To think, not only are you the only one who can write the tale, but you will also be the hero! How fortuitous for you. This could be the making of you, Rhodri, a legend among bards!" Then his look turned thoughtful. "Mayhap you should write the tale now, tonight. You could sing it in Arwystli—you are planning to make haste to Arwystli, are you not?"

"I am," Rhodri acknowledged while accepting a tankard of ale from a serving wench, who gave him a winsome look Nicole couldn't misunderstand.

Then she knew—she *knew*—which part of their journey had put that disconcerting gleam in Rhodri's eyes.

Nicole picked up the tankard the servant had set down before her without so much as a by-your-leave and took a long, fortifying swallow.

Oh, the wretch! Rhodri dare not include their night of passion in his song! Surely he wouldn't—would he? But damn, that's what bards did. They were the keepers of Welsh history, committing important tales to poetry to spread across the land.

But must he tell the *whole* of the history?

Oh, sweet Lord, she would never be able to hear the tale without blushing and running from the room!

"Well, then," Cynddelw said, "you should most definitely begin the writing of it tonight. No bard alive can sing this tale's match! You would be sure to win the chair!"

Far too casually, Rhodri said, "I have not yet decided which events in the journey to include, or not."

"Then you must tell us the tale. Connor and I can aid you in your decisions."

She could imagine her uncle's reaction to certain parts of the tale!

And oh, God, Rhodri was leaving on the morn, off to Arwystli. And if he won the contest, she might never see him again. How would she bear it? To never again see Rhodri ap Dafydd.

She leaned forward, pointedly, toward Rhodri. "I wish to hear the tale when finished. Perhaps there are events I remember differently than you do, or events I feel you should include that you might not consider important."

She was thinking of a certain pig and a twisted ankle, and while she'd only once—moments ago—hoped Rhodri could read her mind, she now *willed* him to understand her meaning.

A flash of chagrin told her he did, indeed, understand her very well. Then he leaned toward her and put his hand over hers.

"My dear princess, you may be assured I remember every event, each word spoken. When the final phrase is written, the last note chosen, you will be the first one to hear the whole of it and give approval. On this I give you my oath."

Nicole swallowed hard, both touched and assured. Rhodri always kept his oaths. She took comfort in his promise, even if he did remove his hand from hers.

"But the contest!" Cynddelw protested. "You will have four days of travel on which to improve both the poetry and melody!"

"Our journey was both long and harsh," Rhodri said. "The heroine of the tale is, as Connor has rightly stated, beautiful, delightful, and compassionate. You will also hear that she has the courage, fortitude, and intelligence worthy of her heritage, and to her I give the right of approval. But that is for another day. Right now, the lady is also weary beyond even a Pendragon's endurance and deserves the comfort of a warm meal and a soft bed."

"Most certes!" With several claps of hands, Connor called back the toothsome serving wench and gave orders for warm food for two and a chamber suitable for a princess of Pendragon. This time the wench found her manners and curtsied to Nicole before rushing off to do Connor's bidding.

The conversation then turned when Rhodri asked of news of other happenings in Wales. She listened with half an ear, unable to pay attention. When her food came, she picked at the bread and broken meats, forcing herself to eat.

Rhodri's duty was now done. He'd delivered her into her uncle's custody. On the morn he would make haste to Arwystli, go on with his own life, pursue his ambition, leave her behind to face her own destiny.

She'd known all along this day would come and had thought herself prepared. She wasn't. For all she'd berated her uncle for putting her through hell, all she could dwell on now were those bits of heaven she'd found in Rhodri's arms.

The wench returned. "My lady, your chamber is ready. I will take you up, if it pleases you."

It didn't please her at all, but she couldn't very well sit in the hall all night simply to hear the sound of Rhodri's voice, be near him as long as she could. She might want to, but even in her morose mood, she recognized how useless and pitiable such an action would be.

So she would be strong and sensible and, on the morrow, have a long talk with Connor about Alberic's order regarding any marriage her uncle might have in mind, and she would face whatever fate tossed her way.

She was, after all, a Pendragon princess.

With all the royal bearing she could muster, Nicole stood and bade good night to Connor and Cynddelw. To Rhodri she needed to say more.

How did one say fare-thee-well to one's own heart?

"I thank you for your excellent escort and wish you good fortune in the contest. I shall miss your . . . music."

Rhodri reached down into the harp's sack, pulled out her circlet, her brother's dagger, and the sack of coins Alberic had given him. He stood and gave them over with no discernible reluctance.

"'Twas an honor and delight to have enjoyed your company all these weeks, my lady." Then he leaned in close and whispered, "You shall hear the music again, Nicole. Soon."

He meant the tale of their journey, of course, and would keep his oath to allow her approval. Nothing more.

"I shall look forward to it, Rhodri ap Dafydd. Fare thee well and Godspeed."

Nicole turned and followed the wench across the hall to the stairs, determined not to choke on her unshed tears.

❧

Rhodri watched Nicole stride toward the stairway to the keep's upper floor, her head high, spine straight, and shoulders squared, as if preparing to do battle, not sleep.

He wished he could climb those stairs with her, tell her there were no more battles to fight. But he couldn't, because he didn't yet have the right.

There was more he'd wished to whisper in Nicole's ear, but the moment of their parting had passed by too swiftly, and the hall wasn't the place for revealing his heart and intent, especially because he must first speak of that intent to Connor.

Still, he wished he could have brought a smile to her lips before she'd walked away, tell her he knew she'd miss more of him than his music.

So he eased back onto the bench across from Connor. Cynddelw had wandered off, leaving the two of them alone.

"Was the journey truly hell for her?" Connor asked.

Not all hell. Interspersed with danger and deprivation were laughter and loving, and those were too precious and private to tell anyone, even in a song.

"I gather you heard Nicole and I were taken to Oxford."

"Somewhat."

Briefly, Rhodri related the events leading to his unfortunate confinement in Oxford Castle's tower, then described how he and Nicole escaped, leaving out Nicole's dealings with Thomas's spirit.

"Being on foot and without coin, and avoiding the roads because of the earl's patrols, lengthened our journey far more than either you or I had planned for." Hoping to leave the tale at that, for now, Rhodri went on. "As events turned out, the delay was a good one for Nicole's sake. Had she been at Glenvair when Gwynedd attacked, she might now be ensconced in Owain's castle at Aberffraw."

Connor gave a long sigh. "The raiders rode in with the intent to kidnap Nicole. The leader was irate that she was not there for the taking, accused me of falsehoods. 'Twas then they fired the grain barn. When I continued to protest that Nicole had not yet arrived, they fired some of the tenants' cottages. And when they fired the manor house, and I still held out, they decided I might be telling the truth. God's blood, by the time they were done, Glenvair was near in ruins!"

Rhodri heard Connor's anger and woe, felt the man's sense of loss, and refrained from asking if he would have handed Nicole over when the raiders lit the first torch. Connor would deny it, certes, but Rhodri couldn't be sure of what Connor might have done when watching flames devour the manor's hope of surviving the winter months.

"Well, Nicole is safe from Gwynedd now, and that is what is important."

Connor huffed. "She will be safer once wed."

So Rhodri, too, believed. The soonest the best, and he had just the man in mind.

"Connor, I was privileged to meet Alberic of Camelen and Darian of Bruges along the way."

Connor's eyebrow shot up. "You went to Camelen?"

"Nay. The two are both intelligent men and between

them made a correct guess at my route to Wales. They were waiting for us when we crossed the Avon." To both his consternation and relief. "As Nicole's brother-by-marriage, Alberic commands me to inform you he is not pleased that you sent me to England and that Nicole no longer resides in Bledloe Abbey. For a time, I thought certain he would take Nicole from me and sweep her off to Camelen. He did not."

Rhodri still wasn't sure why that was so. He still had no notion of what Darian had said to Alberic to sway the baron.

He continued. "Alberic allowed Nicole to continue this journey for reasons of his own, but with a condition. Nicole is to give her wholehearted approval to any marriage you might arrange. Alberic is most insistent she have her choice of husband. He threatens to invade Wales if he learns events play out differently."

Connor huffed. "Alberic has not sufficient men or resources to invade Wales."

"Perhaps not, but Alberic is not without influence, and were I you, I would not test his vow to cut out your black heart if you do not heed him. Besides, I gave Alberic my oath I would ensure you adhere to his wishes."

Rhodri braced for the tirade he saw brewing.

"By what right did you give Alberic such warranty?"

"He gave me little choice! And you do wish Nicole to marry a Welshman, do you not?"

"Certes, but one of my choosing, not hers! By the saints, Rhodri, you overstepped! I will not be bound by an oath given by my bard to a Norman baron!"

Rhodri leaned forward. "You will, Connor ap Maelgwn, or this bard will sing the tale of Alberic of Camelen's generosity and your lack of appreciation for his liberality all over Wales!"

For a moment, Connor's face paled as white as his hair. "A damn vicious threat against the man who raised you, Rhodri ap Dafydd."

Hurtful, to be sure, but apparently necessary.

"Perhaps, but I mean every word."

Connor relented with the wave of a dismissive hand. "Prince Madog has several eligible sons and nephews. Now that Nicole has arrived, we can summon them to Mathrafal. Certes, Nicole will find one of them agreeable enough to marry."

Did Connor believe all he must do is stand the men in a line in front of Nicole for her to make her selection? With a twinge of chagrin, Rhodri admitted that might be the case. The men were all of noble family and possessed land, and a few were even physically appealing. And what man who possessed a dram of sense would say Nicole nay?

However, he hadn't thought Connor would allow Nicole to marry a son or nephew of Madog ap Maredudd.

"Prince Madog is allied with the earl of Chester and will continue that alliance as long as Owain Gwynedd controls more of Powys than he ought. Madog's sons and nephews favor that alliance. I thought you wanted Nicole to marry someone who would not be willing to treat with the English."

"Well, think on it, Rhodri. Prince Madog has sheltered us and will help me rebuild Glenvair. Giving his sons and nephews first chance for Nicole's favor seems only right, does it not?"

Connor's hopes for a grand marriage to unify the

Welsh princes against the Norman magnates of England had apparently changed in the time Rhodri had been off fetching the bride. Now Connor thought to use Nicole to his best advantage. One of Madog's heirs would be rewarded with a Pendragon princess in return for the funds to rebuild Glenvair.

Rhodri would have shaken his head in disgust had he thought it would do one whit of good.

As was the Welsh way, upon the death of Prince Madog, whatever lands the man held at the time would be divided among his heirs, with the grandest share going to the man Madog considered the most worthy. All knew that would be Gruffudd, Madog's second son.

In Rhodri's opinion, two of Madog's unmarried male heirs might stand a chance of winning Nicole's favor. Gruffudd, of course, and one of the nephews, Owain.

Both men would one day have lordships of their own and funds plentiful enough to support themselves and their wives in noble fashion. But would either of them love and cherish Nicole as she deserved? Would they honor her Pendragon heritage as they ought, or use it for their own selfish gains?

Would either of them provide a bard for Nicole to call upon when restless spirits demanded more from her than she could give? Could any bard's harp have the same soothing effect on spirits, or only his? 'Twas a question he had no answer for, and 'twas likely vain and prideful to believe his music alone calmed impatient, demanding spirits.

Damn it, Nicole would be best off marrying a bard. And what better bard than he, who would not only love and cherish her all her days but could help her accomplish what she considered her life's purpose?

Problem was, he had to convince Connor without revealing Nicole's secret ability.

"Connor, I realize I hold no hope of coming into a princedom, but I am of fine Welsh blood and, I believe, have prospects for a secure future. I also realize I am not your first choice of husband for Nicole, but I ask you to consider my suit for her hand in marriage."

To Connor's stunned expression, Rhodri continued.

"Nicole has become precious to me these past weeks. Believe me, Connor, she is all you had hoped she would be, and more. I have said naught to her about my intentions, feeling I must do you the honor of first obtaining your consent."

Rhodri grew more nervous and wary the longer Connor remained silent. He saw the refusal in Connor's eyes even before the man spoke and steeled himself against the words.

"You are a fine man from an esteemed bardic line," Connor began. "I can see you have grown fond of my niece, and I thank you for delivering her to me hale and hardy. But she is not for you, lad. Nicole deserves a husband of established wealth and rank, a nobleman with whom she can make fine, noble sons worthy of the Pendragon heritage."

"I remember another princess of Pendragon who wished to marry a bard. Why would you not approve of my marrying Nicole when you consented to my father marrying your sister?"

Connor took a long sip of ale before he answered. "A mistake I have regretted since the day Nest died. Had I followed my instincts and married her to a noble of Deheubarth, she would not have died so young, and in so foolish a manner."

Rhodri heard both the guilt and the blame. "The river took them. 'Twas nobody's fault—"

Connor slammed his tankard on the table. "By the saints, 'twas your father's fault for giving in to some whim of Nest's! If Nicole must approve of her husband, then approve she will, but I vow 'twill be to a man who knows how to keep a woman in her place!"

With that, Connor rose, unsteadily, and staggered off, leaving Rhodri to count the many times he'd given in to a whim of Nicole's, to remember how many times he'd purposely put her in danger. Too many of both, certes. Yet they'd both survived, even thrived.

He wasn't his father; Nicole wasn't her aunt. 'Twas unfair and ridiculous for Connor to make the comparison, and unreasonable to expect *any* man to keep Nicole in her place.

Further reasoning with Connor didn't seem possible. True, the man had imbibed too freely of the ale and allowed his tongue to wag too loosely. But even when sober, Connor likely wouldn't hear of a marriage bargain between Rhodri ap Dafydd and Nicole de Leon.

But now that he'd voiced his heart's yearnings and argued his case, Rhodri could think of naught else. For the next hour he pondered what he must do and decided how to go about it.

Unfortunately, once more, all depended upon whether or not Nicole would cooperate.

Chapter Eighteen

"N icole. Time to awaken."

She'd been dreaming of Rhodri most of the night. Wonderful dreams. Heartrending dreams. Hearing his voice, so clear and close, calling her from sleep, didn't startle her one whit.

She felt his large, warm palm on her cheek, breathed in his musky scent. Both sensations filled her with a sense of rightness and a longing for things that would never be.

Nicole woke far enough to realize she wasn't dreaming anymore and opened her eyes to a chamber lighted by a single night candle. She peered into the deep-set brown eyes she'd often become lost in.

"Rhodri."

"Do you know how beautiful you are when you first awaken?" He smiled, his thumb brushing over her cheek-bone, thrilling her more than his compliment. "Had I the time, I would write a poem extolling the allure of your sleep-misted eyes."

Except he had no time. He must have come to say a final farewell before leaving for Arwystli.

He shouldn't be in her bedchamber, but in the past few weeks the two of them had shared so much and done so many things they ought not to that one more transgression seemed of little consequence.

Nicole placed her hand over Rhodri's and kissed his palm, glad he'd come but hating to bid him Godspeed and good fortune all over again.

"You are ready to leave for Arwystli? So early?"

"Not as yet. I am of a mind to take you with me, if you will but rise and make yourself ready. What say I kidnap you and we begin a new adventure?"

Stunned fully awake, she rose up on an elbow, hugging the finely woven bed linens against her naked skin. He couldn't possibly be serious about her going to Arwystli with him! Except she sensed Rhodri's urgency when he fetched her chemise and gown from the clothing hook and tossed them on the bed.

Something was seriously amiss.

Nicole sat up fully and reached for her chemise.

"What happened after I left the hall last eve?"

He crossed his arms. "I told Connor about meeting with Alberic, and of his order."

'Twas as she'd feared. Connor had balked at Alberic's insistence that she have the right to approve her marriage.

"So he refuses to give me the right of approval?"

"Oh, Connor intends to allow you to approve, but from a very few number of men of whom *he* approves. I am sure that is not what Alberic had in mind when he allowed you to continue on to Wales. Where are your dagger and circlet?"

Disconcerted over Rhodri's revelations, she pointed to

the mantel over the hearth and slipped the chemise over her head.

Apparently Rhodri was angry with Connor, but in truth, her situation hadn't changed. Naturally, Connor would allow her to choose a husband from only among men he thought suitable.

"You disapprove of these men?"

"Of the men, nay. Of the reason for his choices? Aye! Connor sent me to Bledloe Abbey to fetch a Pendragon princess, who was to join with a Welsh nobleman for the glorious, honorable cause of uniting the Welsh against the Norman magnates of England. 'Twould seem Connor has undergone a change of heart. Now he intends for you to be the prize for the inglorious cause of rebuilding Glenvair!"

She began to understand. "'Tis hardly the ending you had hoped for to end your tale of our journey."

He looked confused for a moment, then smiled. "Hardly. But that is not why I want you to come with me. Those men are not suitable for you for another reason entirely." Holding her circlet and dagger, he sat on the edge of the bed. "You need to marry a bard, Nicole. Someone who can silence disagreeable spirits when needed. Not one of the men Connor named can do more than pluck a string or two."

So he thought she could find a suitable bard from amongst those gathered in Arwystli for the contest. While he competed for the position of *pencerdd* to the prince, he expected her to find herself a husband. Sweet mercy, the only bard she wished to marry sat on her bed, less than an arm's length away.

"We do not know if another bard's harp can perform the same magic on spirits as yours does."

"That we do not." He paused a moment before continuing. "Nicole, we know that together we can aid spirits. Would you consider marrying me?"

They were the precise words she wished to hear. Her heart thudding with joy, Nicole wanted nothing more than to drag him further into the bed and show him how wholeheartedly she would accept him as her husband.

But to agree would put Rhodri in danger and destroy his chance to attain his life's ambition.

She was truly flattered he sought to help her and loved him all the more for his noble sentiment, but she couldn't allow him to give up so much out of a misplaced sense of duty.

She wanted to cry out her misery, and dared not. With as much princess-like dignity as she could muster, Nicole shattered her own heart.

"I thank you for your offer, but if we step beyond Mathrafal's gates, Connor is sure to send men after us. We would again be hunted, this time by Welshmen. If caught, you could spend the rest of your days in a tower cell."

He opened his mouth to utter what she was sure was a protest; she put a finger to his lips to silence his argument.

"You have a dream you have pursued your life long. The lessons, the practice, the poetry, the music—they have shaped you and prepared you for the day when you would play for a prince and earn your chair. If you are hunted, and so cannot perform without fear of being captured, then all you have worked for is lost. You must go without me and earn your chair."

"So you do not wish to go with me?"

She wished to go with all her heart. Bards from all

over Wales would gather for the contest. There would be music, feasting, dancing, and such gaiety as she hadn't experienced since entering Bledloe Abbey.

And she would be with Rhodri. But as much as she yearned to agree, she refused to put her selfish wishes above his well-being.

"I cannot."

Rhodri waved a dismissive hand. "You will be content to select a husband from among the dullards Connor presents to you?"

She inwardly winced. "Not all can be dullards."

He scoffed. "You have yet to meet them. And what of your own life's purpose? Will this husband allow you the freedom to aid spirits—if, indeed, you can convince him you hear the dead speak—or will he forbid you concourse with any but the living?"

"He can hardly prevent the dead from speaking to me. I may have a difficult time silencing their voices when they persist, but I learned how to hide my ability while in the abbey and can do so again."

"If you marry me, you need not hide the rare and exceptional power that is so much a part of you. You could pursue your quest to aid as many spirits as you are able, and I shall help you."

Why must Rhodri's words give both joy and pain? Why did he tempt her so?

"Tell me, what would a prince think of his *pencerdd* spending his days playing his harp in graveyards? You would not keep your position long, I warrant."

"Decidedly not, which is part of the reason we are not bound for Arwystli."

That surprised her. "Then where?"

"Camelen."

"Why ever for?"

He put her circlet and dagger on the floor, then turned to fully face her. "I once believed that becoming a *pencerdd* in a great house was what I most desired. Then we accomplished the incredible at Glenvair. I now believe I have found a grander purpose for my music. Nicole, if you marry a Welsh noble, you may never be permitted to return home to put William to rest and he may plague you for the rest of your days. Both you and your brother deserve to have the matter settled."

William. Sweet mercy, she'd yearned for so long to help her brother seek his peace.

"I have tried so many times to convince William to go to his peace, but he refuses to listen."

"You have never tried to speak to him at the place of his burial, and not when I am playing the harp. Yester noon, you said you heard magic in my music. Certes, is it not time to test how strong the magic might be?"

Nicole tamped down her growing excitement over the prospect. "If I leave with you, we will have the prince's patrols searching for us in Wales and may yet encounter the earl of Oxford's patrols in England."

"Camelen is a mere three days' hard ride. No one will be certain of where we are. I am confident we can reach Camelen without incident."

Could Rhodri be right? Could the two of them, at long last, deal successfully with William?

Magic. She'd been gifted—or cursed—with the ability to hear the troubled dead. Her sister Emma possessed the power to see visions in pools of water. Gwen was the guardian of a potent ancient spell.

Emma required no partner to make use of her ability. Gwendolyn did, and Alberic took his responsibility most seriously. Nicole had never thought she, too, might require a partner to make full use of her gift, but perhaps she did.

Before her sat the one man who she knew not only believed in her gift but was willing to partner her if she would allow. That was why he'd asked her to marry him, so they could uninhibitedly explore the breadth and depth of the magic.

Nicole rose to her knees and wrapped her arms around Rhodri's neck, wishing he loved her as much as she loved him, but finding a morsel of contentment in what they could share together. As his arms came around her in a comforting and stimulating embrace, she felt more sure of her decision.

"You are certain you will not regret missing the contest?"

"Not for a moment. Will you regret not becoming the most favored princess in all of Wales?"

"Never."

Then Rhodri kissed her, and Nicole wondered how the devil they could have spent so much time *talking* while in the same bed.

Her thoughts floated away from William, and from all of the problems they could face both at Camelen and in the future. She dismissed her earlier concerns over his inappropriate presence in her bedchamber, and didn't even wonder over how she had become so blatantly brazen in so short a time.

All she could do was revel in the glorious sensation of Rhodri's mouth on hers once more. Oh, how she'd yearned for his kiss, and more, all through the night.

A night now nearly over.

"How soon must we leave?" she asked in breathless earnestness.

"We have time," he answered, falling back to lie on the bed, taking her with him. "Does my princess wish to explore the differences in making love in a soft bed in a warm bedchamber, rather than on the hard ground in a fern-covered shelter?"

She almost called him to task for calling her a princess, but this time he'd used the title as an endearment, without scorn. And truly, she didn't mind at all being *his* princess.

"Most certes she does!"

The chemise she'd donned was quickly dispensed with, as were Rhodri's garments. Within moments they cuddled under the coverlet, face to face, skin to skin, without any impediment of space in which to enjoy each other.

"An improvement already," she commented. "I do not suppose we can take a pallet with us."

Rhodri chuckled. "Nay, no pallet, but this time we have coin to pay for more comfortable accommodations on our adventure, even if that means a bed of hay in a farmer's barn."

Nicole didn't care where they slept as long as Rhodri slept beside her and, as now, his long fingers skimmed along her curves as skillfully as he strummed his harp.

As he had in a fondly remembered fern-covered shelter, he petted her breasts until they swelled to aching. Her nipples puckered, the nubs going hard and begging for his touch. Understanding her need, Rhodri suckled gently, firmly, tending to her in most satisfactory fashion.

She understood his need, too. The long length of his hard cock pressed against her thigh, eagerly awaiting the coupling to come.

"What can we do in a bed that we could not in the shelter?"

"I can pleasure you properly."

"What we did in the shelter was not proper?"

The corner of his mouth quirked upward in a wry smile. "What we did in the shelter was not at all proper. Granted, we managed a successful encounter, but our positions were all wrong."

"So we will couple differently this time?"

"Differently, but with the same rewarding ending."

Before she could ask what matter the positions if the ending were the same, Rhodri halted her question with another kiss. She drank deeply, her thirst for him unquenchable.

She didn't stop him when once more he insisted upon petting her breasts, her nipples again hardening under the brush of his thumb. Nor did she raise an objection when his hand slipped between her thighs, his fingers sliding into her hot, wet folds, seeking the small nub that responded wildly to his ministrations.

Tongues mated. Hands roamed. Her heart soared with joy, and her body quivered with anticipation.

Nicole took care to intimately appreciate Rhodri's finely sculpted body, from the curve of his rugged jaw, down over the rippled muscles of his chest, and down farther yet to the glorious male member jutting proudly upward from a thick thatch of dark hair.

She took him in hand and was rewarded with a low moan akin to agony.

Sweet mercy, he was hard, his cock a marvel of tempered steel encased in silken skin. Her fascination led to exploration and, to her delight, heightened her own desire.

"If I recall rightly, in the shelter you hinted of further lessons."

"I did." He pulled her up to lie atop him, and she would gladly slide downward to take him inside her did he not roll her onto her back to cover her. "Lie still, and I will show you one of the joys at which I hinted."

He kissed her lips, then jaw, then the sensitive hollow of her throat. Ever downward he slid, pausing briefly to honor each breast before sliding again to sprinkle kisses over her stomach.

She thought he would halt there and retrace his path back to her mouth. She was wrong. He knelt between her wide-spread legs, placed his hands on her inner thighs, and lowered his head to kiss her *there*.

Lie still? Impossible!

Nicole arched into the intimate, intense flick of his tongue. She clenched the sheets, frantic to ease the torment, unwilling to cut it short. Exquisite heat flooded her. Her nether regions begged release.

Her fingers burrowed into his hair, intending to pull him upward, but she perversely held him in place, the sensations too divine to tell him to cease.

But if he didn't halt soon, she would reach her ecstasy without him inside her, and that wasn't her preference.

"Rhodri!"

He didn't misunderstand her command. Within a trice he again covered her, and then, to her utter delight and relief, he filled her. One steady, powerful stroke followed another, flinging her steadily further into an adventure she wished to embark on only with Rhodri.

She matched his rhythm, urging him onward. Breath ragged and heart pounding, Nicole followed where Rhodri led.

Ecstasy came in a bright flash of heat, warming her through, convulsing the sheath in which Rhodri thrust. Never had she known such bliss could be reached until he'd shown her how thoroughly a man and woman could come together.

She lifted her hips, inviting him to seek deeper purchase.

On the next thrust he burrowed to profound depths and stayed there. His head thrown back, the cords of his neck stretched taut with strain, the sweat on his upper lip glistening from exertion, Rhodri surrendered.

The pulse of his release harmonized with hers, and Nicole thought it the most wondrous music to be heard in this earthly realm.

He lowered his head to nuzzle her neck. She wrapped her arms around him, now content to lie still until the last strains of the music faded. There was no place she would rather be. Nowhere she wanted to go. Would that they could lock the door's latch and remain here for hours.

"Ah, Nicole," he whispered, his breath warm against her neck, creating delicious tingles. "You please me beyond reason, woman. Shelter or bed, the result is the same. Your passion is a gift I shall cherish always."

Not a declaration of love. Disheartening, but not defeating. Whether Rhodri came to love her or not, they shared a grand passion for each other and enhanced each other's talents. 'Twas more than many other couples could claim.

"If I had but one wish, 'twould be you had come to my bedchamber earlier."

He rose up on his elbows and grinned, mischief sparkling in his eyes. "I shall keep in mind that my lady is an insatiable minx and strive to ever satisfy her in new ways."

"Say you there are more lessons to be learned?"

"A few."

The night candle sputtered. Rhodri glanced over his shoulder at the now unsteady flame. When he turned back, the mischief had fled. He didn't need to tell her why.

After a last kiss, he abandoned her and the bed. Nicole rolled off the mattress.

They dressed hurriedly in silence. She slipped the dagger into her boot, then looked around for the harp's sack in which to place her circlet and the pouch of coins.

"Did you not bring your harp with you?"

"Nay, 'tis already down in the horse's stall." He draped her cloak over her shoulders and fastened the clasp. "I also pilfered food and a wineskin from the prince's larder. This time we will be neither cold nor hungry."

He made this latest escape sound easily accomplished. Nicole had doubts. Ever since they'd left Oxford, every escape had been harrowing.

"Need I distract a guard or two?"

He shook his head. "We will ride through the gate as soon as it opens for the day. Since the two of us arrived together yester eve, the guards will have no reason to question why we leave together this morn. 'Twill be hours before we are fully missed."

They left the chamber as the night candle gutted out and made their way through the castle's passageways by the sparse light of torches burning low in their iron sconces. Nicole followed in Rhodri's wake down the servants' stairs and out a small door opening into the bailey.

In the hazy light of dawn, Nicole nervously watched for the unwanted approach of the stable master or one of his lads while Rhodri saddled the horse and secured their belongings.

Her wariness wasn't all due to uncertainty over easy passage through Mathrafal's gate, or even over the journey to Camelen. The finality of leaving Wales was niggling at her conscience.

Rhodri seemed at peace with leaving behind his life and his ambition. But how soon before he missed his homeland? How soon before he regretted not competing in the contest? How soon before he wished he'd never heard the name of Nicole de Leon?

He led the horse to the mounting block and looked at her expectantly. Damn, she should probably just get on the horse and allow fate its course. But she couldn't.

Nicole stood before Rhodri, wishing she didn't feel obligated to give him another chance to question his actions, knowing she must.

"I fear you may come to hate me one day. Can you truly leave behind Wales and your dreams without regret?"

"I have you and my harp. 'Tis all I need, Nicole."

"For now, perhaps, but someday—"

"Someday you will cease to worry so much."

He let go the horse's reins and held out his hands, palms up. Without hesitation, she slipped her hands into his.

"I had hoped," he said, "to wait until we reached Camelen for this, but if you need reassurance, I am prepared—nay, most willing—to give you my vow now." He squeezed her hands. "Nicole de Leon, princess of Pendragon, will you accept this humble bard as thy husband? Henceforth, I will honor, support, and cleave only unto thee until death does us part."

Stunned, she could only stare at his spreading grin.

"Unless," he added, "I die before you and my spirit decides to remain bound to this earth to await yours. Then I promise not to bother you overmuch."

Ye gods! Rhodri wanted them to pledge to each other now! In a stable! And why not? Except for one problem.

"We have no witnesses!"

He shrugged a shoulder. "We do not need them, not by either Welsh or English law or custom. If you like, we can repeat our vows at Camelen with your family as witnesses. What say you, Nicole?"

Oh, blessed be! Overwhelmed with love and joy, for a moment she couldn't push words beyond the lump in her throat. When she finally found her voice, she spoke her vows with no less sincerity and conviction.

"I say I could not find a better man in all of Wales or England to accept as my husband. I pledge thee my troth, Rhodri ap Dafydd. I shall strive to be a good wife to you all our days. This I vow."

Their kiss sealed the bargain and promised of more delights to come. But they weren't so lost to the moment they didn't hear the clank of the heavy chain raising the castle's iron gate.

Snugly ensconced on Rhodri's lap, Nicole worried all through the bailey, wishing he'd urge the horse onward a bit faster. And damn if he wasn't right about the guards taking little notice of their passage.

With a sigh of relief, she leaned back into him and relaxed. He chuckled but wisely said naught of her tendency to worry.

Sweet mercy, she was truly going home!

Nicole remembered the day she'd left Camelen, an angry and frightened girl of ten. Now she would return as a married woman, to a Welsh bard no less. Her family would certainly be surprised, and she dearly hoped they would raise no objections. She sighed inwardly, aware that the most strident objection would come from another quarter altogether—a royal one.

She forcefully pushed the worry aside, refusing to allow that thorn to prick too harshly right now.

More than her family's acceptance, she wanted them to like Rhodri, too. She suspected Alberic and Darian had taken Rhodri's measure at the inn and, at the least, gave him their respect and trust, or they would never have allowed her to remain with Rhodri.

Her sisters? Gwendolyn and Emma would likely be happy as long as she was happy. And, truth, all Rhodri must do was play his harp and be his charming self to win them over.

Only one family member wouldn't care about her happiness, the one Rhodri's music must calm if she were to help him.

Her brother, William.

Chapter Nineteen

"Did someone die here?"

Pulled from her musings, Nicole glanced over the peaceful stream where they'd stopped to water the horse and, she suspected, where Rhodri wished to give her a few moments to rest before they rode the last few leagues into Camelen.

She'd taken advantage by sitting on a log to watch the water flow by while Rhodri tended the horse.

"Not that I am aware of. Why?"

"Your thoughts were so far away I wondered if you heard a spirit."

She shook her head. "Nay. I was merely preparing what to say to William."

If he would listen.

"Perhaps the music will put your brother in a mood to hear you."

"Oh, he has always heard me. William simply does not wish to heed reason. I fear he will not this time, either."

If William refused to cease ranting and declined to move on, then she would be forced to leave Camelen.

Rhodri couldn't be expected to play his harp day and night, and William would batter at her, more fiercely than ever before, to kill Alberic.

Rhodri settled the horse near a patch of long grass, then joined her on the log.

"How often does William speak to you?"

"I told you about the first." At Rhodri's nod, she continued. "Then once each year, near Easter, when Alberic brought Gwendolyn to the abbey." She shivered. "Those were always the worst. Alberic would come in to give me a hasty greeting, then take himself off to the priest's hut so I could visit with Gwendolyn. I always hated that."

"So all of William's ranting has been to order you to kill Alberic."

"Not all. He has spoken to me other times, just recently. About a fortnight before you arrived at the abbey, he woke me to say I should leave Bledloe, that my time there was done." She smiled at Rhodri. "'Twas one of the reasons I was reluctant to consider Connor's offer. I truly did not want to obey William. The one time I did he caused me much heartache."

"It has always seemed odd to me that William could speak with you at will when other spirits cannot."

"I assumed it was because he was the first spirit to speak to me, or because I worshipped him as a child. Or because no matter how many spirits I have helped, I have not been able to reach my own brother. The guilt has ever plagued me."

"You have tried."

"And failed, time after time."

"Perchance this time you will enjoy better fortune."

She hoped so. Dear God, she hoped so.

"William is buried in the village church. I believe we should deal with him before we enter the castle."

"You do not wish to see your sisters first?"

With all her heart.

"I wish to deal with William before I see Alberic."

Rhodri rose and held out his hand. Time to go. She accepted his assistance without hesitation, then took the step into his embrace.

"'Twill be all right, Nicole, no matter what happens."

He'd been trying to soothe her worries ever since leaving Mathrafal. To his credit, he'd been right about so much. They'd escaped with ease and encountered no Welsh or English patrols. They'd ridden hard during the daylight and found food and shelter at night, and she now knew what it felt like to make love in a bed of hay.

She held him tighter, because beyond dealing with William loomed a void. She'd tried to peer into it, to see the future beyond, but no vision of her future with Rhodri formed.

They'd married, pledged to each other, sealed their bargain with sweet kisses and rapturous lovemaking. Rhodri would keep his vows, of that Nicole had no doubt. 'Twas his regret of those vows she feared, especially if his music didn't provide her with the means to send William to the afterlife.

She'd not realized until yesterday Rhodri's stake in their success in dealing with her brother. He'd found true magic in his harp's music, and William would be the test of the magic's strength.

If their attempt failed, then Rhodri might begin to wonder if he'd made a mistake by giving up his dreams and then resent being bound to her.

She took heart that his music had so eased the spirits at Glenvair they'd been agreeable to finding their peace. But William's spirit was older, his desire for revenge deep and venomous, and he'd resisted her every effort. He might not so easily succumb.

This area of Shropshire had been her childhood home, and as they rode over the gentle hills and through thick woodlands, Nicole realized how much she'd missed it. So for a while, she concentrated on appreciating the warm sunshine and the autumn-touched trees.

Too soon, and not soon enough, Camelen's walls came into view. The sight of her home took her breath away and filled her eyes with tears.

Stone walls, thick and gray, promised security to all who resided within and protection to all who resided within its shadow. Odd, she'd chafed at the notion of spending her days within the confines of stone walls—all but these. At Camelen she could blissfully reside, even if it wasn't truly her home anymore, but Alberic and Gwendolyn's.

Rhodri ignored the drawbridge and headed for the village, specifically for the church with its square Norman bell tower. The last time she'd been inside was to bury her father and brother.

"Has William said aught to you as yet?"

"Not as yet." Which surprised her a bit. Surely William sensed her presence.

"We will leave the horse by the well. I want to have my harp at the ready the moment you open the church door."

As if his harp were a sword he would wield against an attack. Nicole thought the comparison an apt one.

The village had changed a bit since she'd left. Nearby the church stood newer-looking cottages, the older ones having been burned during an attack on Camelen by a Welshman who'd sought to take Gwendolyn away from Alberic and not succeeded.

Naturally, the children's curiosity about the village's visitors stopped their play, especially when, after Rhodri tied the horse to the well, he pulled a harp from the sack tied behind the saddle.

Nicole didn't recognize any of the little ones, having been gone from Camelen before most of them were born. A few of their parents, who'd come out to see why the children had gone so silent, smiled at her when she nodded at them.

She would love to greet each familiar person, but Rhodri waited, harp in hand. Her homecoming must wait, the joy or pain of the homecoming dependent on a brother who'd been dead for eight years.

Nicole scurried up the stairs, grasped the iron ring, and paused for only a moment before she opened the huge oak door.

The church was dark, musty, and silent but for the strains of silver strings.

You came! At last, you came!

William's excited shouts reverberated through her and, for a heartbeat, she relished the joy she hadn't heard in her brother's voice in a very, very long time. Not since he'd lived. Not since the day he'd picked her up and swung her around, promising to bring her a pretty gift when he returned from the war.

Unfortunately, William's joy wouldn't linger, not when he discovered why she'd come.

Nicole's footsteps echoed ominously as she strode through the empty church toward the altar, a block of white marble covered with an altar cloth, the white linen likely embroidered by Emma. At the foot of the altar were three large slabs fashioned of bronze. Her father lay beneath the center slab, her mother and brother on either side of him.

She swallowed the grief that threatened to divert her from her purpose.

I am here, William.

Who is with you?

Nicole's heart beat a little faster. Rhodri stood beside her, frowning down at the bronze slabs, playing softly.

William must hear the harp, and he was speaking rationally, if a bit irritated that Nicole hadn't come alone.

Rhodri ap Dafydd. Do you remember him from Wales? He is a bard now.

He interfered with us at the inn. Send him away!

Rhodri is my husband. He has a right—

Husband! You are wed to that whoreson?

The insult to Rhodri stung. Nicole crossed her arms. *You are dead, William. You have no say in whom I marry.*

I am your brother. Certes I have a say. No man has any greater right than I! Send him away!

William's intense resentment that she'd married Rhodri, who could interfere with his hold on her, sluiced through Nicole—and the dagger in her boot warmed against her ankle.

Startled, she reached down to pull out the weapon she'd taken from Camelen as a reminder of her brother, feeling the veriest fool for not having realized before now that he'd somehow used the dagger to remain in contact with her.

She supposed her lack of awareness might be somewhat forgiven. For eight years it had lain in the bottom of her box of possessions, under her cot. She hadn't pulled it out until Aubrey de Vere had ordered her to gather her things to make ready for the journey to Oxford.

Ah, the dagger. You must kill Alberic, Nicole. By the love you bear me, you must avenge my death!

She now knew what she must do with the dagger to be free of William.

I will not kill Alberic. I will not be the instrument of your revenge. She bent down and placed the dagger on his grave. *I vow, William, if you do not heed me this time, I will have the dagger buried with you, and you will spend the rest of eternity alone.*

Naaayyy! You cannot desert me!

Nicole steeled her heart against his panic.

You chose your destiny when you chose to follow Father into battle. You died attempting to avenge his death—and lost. 'Tis time you choose again. You must either pass on to the afterlife, or remain here with no hope of being set free. Look to the light, William. Mother is there. Father is there. 'Struth, he likely wonders why you have not followed him.

Nicole knelt and put her hand on the slab beneath which William lay but did not rest.

I beg of thee, William, in the name of the love I bear you and you bear me, hear and heed me well. Find your peace. Your time on this earthly realm is over.

Father, he said softly.

Nicole nearly shouted for joy at this first sign that he was considering moving on.

Follow the light. Go to Father. He waits for you.

The light is so bright, it hurts my eyes.

The light will not harm you. Beyond is peace. Beyond is Father. Go to him.

She wanted to scream at the silence of his indecision, to somehow give him a push toward the light and hope he kept going.

Then he said, *I love you, Nicole,* and he was gone.

Raw grief clenched her heart and bowed her head. Tears welled in her eyes and overflowed. She'd expected to feel relief, perchance joy. Instead, the sorrow pierced so deep, 'twas nigh on as wrenching as losing William the first time.

On a sob, she told Rhodri, "William is . . . gone."

Rhodri knelt down and set his harp aside. "Ah, my love."

She melted into his embrace and sobbed until her throat was raw and eyes were swelling shut. Rhodri held her tight, one hand rubbing her back, while she soaked through the shoulder of his tunic. Finally her tears ceased, and she breathed without a hitch to each inhale.

"There truly is magic in your harp. I could hear him, feel his emotions, but he did not overwhelm me."

"Twice I almost grabbed you to pull you out of the church. I could see how much you were hurting." He kissed her forehead. "The dagger. 'Twas through the dagger he could reach you, was it not?"

"His jealousy warmed the dagger against my ankle. To think, had I not had it in my boot, I might never have made the connection. Did you suspect?"

"Not until you put the dagger on his grave," he admitted. "Then it made sense. What gave him cause for jealousy?"

"You. William did not like that you had the power to affect my relationship with him. I believe he somehow knew that my love for you was stronger than my love for him and realized this time I would abandon him if he did not give over."

Rhodri went still, and Nicole realized she'd completely, perhaps unwisely, handed her heart into his keeping.

Except she wasn't one bit sorry or worried. If ever there were a man she could trust with her heart, body, and soul, that man was her husband, Rhodri ap Dafydd.

He backed away slightly and, with a finger under her chin, raised her gaze to peer into his. What she saw in his deep-set brown eyes thrilled her to her core.

"I love you, Nicole. I dared not hope for more than your affection. Can you truly love me?"

Damn, she wanted to cry again, this time from happiness.

"I love you more than I have ever loved anyone. We are magic, you and I."

Then he kissed her, and Nicole forgot to worry about their future. Whatever the days ahead might bring, she would be with Rhodri, and all would be well. Content to remain kneeling on the church floor; wrapped in his arms for as long as he wished; Nicole's gaze landed on Rhodri's harp.

"I recognized the music you played. 'Twas the song you composed on our journey to Wales. Have you written the words as yet?"

"I had not planned to play it, but when we walked into the church, the music seemed right somehow. Perhaps this melody needs no words."

A special song for a singular event.

Her knees were beginning to protest a bit before he gave her a last squeeze and said, "We should go to the castle. By now your sisters will have heard of our arrival."

Likely. One of the villagers would have run to the castle gate to announce Nicole's return to Camelen. And she so much wanted to see her sisters, to share her happiness.

And the first thing she intended to do was give Alberic a long, joyous hug.

Nicole slipped the dagger back into her boot, the weapon no longer a threat to her peace.

Fare thee well, William.

She received no answer, and that was right and good.

Her hand in Rhodri's, Nicole stepped out of the dark church into the sunlight.

A crowd had gathered in the village green. Villagers and castle folk. Rhys the bard and Father Paul.

Not far from the bottom of the stairs stood Gwendolyn and Alberic, Emma and Darian and, heaven have mercy, Aubrey de Vere, earl of Oxford.

With a triumphant look on his face, the earl thrust out an arm and pointed upward.

"Seize them!"

❧

Rhodri could only stare at the man he'd never expected to see again.

What the devil was de Vere doing at Camelen?

Nicole leaned into his side. "There is a door in the sacristy. We can escape out the back."

Four men garbed in the earl's livery were coming toward him.

"Nay, my love. This is where we make our stand." He shoved the harp into Nicole's arms, stepped in front of her, and drew his sword.

"Call them back, de Vere!" he ordered in the same commanding tone the earl had used. "The church steps are no place for bloodshed. Nor do you wish a stray blade to nick the lady Nicole."

For two heartbeats, the earl held his peace, then ordered his men to halt. With an inward sigh of relief, Rhodri lowered the tip of his sword—a concession, but not surrender.

"You are correct, Welshman. The lady must not be harmed. I am glad you have decided to submit peacefully."

Like hell he had.

"My lord de Vere, you had no right to take us into your custody at Bledloe Abbey. As I see it, you have no right to do so now."

"No right?" the earl blustered. "I sought to keep safe the king's ward, and you unlawfully kidnapped the lady while in my charge!"

From behind Rhodri, Nicole huffed. She peeked around him but stayed behind him. Without his issuing an order. A nice change.

"Rhodri is not guilty of the charge," she informed the earl. "He did not force me to leave Oxford. In truth, I aided his escape."

De Vere's smile for Nicole was patronizing. "There are witnesses to your distress that day, my dear. You need no longer suffer the indignity of the Welshman's company."

The man's tone set Nicole to bristling.

"The witnesses saw and heard what we wished them

to! Truth to tell, my lord, I am rather accustomed to and enjoy the Welshman's company!"

Her answer didn't sit well with de Vere. He clenched his fists.

"I understand you have been through a difficult time, my lady, and so must suffer a misjudgment of good sense. Nonetheless, you are the king's ward and therefore subject to his will. I shall inform him you have been found and leave your fate to his verdict and command."

Now Rhodri smiled. "When you inform the king of Nicole's whereabouts, be certain to include news of her marriage in your message."

Rhodri heard murmurs in the crowd but didn't allow them to divert him.

The earl's eyes narrowed to slits. "Marriage to whom?"

This wasn't the way Rhodri had envisioned informing Nicole's family of their marriage, but that didn't stop him from answering, "To me."

The crowd didn't know if they should be happy or not. One thing was certain, Nicole's family didn't seem the least bit surprised. Truth to tell, a wide grin spread across Darian's face, and he nudged Alberic with an elbow as if to say "There, did I not tell you?"

The disgruntled earl turned to Alberic.

"We shall have the marriage annulled immediately. I am sure Theobald of Canterbury will oblige us. He is still at Nottingham, so is easily reached."

Alberic shrugged a dismissive shoulder.

"If Nicole has pledged to Rhodri, and so is truly wedded and bedded—" Alberic turned to peer up at Rhodri. "Nicole is truly wedded and bedded, is she not?"

Nicole softly gasped at the outrageous question.

Rhodri smiled at this unusual Marcher lord he was coming to like very much. "Wedded and bedded in good fashion, my lord."

His audacious answer solicited a censorious growl from his wife—signaling the need for an apology later—and a nod of approval from Alberic, who continued.

"Then I consider Rhodri and Nicole husband and wife, and they will be treated as a wedded couple at Camelen. Besides, from what you told me of the negotiations in Nottingham, the war is over and King Stephen no longer needs Nicole to make an alliance with a Welsh noble. Since her marriage is no longer of political import, I say we leave the matter be."

Said with a velvet sheath over a steel blade. The earl could have no doubt that if he chose to press for Rhodri's arrest, he would find no ally in Alberic of Camelen.

Rhodri itched to ask what had transpired at Nottingham. If the war was truly over, then King Stephen and Duke Henry must have come to terms, and Henry Plantagenet would be the next man to sit on the English throne.

Bad news for Wales. But as Connor had said several weeks ago, Duke Henry would needs wait for King Stephen to die before he could take the crown. Perhaps there was time yet for the princes to come to some agreement on the defense of Wales, and Rhodri wished the current king of England a very long life.

But the news was good for Nicole. With no Welsh alliance necessary to sway the outcome of the now ended war, King Stephen no longer needed Nicole for political reasons. She wasn't as important to him as she'd been mere weeks ago.

And none of that mattered if de Vere didn't surrender

his claim on Nicole or decide not to arrest a certain Welsh bard. The earl's stiff spine and sour expression didn't bode well.

But what else could the earl do, given Alberic's stance? And given the large numbers of soldiers at Alberic's immediate command. With his small escort, Aubrey de Vere couldn't hope to win a challenge of arms. Rhodri could almost smell the earl's inevitable retreat.

De Vere scowled at Alberic. "The king will not be pleased that one of his wards has been defiled, but as you say, the king no longer has need for Nicole to marry a Welsh noble. I shall inform the king of her marriage and whereabouts and allow him to decide whether or not to take further action."

Nicole grumbled quietly. "I was not defiled."

Rhodri smiled at the complaint but was willing to allow the earl his opinion if only he would leave!

De Vere said a curt fare-thee-well to Alberic and bowed courteously to Gwendolyn before stalking off, his escort scurrying to catch up.

Nicole shoved the harp into his arms and wasted no time in flying down the stairs and leaping into Alberic's arms. The crowd finally cheered, thinking Nicole thanked Alberic for sending the earl on his way. Rhodri knew better. For the first time in eight years, Nicole could look on her brother-by-marriage without William screaming at her to do murder.

Then Nicole squealed and launched herself at her sisters. Gwendolyn, strikingly beautiful and willow slender—so she must have given birth. Emma, rounder and softer but no less beautiful in her own right.

But his thoughts and love were only for Nicole, the

mostly convent-raised hoyden to whom, in Rhodri's opinion, no other woman could compare.

They'd done well in the church. His harp *did* hold magic, his music allowing Nicole to, at long last, help her brother find his peace. While Rhodri took pride in the accomplishment, he was even prouder of Nicole. Watching her contend with her belligerent brother had shredded his heart. Hearing her confession of love had made him whole again.

Content to allow Nicole her reunion with her sisters without his interference, Rhodri slipped the sword under his belt and, armed only with his harp, descended the stairs to where Alberic and Darian stood and also fondly, patiently watched the sisters celebrate their reunion.

Alberic readily accepted Rhodri's outstretched hand.

"'Twas good of you to bring her home," Alberic said. "I thank you for the service you gave her, in the church."

He shouldn't have been surprised Nicole had immediately explained to Alberic, during their embrace, how she could now greet him without pain.

"Believe me, Alberic, I could do no less. May I assume both Gwendolyn and the new babe are doing well?"

A proud grin lit his face. "Babes. A boy and a girl. A surprise to us all. And, aye, all are healthy."

"My felicitations, my lord, and my thanks for your support against the earl."

"I had little choice," he said without a hint of ire.

"You could have begged favor for Nicole and allowed the earl to have me."

"Nicole would have fought to save you, and one does not lightly dismiss the desires of a Pendragon princess."

Darian chuckled. "Nay, one does not. They are, all three, strong-minded women."

Strong-minded, perhaps, but also loving and fiercely loyal to those they loved. So, too, were their husbands. Why Alberic and Darian had allowed Nicole to leave the inn in the company of a man they didn't know, Rhodri had never quite understood.

"At the inn, you allowed Nicole to accompany me to Wales. I never came to any conclusions as to why."

Darian waved a dismissive hand. "When you told us that Nicole had spoken to you of her gift, I realized destiny had already taken a hand. She would not have revealed her abilities, particularly with regard to William, if she did not already love and trust you. She had already chosen you, whether she knew it at the time or not. 'Twas the same with her sisters and us."

"Your wives, they have powers similar to Nicole's?"

Alberic answered. "Somewhat, but that is a tale for later, when we are all together, with no one else to hear. 'Twill require a stretch of belief on your part, and an oath to tell no other."

"You may have that oath now."

"Then we welcome you as our brother." Alberic lightly cuffed Rhodri's shoulder. "What say we celebrate the day's success with a tankard of ale?"

Oh, that sounded grand, but he had one more thing to do before he could celebrate.

"Not as yet. I made a promise to Nicole I should like to keep now. While I assure you she is truly wedded and bedded, she worries that there were no witnesses to our vows. As long as her family is all gathered and a priest at hand, I should like to lay her concern to rest."

Alberic glanced over his shoulder. "Father Paul, your services are required. Rhys, perhaps you can take charge of Rhodri's harp for the nonce. There, I have done my part. All that remains for you to do is tear Nicole away from her sisters."

"Oh, I believe this is one time she will cooperate."

The comment elicited laughter from both men he could now call brother. He'd married Nicole and gained a family, a blessing he hadn't foreseen.

He handed his harp over to the tall, lank, gray-haired Rhys, Camelen's bard, whom Nicole had mentioned a time or two.

Rhys plucked a string and smiled at the harp's voice. "Do you mind if I play?"

"Not at all."

His hands now free, Rhodri strode over to the women and placed his hands on Nicole's shoulders. "My ladies, if you would be so gracious, I should like to borrow Nicole for a moment."

Nicole turned around to gaze up at him. "Why for?"

"We now have witnesses."

She glanced around at the crowd, her family, and at Father Paul awaiting them at the top of the church's stairs.

Beaming, Nicole placed her hand in his. "You can write the song of our journey now. This is a fitting ending to our adventure, do you not think?"

"Ah, but a new adventure begins. I love you, Nicole de Leon. I should have told you long before today. I wish—"

She put a fingertip to his lips. "Better today than never, and I think today simply perfect. I love you, too, Rhodri ap Dafydd. What say we declare that love before all and sundry?"

Without a qualm, Rhodri cooperated.

ABOUT THE AUTHOR

SHARI ANTON's secretarial career ended when she took a creative writing class and found she possessed some talent for writing fiction. The author of several highly acclaimed historical novels, she now works in her home office, where she can take unlimited coffee breaks. Shari and her husband live in southeastern Wisconsin, where they have two grown children and do their best to spoil their two adorable little grandsons. You can write to her at P.O. Box 510611, New Berlin, WI 53151-0611, or visit her Web site at www.sharianton.com.

THE DISH

Where authors give you the inside scoop!

❤ ❤ ❤ ❤ ❤ ❤ ❤ ❤ ❤ ❤ ❤ ❤ ❤ ❤ ❤

From the desk of Larissa Ione

Dear Reader,

Growing up, I wanted to be both an author and a doctor. Too bad I suffered from an unfortunate tendency to pass out at the sight of blood. For some reason, doctors fainting in emergency situations is frowned upon. Go figure.

So I concentrated on my first love, writing, but I never got over my fascination with emergency medicine. A few years ago, I swallowed my squeamishness and earned an Emergency Medical Technician certification in order to help me accurately portray the medical heroes and heroines I love so much.

Something else I love is the paranormal, so when I decided to follow my heart and write dark supernatural tales, I still couldn't let go of those hot doctors and paramedics. I wanted them to play a large role in my paranormal novels, but how? How could I combine medicine and the paranormal?

The answer came to me while watching an episode of *Angel*, when my favorite broody vamp got hurt. My poor baby! He needed medical attention, stat. But really, where could demons, vampires, and werewolves go for help?

To a demon ER, of course!

PLEASURE UNBOUND (on sale now), the first in a series of novels set in and around an underworld hospital, is the result of both my interests and my addiction to TV shows such as *ER*, *Grey's Anatomy*, and *Buffy the Vampire Slayer* (and okay, maybe my fangirl crushes on George Clooney, Patrick Dempsey, James Marsters, and Joss Whedon).

In PLEASURE UNBOUND, you'll meet Tayla, a tough, street-savvy demon slayer who lands in a demon hospital under the care of a sexy incubus surgeon named Eidolon. When a sinister plot forces them to work together in order to learn the truth behind a rash of killings that threatens both demons and slayers, Tayla and Eidolon find that the biggest danger of all is to their hearts.

I hope your visit to Underworld General proves to be the most pleasant trip to a hospital you've ever experienced. Happy reading!

Sincerely,

Larissa Ione

www.LarissaIone.com

♥ ♥ ♥ ♥ ♥ ♥ ♥ ♥ ♥ ♥ ♥ ♥ ♥ ♥ ♥

From the desk of Wendy Markham

Dear Reader,

When I wrote THE NINE MONTH PLAN five years ago, I never dreamed the book would kick off a series. Then I began hearing from readers who could relate to the loud, loving, laughing Chickalini family and wanted to know whether Nina's siblings would find their own happy endings.

In my latest novel, THAT'S AMORE (on sale now), Ralphie—now a newly orphaned adult in the wake of his father's passing—must come to terms with a broken engagement, the upcoming sale of the only home he's ever known, and an unwanted attraction to a woman who's all wrong for him. What he doesn't know is that Daria Marshall's presence in his life may not be entirely accidental. Daria can see dead people—including a sad-eyed spirit who seems to have led her right to the Chickalini doorstep.

Writing this latest installment was like coming home . . . and not just because I'm so familiar with these characters and their cozy, more-shabby-than-chic Queens rowhouse. The thing is, now that I'm a married mom living in the New York City suburbs, I frequently find myself nostalgic for my own small-town youth almost five hundred miles away—and for the loving extended family that is never far from my thoughts.

Simply put, writing about the Chickalini family brings me back home again.

Raised in the heart of western New York's snowbelt, I had parents who were married at twenty-one, had me at twenty-two, and strolled hand in hand through four-plus decades of marriage. Our sprawling Italian/Sicilian family—dozens of aunts, uncles, and cousins, plus all four grandparents—lived within a few treelined blocks of our Queen Anne Victorian. Family and friends dropped in at all hours and were greeted with coffee and cookies or wine and cheese. We celebrated milestones at Holy Trinity Roman Catholic Church and holidays around noisy, crowded dining room tables laden with food.

There were times when all that togetherness got on my nerves, as it does on Ralphie's. But like Ralphie, Nina, and their siblings, I learned the hard way about the importance of family, and tradition, and holding on—and letting go.

My beautiful young mom was tragically taken from us, much too soon, a few years back. Gone, too, are two of my grandpas, a grandma, cousins, and countless old friends. But they all live on in my heart, and every now and then, they are captured in a fictional glimmer right here, in the pages of the Chickalini family books.

Cent'anni!

Wendy Markham

www.wendymarkham.com

♥ ♥ ♥ ♥ ♥ ♥ ♥ ♥ ♥ ♥ ♥ ♥ ♥ ♥ ♥

From the desk of Shari Anton

Dear Reader,

There's a moment during the writing of a book when an author knows she's telling the story she's supposed to tell. For some authors, this sublime moment of serendipity occurs in the initial stages of plotting. For me, these pleasant, priceless discoveries tend to happen when I'm writing the first draft of my books.

Each time that moment happens, I'm relieved at my good fortune and thankful for a cooperative muse who always seems to know I'm headed in the right direction even when I'm doubtful.

Such a moment happened while I wrote MAGIC IN HIS KISS (on sale now). I knew all along that Rhodri ap Dafydd, the hero of my story, was a talented Welsh bard. But I didn't realize the importance and significance of his music until I wrote the scene where Rhodri is composing a new song on his harp. I knew then what course his life was meant to take, and why he was the perfect hero for Nicole de Leon.

Of course, at that point in the story, Rhodri doesn't realize how important his music will be to Nicole's life work, and Nicole has no idea that because of the magic in his music Rhodri is destined to be her life's partner. At that point in the story, they aren't even sure they like each other! But, of course, they are bound together by the music, by destiny, and by love.

It's always fun to watch a story unfold. An author sometimes blindly follows the lives of the characters to discover where they're going and why, just as a reader keeps turning the pages of a good story to learn what happens next. The experience for both of us can be (dare I say it) magical!

Enjoy!

Shari Anton

www.sharianton.com

Dear Reader,

While writing the Magic trilogy, I learned a lot about psychic powers and had a great time imagining how, if one had such powers, they would affect a person's everyday life.

I can't say that I, personally, would like to have the power to recall King Arthur from the dead like Gwendolyn in MIDNIGHT MAGIC, to look into water and see visions like Emma in TWILIGHT MAGIC, or be able to hear the dead like Nicole in MAGIC IN HIS KISS. However, I'm glad these three sisters didn't mind my inflicting them with those powers so I could vicariously explore the possibilities!

I hope you enjoyed their stories and my brief dip into the world of the paranormal.

Happy Reading,

Shari Anton